A Match Made at the Museum

Abbie L. Grubb

To Tony, whose joy lights up my life every day.

And to Ken, my own match made at a museum.

Chapter 1

Evelyn lifted her cup to her lips and sipped as she surveyed the room. Her mother and father were perched on opposite ends of their pale green settee. Mama's cup of tea remained untouched as she regaled her youngest son, John, with the latest gossip from her morning visits. Papa faced the other direction as he and their eldest son, James, discussed the estate while snacking on cakes and ignoring the tea grown cold beside them. Evelyn occasionally interjected into both discussions, but was, for the most part, silent.

She set her cup down and flipped through the pages of *Ladies Monthly*, reading and admiring the sketches of dresses, bonnets, and gloves. She avoided comparing her own attire to that of the pages, knowing she would not like the comparison. She bit back an unbecoming sigh before it could escape and earn a frown of reproof from Mama, but she could not refrain from glancing between the door and the time piece on the mantel. At long last, the clock hands cooperated, softly chiming the 4:00 hour. She stood, smoothing her yellow muslin gown and saying her goodbyes to her family.

"This was lovely, but I have some things to attend to before our evening activities. Please excuse me."

Her mother shot her a perfunctory smile, pausing long enough in her tales to address her middle child. "Of course, dear. We will depart at 7:00 for the Talbot's party, so be sure to be ready. And please wear your cream gown with the pink flower embroidery. It is such a becoming cut on you," she decreed.

"Of course, Mama. Marie has already laid it out." She smiled at her mother and looked towards her father and James, but they were deep into a debate on the merits of stable design and paid her no heed. She slipped from the room and moved swiftly to her bedroom. Within minutes she had captured most of her voluminous, and often unruly, red curls into a straw bonnet, scooped a satchel from the bottom of her wardrobe, threw a pelisse on for warmth, and made her way down the stairs. She ran out the rear doors and onto the grounds, pulling her wrap more tightly around her to block the chill in the air, and moving in the direction of the gardens.

Decades before, her grandfather had built a small walled garden behind their townhouse. While the house was made of a bold red brick, the garden's walls were constructed of a rough-cut gray stone quarried from the north of England that provided a solid buffer from the wind. Once through the black iron gate, Evelyn breathed deeply as the chill abated and silence enveloped her. She continued a determined pace between the rows of waist-high hedges, small overhanging flowering trees, and a wide variety of blooming flowers that had all been planted for her grandmother as a wedding gift.

She slowed finally as she came to the far end of the garden where a covered pavilion provided shade over several small benches. Honeysuckle vines had been allowed to grow unchecked up the columns supporting the structure, and she inhaled their sweet scent as she sank onto one of the benches.

"One hour," she whispered, as she pulled a stack of papers from the satchel she had brought with her. She drew a pencil out and shuffled through the sheaf of papers to find a clean one. She stared briefly into the distance then began to write.

She had not moved from her spot when her lady's maid, Marie, came to find her well over an hour later.

"Begging your pardon, Miss, but your mother has sent me to ensure that you're ready for the party on time." The young woman bobbed a small curtsy as she greeted Evelyn, apologetic for having interrupted her serene afternoon respite.

Evelyn started at the sound of the girl's voice, but smiled when she looked up.

"Not at all, Marie, you did the right thing coming to find me." Setting down her pencil, Evelyn flexed her fingers and stood, stretching as she did so. "How long have I been out here?"

"According to Lady Berkeley, you left tea nearly two hours ago." She craned her neck to try to catch a glimpse of the writing on the pages strewn about the bench and asked in a whisper, "Have you made much progress?"

"Two hours!" Evelyn exclaimed, "I feel as though I have been here no more than half an hour!" Turning her back on the expectant look of her companion, Evelyn gathered her pages and pushed them back into her bag. "We must make haste."

Once all her pages were secured, Evelyn turned to look at Marie. "He proposed!" she declared, grinning at the young woman.

"He did not!" Marie exclaimed as her face lit with enthusiasm.

The two girls moved towards the house talking excitedly about the fictional characters and plots that Evelyn had been writing for months. The women came from different stations but shared a bond born of years of personal interactions, trusted confidences, and a love of good storytelling. Marie had been the first audience for Evelyn's stories when she was just a girl scribbling tales of animal adventures in the garden and making up ghost stories to frighten them both. The development of a true talent for words had led Evelyn to spend nearly every spare moment writing. She had been crafting love stories for Marie's entertainment for several years now, along with silly anecdotes about society, personal reflections on her family, and even occasional forays into political topics. As she passed more and more birthdays unmarried, she had found her writing to be a way to create the life she hoped to find one day; it had thus far remained elusive.

"You will have to wait until tomorrow to find out what happens because I must ready for dinner, but I think you will like the ending for our heroine," Evelyn promised.

"I'm not sure I shall sleep a wink if I can't hear what happened, but I suppose I'll have to try," she moaned.

When they reached her room, Evelyn carefully placed her satchel back in its hiding spot behind a false bottom in her wardrobe. Marie prepared Evelyn for the evening and their activity distracted them both from their earlier conversation. Within an hour, Evelyn pulled the door closed behind her and headed down the grand staircase to join her family. As requested, she wore her mother's favorite gown of cream silk with an overlay of pink embroidered flowers. A string of pearls that had been a gift from her father lay at her throat, and her red hair was gathered on top of her head in a somewhat artistic cacophony of curls adorned with white flowers. A few tendrils fell to each side of her face in the current fashion, assuring everyone that her mother was well-versed in the latest styles. While Evelyn was far from ungrateful for the amount of care her parents paid to her image, she did wish they paid as much attention to her as they did to her attire.

"Let me go light the way," she whispered as she caught sight of herself in a mirror. With the light colors her mother favored coupled with her pale complexion and bright hair, she could not help but feel that she resembled a candle. Even her brother John had nicknamed her "Blaze," in their childhood. She had not appreciated the moniker.

"Don't you look lovely," her father exclaimed when she descended the stairs. Her mother looked her over and gave an approving nod, adding, "You are sure to garner attention wearing the latest fashions." Lady Berkeley preened her own recently acquired gown as she said these words, no doubt assuming the same could be said of her.

"Are you sure I am not too washed out in such colors?" she asked her mother as a footman handed over her gloves and assisted her into a pale pink spencer.

Her mother did not even look at her as she answered, "Nonsense, your gown is of the highest quality materials and made by the best modiste in town. Anyone can see it is beautifully made and of the latest fashion."

Evelyn looked to her father for any sign of support, but he was studiously avoiding her eye as he donned his gloves and hat. She couldn't blame him for his lack of response. It did him no favors to contradict his wife on matters of fashion or domestic affairs. He had learned that at least in their nearly 30 years of marriage. Making a mental note to try to avoid catching sight of herself in any mirrors, she followed her mother and father out the door and into their waiting carriage.

After arriving at the Talbot's brightly lit townhome and performing the perfunctory greetings in the receiving line, Evelyn moved away from her parents and weaved her way through the crowded second-floor rooms to find a spot near the refreshments. The spot was out of the way of the many guests, but still offered a good view of the dance floor and the crowd. She scanned the room for her two best friends, twin sisters Sophia and Charlotte Montgomery, but saw no sign of them or their mother.

Unbidden thoughts of Charlotte and Sophia's older brother William came to mind. Though she told herself she was looking for her friends, she knew she hoped to catch a glimpse of him as well. Her shoulders sagged slightly at the thought and she sighed, then caught herself and replaced her frown with a pleasant, albeit fake, smile lest Mama catch her at less than her best.

As if drawn by Evelyn's quick slip of decorum, Lady Berkeley appeared next to her and pressed a surprisingly sharp elbow into her side as she whispered far too loudly, "For goodness' sake, child, smile; the Duke of Ravenwood is approaching."

Glancing to where her mother gestured, Evelyn saw the tall, dark-haired gentleman approach and dipped into an appropriate curtsy before looking up into his pleasant and smiling face. His looks could not be described as classically handsome as his nose was a bit too large and his hairline had begun receding at a young age, but his smile was quite charming. Many women would argue that his title made up for any physical deficiencies.

"It's such a pleasure to see you, Your Grace. How is your mother faring these days?" Lady Berkeley glowed under the attentions of the titled gentleman as he returned a small bow and bestowed a smile on the two ladies.

"Your Grace, it's a pleasure to see you again," Evelyn said, with a sincere smile.

The Duke took her hand and lightly pressed a kiss to it. "My mother was quite well when last I saw her before returning to London for the Season. She was somewhat disappointed to remain behind, but she is not as spry as she once was and now prefers the quiet of home to the excitement of the city."

"Oh, I shall write her first thing tomorrow and fill her in on all the news of Town. She was my dearest friend growing up, as I know you know, and it pains me not to see her this year," exclaimed Lady Berkeley, clasping her hands dramatically in front of her.

"She will revel in every word," he assured her. "She has seemed a bit lonely of late. A letter from you will be just what she needs."

Evelyn was not sure her mother could beam any brighter at the high praise from Ravenwood. "And what about you, sir? Are you enjoying the rigors of the Season compared to the quieter life of the country?" Evelyn asked him.

"The pace and bustle can be wearying at times, but I do enjoy the Season. Just as I begin to feel it might be too much, I find it is time to head home again! It is the perfect cycle!" he surmised.

As they all surveyed the crowded room, Lady Berkeley spoke again. "Have you any plans to marry this Season, Your Grace?"

Evelyn barely hid her amusement and embarrassment at her mother's rather direct question. The Duke laughed it off, no doubt used to such meddling mothers.

"No ma'am; I find myself a bit young to consider marriage quite yet. Besides, how could I find anyone who lives up to the fine example your daughter has set as my friend these last years!"

Evelyn laughed along with Ravenwood but found her fake smile returning. After several more moments of conversation, the Duke excused himself.

Lady Berkeley moved away from Evelyn as soon as he had, and Evelyn moved towards the refreshment table for a lemonade. She watched the passing crowds and was greeted by warm smiles and nods from many acquaintances. A few stopped to speak a word or two of greeting.

As she sipped her lemonade, she thought back on her second Season when the Duke had been a regular visitor at their home. She no longer felt any embarrassment about the feelings she had thought she held for him, and she certainly no longer held any tender sentiments. Yet, she still had no explanation for his many weeks of visits during that Season that did not result in the offer of marriage her mother had so desperately hoped for.

She had no more formal Seasons after that year, though she continued to travel with her parents to London and attend a number of social events each year. She ignored the pitying looks from others and instead focused on family and friends. She was grateful that Charlotte and Sophia, who were younger than her, came out during what would be her third year in town and helped to secure invitations and provide company at many of their shared events.

The Duke of Ravenwood had been replaced by Lords Bertram and Allen during her next summer. The former was a very pleasant Baron who had called on Evelyn regularly until his betrothal to Miss Amelia Carter was announced. Lord Allen had paid regular visits as well, and they had enjoyed many walks through the garden discussing their shared love for literature and nature. She had hoped his attentions would continue after the Berkeleys had left London, but instead, she heard of his Christmas betrothal to the young widow, Mrs. Hope Reynolds.

Though she had not thought it possible, the callers had increased during her fourth year with what her mother had initially called an "embarrassment of riches." She had been regularly invited for rides through Hyde Park and had never lacked for visitors during social hours. Still, not one of those callers had sought a conversation with her father; not one had even expressed an intention towards marriage.

She had seen her former callers throughout the following Seasons; she could hardly avoid them, nor did they seek to avoid her. Rather than awkwardness or guilt for having engaged her hopes, all spoke fondly of her and their friendship. But none had loved her. If she was being honest with herself, she had not loved any of them either, but she had thought herself capable of it several times.

She shook her head to dispel her morose thoughts and sipped her lemonade. Such thoughts had occupied her for months. After last Season, she had analyzed each interaction and conversation for any sign of error on her part.

"Perhaps you are just too friendly," Charlotte had said, trying to make her feel better. "Our Mama always says, 'men enjoy a hunt, whether it is for foxes or women!'"

"You are the prettiest girl in any room," her father had said during her first Season. "Any man would be lucky to have you," he said during her second Season as he had pressed a kiss to her cheek. His reassurances had stopped after her third year.

"Perhaps it is because you talk too much," John had suggested when he had found her teary-eyed and missing Lord Allen's conversations and company.

"Perhaps it is because you do not talk enough," James had theorized the next year.

Evelyn smiled and nodded politely at a couple who walked by arm in arm. The striking young lady had shared her coming out the same year as Evelyn. She had since married and produced an heir for the handsome man she clung to as they paraded across the floor. Evelyn observed their obvious contentment with one another and envied the relationship.

She was soon distracted by the approach of a heavy-set man of average height and short blond hair. His clothes were of the latest fashions, albeit a bit too tight across the middle. He smiled at Evelyn, reaching for her hands as he approached. He leaned over, brushing a kiss lightly across the back of her gloved hands.

"My dear Miss Berkeley, how are you this evening?" he asked in a booming voice, causing a few heads to turn in their direction.

Evelyn smiled as she pulled her hand back, and set her cup on the tray of a passing servant.

"I am doing quite well, thank you," she replied dipping a small curtsy. "And how is your wife, Lord Allen?"

"Oh fine, fine, you know. We welcomed our first child just weeks ago," he answered with obvious pride.

"Congratulations to you both!" Evelyn exclaimed, truly happy for him.

"Yes, yes, it is quite exciting. Might I ask you to join me for this dance?" he asked, raising his eyebrows slightly as he looked at her expectantly.

"Of course, I would be delighted," she answered, slipping her hand into his. He led her onto the floor to find their place among the others lining up for the reel.

And she *was* delighted. He was a pleasant dance partner, although by the end of it, he was breathing heavily so their conversation necessarily lagged. They never struggled for conversation during the following supper, however. They discussed the latest publications and his current redesigns of his estate gardens. This was not their first such occasion of friendly dancing and conversation at parties and balls throughout the Season, and Evelyn did truly enjoy his company.

After one of their many conversations, Charlotte and Sophia had peppered Evelyn with questions about Lord Allen. "Has he ever tried to lay a hand on you?" Sophia had asked. "Does he flatter you with compliments?" queried Charlotte. Evelyn had assured both ladies that his behavior was never untoward or inappropriate. He spoke lovingly of his wife, engaged multiple people in their conversations during supper, and treated Evelyn with the utmost respect and appropriate social decorum. As Evelyn had come to realize, he just wanted a friend.

After supper, Lord Allen escorted Evelyn back to her mother in the ballroom.

"Lady Berkeley, a pleasure to see you as always," he said in greeting as he approached the older woman.

"Ah Lord Allen, the pleasure is mine," she said tersely giving him a tight smile and the briefest of nods.

Lord Allen seemed not to notice the slight and turned his attention back to Evelyn.

"My dear, it was such a joy to share the supper hour with you. You always have such fascinating insight on the latest publications."

"Thank you for the invitation and kind words, Lord Allen," she replied, "and I wish you the best of luck on your new garden plans."

With another smile and a small bow, he turned away and Lady Berkeley huffed her displeasure. "Why you still entertain that man is beyond me," she fussed.

"Mama, be kind," Evelyn scolded from behind her fan. "He is my friend."

"Humph. Friendship is well and good, I suppose, but I still do not understand why he married that other girl when he could have married you." She did not wait for an answer before waving down a friend and moving across the room to join other conversations.

Evelyn sighed again, wondering when she had become the sighing type. She had no answer to her mother's question. She had asked herself the same thing on multiple occasions, but no answer was forthcoming.

So, she had decided to write herself a different ending instead.

After her disappointment over Ravenwood, she had written a Gothic novel in which the hero left the heroine for another only to realize too late that she was his true love. Upon his return to beg her forgiveness, he found she had died of a broken heart just a week earlier.

When Lord Bertram had announced his betrothal, she had written a humorous tale in which a man proposed to a woman beneath his station just to spite his father, but they fell in love and lived happily together as husband and wife.

Lord Allen's marriage had inspired a moral tale in which a man loved a poor maiden but left her for a wealthy woman, only to spend the rest of his life in a miserable loveless marriage, bemoaning his lost love.

Obviously, her stories did not always directly reflect reality, but

Evelyn found writing to be the catharsis she needed. While she had always enjoyed writing, it had become a passion in recent years. In her writing she was heard; in reality she often felt that no one was listening.

Her mother's voice drifted across the ballroom, pulling her from her reverie. "Evelyn *loves* whist; I'm sure she will partner you."

Evelyn stopped herself just short of another sigh. Her mother made a not-very-subtle gesture to come closer from the other side of the room.

"I despise card games," she whispered to no one as she moved closer to her mother. She directed a fake smile towards the group surrounding Mama.

"These lovely gentlemen were just saying they will be at the Montgomery's dinner later this week and would like nothing more than to join you for a round of whist after supper."

"I would be delighted to join you," she assured them all, now dreading the dinner party and wishing she had the courage to tell her mother she hated whist.

Chapter 2

The room was peaceful in the morning twilight hours as Oliver watched his grandfather's chest rise and fall. A fire crackled in the grate, mingling with the sounds of his uncle's snores from the corner where he had fallen asleep propped up in a chair. Family and local friends had been passing through the sickroom for the last several days as the end drew near for the elderly gentleman.

Oliver looked at the hand he held along the edge of the bed. What had once been strong was now frail, a mere shadow of the gregarious and confident Sir Anthony Moreland who had been such a pillar in his life. Each summer, Christmas, and various holidays had been spent here at Longwood, trailing behind his grandfather and hanging on his every word.

He squeezed the hand gently and smiled as he recalled fond memories of riding lessons, walks in the garden, and games of hide-and-seek in the halls of the manor home. And the stories. It was his grandfather's stories that had brought him here three months ago, determined to capture as much as possible before his grandfather slipped away. What had been fascinating to him as a young boy had become his obsession as a young adult. His youthful hero worship had grown into an affectionate admiration through his teenage years. Attempting to find his own way into adulthood had yet again changed Oliver's perspective as he sought to understand and emulate the older gentleman.

"I will never understand how you endure his rambling for so long," Oliver's father had commented years before. "As much as your mother adored him, even she would tire of his stories long before you did." While his father was certainly not displeased with the closeness Oliver and his maternal grandfather shared, he never fully understood it. He even expressed surprise that Oliver would wish to continue his visits to Longwood after his mother had died.

He let go of the older man's hand and rested it beside him on the bed before standing and stretching to remove the tightness and knots that hours in a wingback chair had caused. He walked over to the window that faced his grandfather's bed and pulled back the curtains to look out over the estate. Hints of early sunlight illuminated the gardens below and the rolling hills that spread out towards the town of Stockton. He raised his eyes, looking past the horizon imagining the world beyond. Despite the beauty before him, the distant lands where his grandfather had once stood called to him in a way that no region of England ever had.

Coughing from the bed drew his attention and he let the curtain fall back in place and crossed the room in long strides. His dark hair fell across his face as he looked down and he pushed it back away from his spectacles to better see his grandfather. His figure seemed so small beneath the bedclothes that had been piled high to ward off the winter chill. His grandfather's similar dark hair splayed across the pillow like a halo framing his face. The cough subsided and his breathing returned to the slow shallow breaths that had filled his last days. His eyes remained closed despite Oliver's wish for one last look into their stormy gray depths. The doctor had assessed him last night and warned that he likely wouldn't make it through the day. Oliver had vowed to himself to remain at his side to the end; while there would be no recovery, he did hold out hope that the dying man might awaken one last time.

His uncle and his grandfather's only son, Jackson Moreland, stirred in the corner, no doubt awakened by the coughing. He, too, stood and stretched before making his way to the bedside opposite Oliver. "No change I see," he said unnecessarily. He straightened the covers on his father's chest before turning away from the bed. A former soldier, life-long bachelor, and a constant companion to his father for the last 10 years, Jack was struggling with the impending loss worse than anyone. He vacillated between bouts of uncontrollable tears, morose silence, and abnormally upbeat chatter as he attempted to process his grief.

"No, no change," Oliver confirmed. "Shall I ring for breakfast?"

"That sounds delightful, my boy," Jack responded as he paced the room, absentmindedly picking things up and setting them down again.

Oliver rang for a servant and returned to his seat, watching his uncle with a bemused smile. The man had never boasted the tall muscular figure of his father even in his youth, but his stocky frame had only become wider as he aged. His unruly dark hair marked him as a Moreland, but he otherwise took after his mother's side. During his stint in the King's service, his men had affectionately compared him to Napoleon. According to Jack, there could be no comparison because "Old Boney" had been caught, and he himself would have never, but he handled the teasing well. Jack stood before his father's dressing table, pushing around his belongings, lining up his shaving tools first one way then the other. After rearranging the table, he moved across the room and looked out the window as Oliver had done.

A maid entered in response to Oliver's summons and left again to fetch a breakfast tray upon his request. A footman then entered and stoked the fire, coaxing warm flames from the dying embers. When the maid returned, she set the tray on a small table near the window. She poured two cups of tea, opened the curtains fully to illuminate the breakfast table, and withdrew. Given the new focus, both men converged on the tray and assembled small plates of bread, butter, jam, and eggs.

Jack and Oliver fell into an amiable silence as they ate, one facing the view from the window and the other facing the elderly man's bed. Oliver added sugar and cream to his tea and took a sip as he looked towards the bed. Jack held his steaming mug in his hands and gazed out over the estate that would soon be his.

"I've been meaning to talk to you lately, my boy," began Jack after several bites of bread. "After...well, you know, this estate will be mine and I will have to step into the role fully for the first time. Father certainly taught me all he thought I would need to know to care for the land, but he always took the lead. It will be a lot of responsibility and a lot of work. Not that I'm afraid of work, mind you."

Oliver smiled encouragingly at Jack, unsure where he was going with his musings. "Of course not. You have never run from honest work in your life," Oliver assured his uncle.

"Yes, well, some may say the same about you." He looked affectionately across the table at the nephew who often seemed more like a son.

Oliver smiled at the man and joked, "I have them fooled then!"

Jack grinned then turned serious again, pausing before asking, "What are your plans, son?"

Oliver's insides tightened at the question he dreaded. He was not his father's heir. That privilege was claimed by his oldest brother, Edward, and he had been the apple of their father's eye from birth.

He was not his father's spare, either. That distinction was his brother Andrew's, and he had chosen a peaceful and protected life in the Church; should the need ever sadly arise, he would be a healthy and hale heir-replacement.

While both of his brothers could claim a relationship built of fondness and mutual respect with their father, Oliver had never felt such a connection. After his father remarried, there was even less of one and he had begun spending more time with his late mother's family.

He had hoped to follow in the footsteps of his grandfather and uncle by becoming a soldier, however his father's refusal to purchase a commission and, ultimately, his own deficient eyesight, had ended that dream. As a result, he had yet to settle on any true occupation or path.

"My plans?" He glanced at the ceiling, then out the window. "My plans are...undetermined as of yet," he finally said.

Embarrassed at this lack of direction, he avoided looking at Jack. His uncle had never wavered from his path. Despite being his father's only son and heir, he had left home young to be an officer, resigning his commission after more than two decades of honorable service and returning to Longwood. He had shifted his service from King and Country to learning estate management. Despite his wealthy origins, Jack truly did not shy away from work. He rose with the household staff most days and regularly worked the fields during harvest, repaired cottages, or assisted the tenants with any other needs that arose.

Oliver had no fear of hard work, either, but he found himself more at home in libraries than in fields. Despite being the third-born son, his father's wealth had allowed him the same education his brothers had received, first at Eton then Cambridge, where he had spent several very happy years pursuing research in the classics, history, and antiquities. In the last year before being summoned to his grandfather's bedside, he had begun to focus his studies on the experiences of the British Army. Given Jack's years of active service to country and estate, Oliver worried that he would not understand his desire for continued research and writing. It was not traditional work for a man of his station, so Oliver decided to keep his burgeoning plans to himself for the time being.

Jack tipped his head to the side and looked at Oliver, as if he knew he held back, but ultimately chose not to push him for more explanation.

"Whatever you decide, I hope you know that you always have a place here at Longwood. I have no children of my own as you know, and do not plan to at this point in my life. I have other nephews, of course, but none that I like so well as you, if I'm being honest," Jack explained. "I'd like nothing more than for you to stay here and learn the property as it is my desire to name you as my heir."

At this unexpected statement, Oliver looked at his uncle with surprise, "Me?" he asked. "Would Grandfather approve of that decision?"

"Who do you think suggested it?" Jack asked with a grin.

"I...I'm not sure what to say, Uncle, but I thank you truly for the offer," Oliver stuttered. "It pleases me no end that both of you would think me capable of caring for this great place." Oliver was both embarrassed and surprised to find himself swallowing to dispel a sudden lump in his throat as he looked between the bed and the man across from him in gratitude. No one else had the confidence in him that these two men did, and no matter what his future held, he did not want to disappoint them.

Jack watched him expectantly, waiting for an answer.

"I want to explore an...idea I have had lately," Oliver began, "but I will consider your invitation and let you know my decision soon."

Jack stood, setting his napkin beside his plate and brushing crumbs from the front of his jacket. "The choice is yours," he said with a smile. "But remember, we do not get younger, my boy; do not let life pass you by while you chase after will-o'-the-wisps. I'll not tell you how to live your life, but I will tell you that it is a satisfying day when you have worked the land for the good of your property."

The older man clapped Oliver on the shoulder as he moved towards the bedroom door.

"Thank you, Uncle. For everything," Oliver called to Jack, who left the room, acknowledging his words with a small backward wave.

How could a man so steeped in the importance of hard work and duty understand his desire to research and learn for a living? Not only was it considered beneath his station, but to a man like Jack, it was a pursuit more suited to a hobby than a career. Oliver sighed and stared out the window. The irony of his circumstances was not lost on him. While he wanted to tell the stories of soldiers like his grandfather and uncle and other men who gave of themselves for their country, those same men would not likely view a profession of research and storytelling favorably. And what of his dreams of a life in America? Oliver stood from the table and moved towards the window, staring unseeingly at the estate.

Two months later, Oliver again stared out a window, oblivious to the traffic on the street below. Though his grandfather had passed, and Jack had fully assumed ownership of Longwood, he still had not given an answer to his uncle's request to stay at the estate. Oliver had left for London after the funeral explaining that he would help tie up any loose ends of his grandfather's will. It wasn't a complete falsehood, as he had visited with solicitors and several bank representatives within the first two weeks of arrival, but the loose ends were long since tied neatly in a bow.

He ran his hands through his hair and looked down at the papers strewn across the desk in his study. The small townhouse he was renting was nothing extravagant, but the room was well-appointed with large dark furniture and two full walls of shelves to hold his large collection of books. He claimed it was the placement of his study so near the street noise that had prevented more progress on his writing, but he knew he was only fooling himself.

He picked up the top paper and read his scrawl. "'Captain Anthony Moreland led 346 troops against the American militia in New York. His bravery made him beloved by his men. His wisdom inspired others to follow him, even to death. His commanding officers often said he was one of their best assets.'"

Oliver groaned and sank into the seat behind his desk. His grandfather was everything he had written, yet it was so flat on the page. It conveyed none of the spark that had captivated him as a boy. He had seen men laugh uproariously at campfire tales and sob over the losses they had endured. He knew of some men who refused to even speak of their worst experiences because the pain was too deep. Yet his words were stilted, dry, and emotionless on the page.

He removed his spectacles and leaned back in his chair, scrubbing his hands down his face in frustration. He felt like he had not moved from this spot in the last two weeks, yet he had nothing to show for his efforts. His household staff had ensured he was eating and sleeping at semi-regular intervals, but his entire focus had been on committing his grandfather's stories to paper. He had written down notes, researched campaigns, and visited with Grandfather's men-at-arms both in the past and again not so long ago. He had solicited interest in the idea of developing a soldiers' home, but he had realized quickly that he needed more. He needed something he could place in an investor's hands that would convince them of the worthiness of his proposal and, thus far, he had been incapable of writing it.

He stood and moved away from the desk, again running his hands through his hair, and leaned against the window to watch the bustle on the street below. He knew that there were those in the crowds who needed help, and he knew there were those who had the means to help them. He wanted to use the war stories of his grandfather and other men like him to create a fund that would provide support for the men who had returned from the continent to debt and poverty instead of adulation. It was common knowledge that many enlisted men joined the fight with the goal of elevating themselves, but that was a dream out of reach for most who enlisted from the working classes. His grandfather had been among the fortunate, a son of a titled landowner who could return to a life of ease on one of his father's properties. Many were not as fortunate as his grandfather and uncle. There was the Chelsea Royal Hospital, of course, but its reach and resources were limited. He wanted to try to meet the needs of those who had exhausted their other options and had still come up lacking.

He tried not to dwell on the casualties, but some stuck with him. As it had so many times before, his mind drifted to Jacob Stafford. Stafford had been his best friend in his first years at Cambridge. Though he came from a lower station, his grandfather having been a blacksmith and his father a sailor in the Navy, Jacob had earned a scholarship to attend the university and had hoped to dedicate his life to the church. He never got the chance. During their second year, he was called home to care for his father and he never returned. Oliver had visited him later that year and what he saw had changed him. The elder Stafford had sustained horrific burns to one side of his body in an engagement with a French frigate while on board the *HMS Amelia*. Though nursed well enough to return home he never fully regained his health or mobility.

Oliver had tracked down Stafford's home address through school records and had arrived at the small cottage on the southern coast with no warning. After he learned of the situation, Oliver stayed at a local inn for several weeks and helped where he could, but it became clear quickly there was little he could do. What had surprised Oliver the most was not Jacob's departure from school nor his decision not to return, but rather the fact that there was little to no assistance offered to the family. He had a sixteen-year-old sister and a fifteen-year-old brother, both of whom had been maintaining the family farm with small amounts of money sent home from their father and occasional financial assistance from their grandfather when needed.

Oliver had left after a rather heated argument with Jacob that had made Oliver feel ashamed of himself for his naiveté about the precariousness of the financial situations for many below his station. Oliver had certainly never been one to shirk his responsibilities, whether to family or to school, but he had also never been in danger of poverty or losing his home. As such, his solutions looked to others—family members or the Navy—to provide for Jacob's family, but Jacob had known what Oliver did not. There was no relative that could help them, and no one at the War Office was going to go out of their way to ensure the family of an injured sailor was cared for. Jacob put aside his desire for a life in the church and took over the family farm.

That had been five years ago. Oliver and Jacob exchanged letters a few times a year and Oliver had even visited again a few years ago, but their relationship was not the same. Oliver longed to help but had little capital to his name and knew Jacob's pride would not allow more than an occasional basket of treats sent from London. He had returned to Cambridge with a renewed sense of responsibility to make something of himself and with the seed of an idea. The intervening years had fostered a continuing sense of self-reliance in Oliver and the burgeoning idea had grown into an obsession to build a soldiers' home.

A small cough sounded from the door and he started before turning to find his butler, Jennings, in the doorway. "My apologies for the intrusion, Mr. Marten, but Mrs. Webb requested that I ensure you ate supper while it was still hot. Shall I have someone bring you a tray?"

His housekeeper, Mrs. Webb, would ensure everyone passing on the street was fed a hot meal at her table if it were up to her. Her terse manner and rigid attitude towards cleanliness were intimidating to some of the younger and newer staff members, but Oliver had known her since he was a child and knew a soft heart hid beneath the brusque demeanor.

He ran his hand through his hair again, surprised that it was already so late in the day. Now that it had been brought to his attention, he realized the shadows in the room were increasing and that he was quite hungry. "Please ask Cook to send a tray up to my chambers and I will eat there. And be sure to thank Mrs. Webb for me."

Jennings bowed and left, pulling the door shut behind him.

Oliver gazed once more out the window into the distance where he imagined he could see the tops of the sailing ships in the harbor. Once he had the soldiers' narratives written down, he felt sure he could convince others of his plan's value. He could help secure a future for men who had given up everything to serve. He could provide a direction for himself at the same time. If only he could tell their stories.

Chapter 3

The stately British Museum appeared ahead of them as Evelyn walked arm in arm with her friends down the street amidst a sea of passersby. The château had once been home to the Duke of Montagu, but now its parlors held Egyptian Mummies and musty archives rather than afternoon callers. The Museum had opened decades before and this was certainly not Evelyn's first stroll across its large courtyard and grand interior.

"It shouldn't be too hard to find him," Sophia remarked as they mounted the steps.

Charlotte finished, "He's nearly always in the Reading Room."

The three ladies entered the building and nodded at the clerk, who returned the gesture with a smile. The Montgomery sisters regularly visited their brother in his favorite refuge, often on missions just like their current one.

Evelyn marveled at the displays as they walked the halls. Wood shelves held thousands of volumes of books on the first floor, giving the impression of a library as opposed to a museum. In addition to his responsibilities caring for their estate and serving in the House of Lords, her father had a love of antiquities that had brought them to the British Museum many times in her life. She would spend hours in the galleries with him, admiring the Greek and Roman statues. He had certainly passed on his love of the arts and established a bond of love between them at the same time. As a daughter born between two sons, the heir and the spare, Evelyn had never been as close to her father as her brothers were, especially as adults, but she was the only one of them to have the memories they had made on their trips here when she was a child.

They moved through the numerous shelves of books to a large staircase. Holding tightly to the railing as she mounted the steps, Evelyn took in the large depiction of Phaethon and Apollo on the ceiling above. The ladies walked across one of the first gallery rooms full of large cases with objects from the Americas and New Zealand on display. The twins paid little attention to the cases, having no real interest in their contents, but Evelyn lagged behind looking over the trinkets and artwork from distant lands. She could not imagine traveling so far or living somewhere so foreign when England was all she had ever known, but the art intrigued her nonetheless.

Just ahead of her, Charlotte and Sophia pushed open the doors to the Reading Room. Breathing deeply, Evelyn inhaled the familiar smell of old books, ink, and dust that greeted them upon entry. Sunlight filtered through the windows, illuminating the shelves piled high with boxes that surrounded the tables and chairs in the center of the room. The room seemed empty upon first glance, but a steady sound of tapping revealed a presence.

Evelyn looked toward the noise and saw blond hair just visible above an array of boxes spread across a table in the corner. Moving closer, she saw the fingers of a finely manicured hand tap a rhythm on the table. Eyes she knew to be blue scanned yellowed pages that were covered in a looping script. She watched as he paused to write his own scribbled notes on a separate page.

As she observed the peaceful scene, Evelyn doubted herself for the millionth time since devising her plan. *There's no way he will ever stop seeing me as a friend, or worse, a sister, and consider me for a wife,* she thought. Having known Sophia and Charlotte since childhood, she had always been friendly with their older brother William as well. But she had recently devised a plan that would take them beyond the level of friendship. As she approached her fifth year in town unmarried, she had become increasingly anxious at her lack of offers. She had not lacked for suitors, but all had eventually moved on with no explanation. While her personality or her dowry-or both-had been enough to draw interest, it had never been enough to secure her an offer of marriage.

"William, what in Heaven's name is all over your hands?" Charlotte moaned, bringing Evelyn out of her thoughts.

Startled, the man in question dropped his pages. He looked up at his sisters and down at his ink-smudged hands, raising his shoulders guiltily as he reached for a handkerchief. His efforts to clean the worst of his fingers succeeded only in soiling the linen and he gave up the useless battle. His eyes gleamed with good humor as he surveyed his younger sisters, who both glared at him in return.

"Come girls, wouldn't you like to give your dear brother a warm hug?" He pushed back his chair and moved towards the young ladies with his hands outstretched before him.

Sophia squealed in a most undignified manner and moved behind Charlotte, holding her in front of her as a shield. Their glares turned to laughter, as they moved backwards to avoid his gestures, until he stopped the charade, dropping his hands to his sides and laughing with them.

He smiled fondly at his sisters and turned to Evelyn to offer a proper greeting. He bowed slightly at the waist and grinned as he spoke. "It is always a pleasure to see my *favorite* sister. How is your family, Evie?"

Evelyn nodded a greeting and smiled at his use of her nickname. "My Mother and Father are both well, as are James and John. James has just returned from our country estate, and I'm sure he would be pleased to hear from you."

"I'd love to see him again and perhaps beat him at a few games of chance!"

"You know Mother hates when you talk of such things. It really is most shocking." Sophia scolded her brother in words, though her tone remained teasing.

"What missive does Mother send today?" he asked. He leaned casually against a table, his arms crossed comfortably across his brown waistcoat. Despite his rather unconventional academic interests, no one could accuse William of sacrificing fashion expectations to his hobby. His clothes were cut of the finest fabrics, tailored to his lean frame in all the most flattering styles and colors.

"She requests your presence at dinner tomorrow night. You and Adam both," Charlotte answered.

"I think she wants to discuss our plans for the upcoming weeks," Sophia added. "Apparently we were not 'successful' last year and she wants to enlist your assistance in finding eligible young men who are willing to attach themselves to us." Sophia peered down her nose in an imperious manner, mimicking the higher-pitched voice of her mother as she spoke. She followed the sentence with a dramatic flick of her fan to punctuate her mock annoyance.

"Mother misses you," Charlotte said, in a much gentler tone. "While I agree she may also be disappointed that at least one of us did not marry last year, she has hardly said so in as many words."

"One of us?" cried Sophia. "I have made it perfectly clear to anyone who will listen that I shall not marry until you do. I shudder just thinking about having to live apart, let alone if you are still at home with no new husband and family of your own." The outspoken twin instinctively reached for her sister's arm and looped hers through it, drawing her closer.

"I love you too, Sophia," Charlotte soothed with a soft laugh, squeezing her sister's arm.

"I don't know what your mother is worried about," Evelyn interjected into the sisters' banter. "You both had dozens of men calling all last Season. I am sure you will both receive offers this year."

"Not if Sophia scares them all away!" William laughed. His gaze on his sisters held fondness, even while he teased further. "Any two men would be terrified to offer for the both of you out of fear that one would die from too much talking and the other from not enough!"

He turned to Evelyn before either woman could contradict him, and asked, "And what of you, Evie? What are your thoughts on the upcoming Season?"

Evelyn froze, her mouth slightly open in an unbecoming manner. *I hope to make you see me as an eligible wife*, hardly seemed an acceptable answer, though it was exactly what she hoped.

Evelyn had spent weeks last year in despair over her failed Seasons. Eventually, her optimistic disposition had won out and she had emerged from her despair with a plan. She had mentally compiled a list of eligible men and narrowed it down to those she felt were most likely to return her interest. From there she considered everything from social rank to fashion sense and temperament and had concluded that William was her best choice. She could not remember ever having had any truly meaningful conversations with him, nor did she think they shared many interests outside of the museum, but she was desperate.

"Do you think any two men will fall for my sisters?" he prompted. He looked at her with an odd expression and she realized she had taken her thoughts in a far different direction than he had intended.

Evelyn pasted on a smile and forced a light laugh. "I think any man would be lucky to lose his heart to one of them. I only hope that he meets the approval of the other, or he may as well consign himself to an early grave." She turned her eyes to the twins, still standing arm in arm and grinned.

They all laughed. Sophia's fun-loving antics as a child had rivaled those of the boys on her father's estate. She was quick to laugh and to play tricks on her family members, but nothing would raise her ire so fast as an unkind word towards her twin.

William walked to the door ushering the girls ahead of him. "Tell Mother I will see her tomorrow and will try to bring Adam with me as well. And ask Cook to make me some of the tarts I love!"

Charlotte stood on her tiptoes and pecked his cheek, "Of course, Will. Mother will be pleased." She smiled at him, content that they had succeeded in their simple mission.

As they moved to leave the room, the doors ahead of them

opened. A dark-haired man wearing a modest blue coat and spectacles pushed into the room with a stack of papers in his arms and paused when he saw that it was occupied. His hesitation, however, was short-lived as recognition lit his face with a smile.

"William Montgomery! I haven't seen you in ages!"

William rushed towards the gentleman with a matching smile and clasped his hand in greeting. "Why does it not surprise me that I should find my most bookish friend in a reading room! Oliver, my friend, you should be gracing the parlors and ballrooms of London, not the libraries!"

"I might point out that it takes two to meet in such a place," the man retorted. "But I am so pleased to see you, I won't even argue with you over which of us was more bookish!" he teased.

As both men laughed, the newcomer turned his intense dark eyes towards the ladies behind William. Noticing the shift in his attention, William turned around and gestured to the women.

"Have you met my sisters? I guess not given your proclivity for libraries over ballrooms," he answered himself before the other man could respond. "Mr. Oliver Marten, allow me to introduce you to my twin sisters, Misses Sophia and Charlotte Montgomery."

The women dipped into curtsies and smiled at the man. "It is always a pleasure to meet one of William's school friends," Charlotte said.

"Yes, so that we might pepper them with questions about Williams's behavior when he was at school," Sophia added with a smirk.

"I'd be happy to regale you with stories of your brother's escapades at Eton, though truly neither of us got up to as much trouble as some of our classmates. You may tire quickly at how many tales begin or end in the kitchens." Despite the lighthearted words, his tone was reserved as if he was unsure if he should join in the banter.

"We may be bored with the stories, but we would certainly not be surprised. William has always had quite a sweet tooth," Charlotte teased, smiling at her brother.

As they laughed, Oliver looked at William and remarked, "I don't remember you having another sister. All of your tales of home featured either the twins or your older brother. Adam, right?"

"My apologies for the oversight, but your memory is correct. I sometimes forget that Evie is not related because she has been like a sister to all of us for so many years." William turned an affectionate look on Evelyn.

"Mr. Marten, this is Miss Evelyn Berkeley. Our family lands border one another, and so our families have been close for many years."

She smiled, but inwardly groaned at his second sister reference of the day. Sisters were not marriage material. She was going to have to change his perspective if she stood any chance.

Evelyn dipped an appropriate curtsy in response to Oliver's small bow, but her full attention remained on William. "Come now, we are no longer children, William! We are more like friends than siblings, surely!" she countered, placing her hand lightly on his arm. Her voice sounded unnaturally high and light, even to her own ears, but she desperately wanted him to view her as an eligible young woman, not as a sister.

William appeared unaffected by her act. He distractedly patted her hand on his arm before turning his attention back to Oliver.

"What brings you to London and the Reading Rooms?"

Was it her imagination or did Oliver look guilty as he glanced down at the papers in his hand? Evelyn watched him as he shifted the stack behind his back and rocked on his heels. "I am as 'bookish' as ever, as you say," he responded with a slight grin. "I am currently reading up on our military exploits across the water. I write and occasionally speak on our involvement on the Peninsula...and in the Americas." The latter seemed almost an afterthought. "My father despairs of my ever leaving Cambridge and has given me up as a lost cause."

"So you are here in London, then? Fantastic! You must join us for dinner tomorrow. My mother has just sent the girls on a quest to fetch me and Adam home for the meal; it would be much more fun with your company. You will let Mother know, will you not, ladies?"

"Of course," responded Sophia, beaming at Oliver. "Mama will be happy to have you along with Will and Adam. And Evelyn, you must join us as well to round out the party. We will have such fun!" Sophia delighted at the idea of such a lively evening rather than a dull family dinner.

"Well, it's settled then." William clapped his hands together and smiled at his friends and family.

"Since your sisters are confident it will not be an imposition, I would be honored to spend the evening with your family. And Miss Evelyn, of course." His piercing gaze took in all those gathered, adding another slight bow to Evelyn as he spoke.

Evelyn gave him a tight-lipped smile in return but quickly turned her gaze towards her friends. "Ladies, shall we continue with our plans for shopping? Surely the men have more important things to do now than to continue exchanging pleasantries with us!" Evelyn moved towards the door behind Oliver and pulled it open. Sophia and Charlotte each squeezed their brother's hand on their way past and acknowledged Oliver with a nod. Evelyn followed her friends out of the room and could hear the men's voices in conversation as the door closed.

"What a handsome dinner companion," Charlotte commented in a quiet voice as they moved through the echoing chambers of the museum back down to the first floor.

"If you like the tall, dark, and brooding sort, I suppose." Sophia cocked her head to the side considering the statement. "I much prefer a lighter and less serious look, if I'm to describe my preference. What did you think, Evie?"

"Oh, I agree with you, Sophia. He is handsome enough, certainly, but I'd like someone with whom I feel more at ease. He was so serious. It's a wonder he and your brother were friends given William's light-hearted nature."

"Let us not be too quick to judge," Charlotte chided quietly as they approached the door. "Surely Will is a good judge of character so I will reserve my opinion for when I've come to know him better."

Feeling slightly chastised, Sophia and Evelyn were silent as they exited into the bright morning sunshine. While Evelyn had no strong feelings against him, she had no interest in getting to know Oliver better. With her sights set on marriage, she sought only a way to convince William of the merits of her plan.

Chapter 4

Evelyn's eyes widened as she looked at her reflection in the mirror when Marie stepped away. "My hair looks lovely, Marie," she commented, choosing to focus on the positives of her reflection instead of her pastel pink gown. She smoothed the front of the gown and turned to the side to see herself from all angles. No matter which way she turned, the overall effect was of some sort of sweet confection that might be sold at Gunter's. The pink underlay of the skirt was covered with a lighter pink lace accented with far too many small white flowers. Between the dress itself, the pink flowers Marie had woven into her coiffure, and her flame-red hair, Evelyn looked as though she would taste of cinnamon if she actually were a confectionary.

"Why do you not request different colors, my lady?" Marie spoke softly while tidying the vanity to avoid eye contact.

Although her mother would admonish the girl for such thinly veiled criticism, Evelyn knew it came from a desire to help.

Evelyn pasted on her society smile and forced Marie to meet her eyes. "It is not worth the fight, Marie. I used to...but Mother always said she knew best what society wanted. According to her," she adopted a high-pitched voice, "pink is the best color for a demure young lady of the highest standing looking to engage a husband." She twirled for effect in front of the mirror and laughed. "I am not sure I am either demure or young, but I *am* still trying to engage a husband." She looked back at Marie, touched by her concern. "Do not worry, Marie, it makes her happy to feel that she is helping me in the only way she knows how. It is far easier to go along with it."

Marie did not look convinced but said no more on the subject as Evelyn grabbed her reticule from her bed and headed downstairs. A footman met her at the bottom of the stairs and informed her that the Montgomery carriage had just arrived. She put on her gloves and bonnet as she exited, nodding at the footman who helped her into the vehicle.

Charlotte and Sophia's smiles greeted her moments later as the same footman helped her down at the door of their townhouse. The sisters looked beautiful in complementary dresses and matching hairstyles that pulled their hair back elegantly in an intricate pile of curls with ribbons and flowers woven throughout. Charlotte's rose-colored gown featured delicate green trim work at the bodice and cuffs, while Sophia's was identical in all but color scheme; hers featured rose accents on a green gown.

Evelyn smiled at their different yet coordinated choices of dress and thought how wonderful it must be to have such a closeness with someone. She loved her family, but never felt such depth of connection with any of them. Her brothers were kind to her, but neither one would ever seek her companionship over that of either each other or their school friends. Her mother focused on imparting social and domestic expectations and attempting to get her successfully married, yet she paid little attention to her daughter's hopes and dreams for her own future. Evelyn often wondered what it would be like to be first in someone's estimation rather than second or third.

The twins separated as Evelyn moved up the stairs and each took one of her arms to lead her inside. A young man took her gloves and bonnet as she entered, then the three proceeded up the staircase into the family drawing room where the immediate family was already gathered. The cheery room was lit by the late afternoon sun streaming through the wide windows facing their small garden behind the townhouse. Tall ceilings gave the reasonably small room a sense of being larger than it was. Evelyn moved towards a settee arranged within a cozy circle around the center of the room. Lady Montgomery was seated in a wingback chair and Evelyn leaned down to grab her hands and bestow a kiss on the cheek of the mother of her best friends. She nodded to Lord Montgomery, who stood quietly behind her in front of the fireplace, allowing his wife the attention she so enjoyed.

"Evelyn, it is so good to see you," she cooed as if she had not just seen her the previous week. The matriarch wore a stylish gown of deep purple trimmed with lace and an elaborate matching turban that completed her rather dramatic look. She fanned herself as she held court from the central position in the room. Evelyn smiled at her reception and perched on the edge of the settee while trying not to be obvious as she looked about for William.

"How are you, Lady Montgomery? Is the Season treating you well?" she asked politely.

"Oh tolerably, I suppose. We are so busy with visitors and invitations nearly every day it seems. How I long for the quiet of the country." She glanced up as the door opened and three gentlemen entered the drawing room. "Ahh, I see my boys have finally decided to grace my doorstep." She closed her fan and rapped it on her hand for emphasis sending a glare across the room, though it seemed her ire did not quite reach her eyes.

The tallest of the three quickly moved towards Lady Montgomery and dramatically went down on one knee before the older woman. His clothing was of the finest cut and colors, marking the wealth of his family. He wore brown breeches and a dark blue jacket with neatly arranged blond curls just barely brushing its collar. His blue eyes sparkled as he bowed before his mother.

"Will you ever forgive me, Mama, for daring to move out of your loving home?"

"Oh, stand up you silly boy," she replied, laughing. She thumped her fan on his knee as she spoke, and he stood, kissing her cheek as he did so.

Evelyn smiled at the antics of the oldest Montgomery child. He had always been kind and protective of his younger siblings and had risen to the responsibility befitting his inheritance from a young age. He had become betrothed just weeks before to a beautiful woman whose family hailed from their home county. Evelyn had always admired Adam's confidence and the way he seemed to know how to act or what to say in any situation. She had never been as close to him as she had the twins, of course, but she had looked up to him nonetheless.

Her gaze moved to William who stood with Oliver just inside the door, watching the encounter with a smile. She studied him while she knew he was not looking her way, and pondered how she could alter their relationship enough for him to see the merits of her plan. As she deliberated, she felt the unmistakable sense of someone staring at her and shifted her gaze to Oliver. She blushed as their eyes met and he ever so slightly arched a dark brow as if to acknowledge that he'd seen her obvious perusal of his friend. Evelyn quickly looked away from the judgment in his demeanor and joined in the laughter at Adam's behavior.

William moved towards his mother with Oliver at his side and both gave a simple bow to Lady Montgomery.

"Mother, you remember my friend from school, Mr. Oliver Marten." Oliver reached out to take her hand, bending low over it in greeting.

"Of course," she exclaimed. "Mr. Marten joined us for two weeks one summer when you were both still in school. What a pleasure to see you again, sir. What have you done since last I saw you?" She gestured to the seat on the other side of her, and Oliver lowered onto the chair.

"He is getting up to no good, of course," William interjected before he could answer. "I found him at the British Museum yesterday."

Lady Montgomery frowned at her son, "Let him speak, young

man. How is your family? They live at Blackwood Hall, if I remember correctly."

"Yes, ma'am. That is, my father and stepmother are at Blackwood Hall. I had been residing at my grandfather's estate, Longwood, up until his passing earlier this year. I decided, after the appropriate time of course, to come back to London for the Season." A shadow passed over Oliver's face as he spoke of his family, but it passed quickly and he turned to William and quipped, "Your son interrupted me as I was trying to research family business, as a matter of fact." A slight grin turned up the corner of his mouth, making him appear less serious and more approachable.

"Family business?" William retorted, "Family stories, more likely."

"I am looking into some family history," Oliver explained at Lady Montgomery's questioning look. "My grandfather was quite the storyteller and I'm looking into some records to see what information I can find to corroborate his tales. Quite boring stuff, I assure you, but good for posterity. And what of you, William? I never did find out what you were doing knee-deep in ancient manuscripts."

"Nothing quite so glorious as battle records, I assure you," William quipped. "I was looking into the political history of the English monarchy and its positions on...oh, never mind, it is boring politics not fit for ladies' ears. Oliver and I can discuss our interests later. Ladies, what did you most enjoy at the museum?" William looked directly at Evelyn, Charlotte, and Sophia in turn, obviously hoping to redirect the conversation.

"The jewels!" chimed the twins in unison.

William narrowed his eyes as if scrutinizing the girls. "Do I need to alert the guards to double-check their inventory?"

Sophia looked everywhere but at William and put her hands behind her back. "I have no idea what you could possibly mean," she stammered.

Charlotte playfully slapped her sister on the arm as everyone laughed.

William looked towards Evelyn. "And you, Evie? Do you enjoy the diamonds as well?"

"The diamonds are impressive for sure, but my favorites are the Egyptian mummies," she replied with eagerness. "I am fascinated by the thought of who they once were. What were their lives like? How did they die? I could examine them for hours just imagining their lives."

Charlotte, Sophia, and William laughed at her enthusiasm, bringing another blush to Evelyn's cheeks.

"Yes, I know," she laughed. "It is rather silly to make up imaginary stories based only on the remains." She looked down at her feet, regretting that she hadn't sat facing the clock, so she would know if dinner would be announced soon enough to divert all attention away from her. She risked a glance at William, but he had moved into conversation with his brother across the room. From the corner of her eye, she caught Oliver watching her watching William. And again, he arched that same blasted eyebrow.

She attempted a haughty and disinterested look and turned to engage Charlotte in conversation, but not before she caught what looked like a smirk on Oliver's face.

After a few more minutes of friendly chatter, Lady Montgomery signaled and she and her husband led the way into the dining room, followed by the twins with their brothers, leaving Evelyn and Oliver to bring up the end of the line. He approached her and held out his arm, which she politely took for their brief walk through the halls, moving away from him once in the dining room. The Lord and Lady sat at opposite ends of the table, with Adam and William on either side of their father. The twins sat next to William, and, despite her attempt at distance, Evelyn found herself next to Oliver for the duration of the meal.

As a footman pulled out her chair, she frowned as she tried to figure out how she could engage William from so far away. If only he, rather than Oliver, had escorted her in. There was nothing wrong with Oliver, he was simply a distraction from her goal. Besides, he seemed so serious. Evelyn had seen him frown or smirk more often than anything else so far, so it did not seem that he would be enjoyable dinner company.

By halfway through the second course, Evelyn was convinced she was right. Charlotte and Sophia conversed primarily with one another, bringing her in occasionally only to settle a minor disagreement over invitations, dress fashions, or society gossip. When she turned to Oliver to ask him questions about himself, his answers were disinterested at best.

"Your family is from Suffolk?" She asked.

"Yes, our estate is not too far from Ipswich." He put a bite of duck in his mouth as if to punctuate his sentence.

She waited for him to finish, then asked, "And do you like the country or do you prefer being in Town?"

He paused and looked at her as if trying to ascertain why she continued to speak to him, then responded, "I like the country, but I need to be in London for now."

"Ah yes, the family records. What type of stories did your grandfather share that caught your interest?" she asked before he could take another bite.

His brow furrowed, but he answered, "He told of his time in His Majesty's service."

She continued to look at him, waiting for some sort of elaboration, but he took another bite and looked away.

Undeterred, she pushed on. "What is it you hope to learn from the records?"

He wiped his mouth with his napkin before leaning close and whispering, "What is it you hope to learn with this line of questioning given your obvious intentions toward William?"

As she sat in shock, she felt her mouth drop open and quickly snapped it shut, bringing her napkin to her face to cover her discomfiture. After a moment she quietly replied, "I have no idea what you mean. William and I have known one another for years so any attention I may give him is that of a long-time friend, nothing more. Not that it is any of your concern," she added.

She ate her third course in angry silence while Oliver spoke briefly with Adam on his other side. She studiously avoided looking in William's direction for the next half hour, focusing instead on Lady

Montgomery, who wanted to discuss the latest assortment of laces she had seen at her modiste the previous week. While not the most exciting topic, it was easy to keep up an agreeable commentary while she elaborated on the proper number and type of ribbons that should adorn one's bonnet for various social outings.

When dessert was served, Lady Montgomery exchanged her interest in ribbons for pastries, allowing Evelyn to quietly enjoy her own sweets.

"I did not mean to cause offense," Oliver whispered from over her left shoulder. "A young lady such as yourself could do much worse than a man like William...though he can be a bore when he drones on about politics."

Evelyn glanced at him and found he was actually smiling. It was only a slight smile, but it did make him seem a little more agreeable.

"I do not find him to be a bore," she retorted, immediately regretting her response for its implied admiration. She flushed again, and added, "He is my friend."

"He is my friend too, but he can still be a bore. I simply mean that any young lady who marries him will need to be prepared for much rambling," he grinned. He lowered his voice and added, "I think he simply enjoys hearing himself talk."

Evelyn didn't know if it was the accuracy of the statement about William or the full grin on Oliver's face, but she could not help but smile herself. Even as a young man, Charlotte and Sophia despaired of his "lectures," when he read something new and insisted on sharing it with them. "Any young woman in love with him would surely be happy to listen to him 'ramble,' as you say." She assured him.

"In love? I thought you said he was your friend?" His grin was now back to a smirk as he raised his glass and took a drink.

"I did not say *I* am in love with him, I simply said a woman who married him would no doubt be in love and would therefore enjoy his interests." It seemed she was to spend the duration of this dinner flushed, no matter how she tried to calm herself with her own small sips of wine.

"Would she? Are you so sure that he will marry for love? In my experience, it is better to marry for security - both his and hers - than for any false notion of love." All sign of a smile was now gone, replaced by the furrowed brow. Was the man ever happy?

"Why would he not marry for love? Adam's betrothal is a love match and William certainly still has time to find a woman who loves him as he loves her," she argued.

"And are you sure that is not you?" Oliver queried quietly with the arched eyebrow she was quickly growing to despise, before turning away to question Adam about the upcoming hunting Season on the Montgomery's country estate.

Evelyn finished her dessert in silence and this time did not avoid letting her gaze move towards William. Did she love him? She could, she supposed. She thought of her mother and father, who still seemed fond of one another after decades of marriage, but she had trouble replacing their faces with hers and William's as an older married couple. She thought of her favorite novels and their descriptions of love. Certainly, there were no fireworks when he was near. She felt no butterflies in her stomach, and she had never forgotten to breathe when she looked at him—or anyone else, for that matter.

She sipped her wine as she thought about her plan. She wanted to be married, and she felt William was her best chance. Of course, she would prefer a love match, but she could be happy in a marriage of convenience. Couldn't she? She thought again of the books she had read and smiled as a new idea dawned. She could write her own story. She would write a love story for herself, with William, and then do everything she could to make it come true.

She glanced down the table, itching to retrieve the papers from inside her reticule and begin writing. She was pleased to see Lady Montgomery set aside her napkin and stand signaling the end of the meal. Everyone quickly followed suit and the group moved collectively into the drawing room.

"I hope you ladies do not mind if we stick around this evening. Given our small numbers, I am sure we do not need to stand on formality. I for one am up for a game of piquet. Who will join me?" Lord Montgomery's suggestion met no opposition from the small gathering. The staff arranged several tables and Lord Montgomery soon squared off against Adam, William against Oliver, and Charlotte against Sophia. Lady Montgomery, much like Evelyn, was not a fan of piquet and contented herself to sit in front of the fire and only watch the proceedings with vague interest.

"And what of you, Miss Berkeley? Do you not play cards?" asked Oliver.

"I am not a fan of most card games," Evelyn responded, "though I do play on occasion; however, it appears tonight that my presence is superfluous." She smiled as she took a seat in a comfortable chair drawn up to a small table by the window.

"Superfluous?" Charlotte cried. "You are *not* superfluous, my dear, you are simply a bonus to our small party."

Evelyn smiled at Charlotte's attempt to make her feel included. She needn't bother though; Evelyn was used to feeling like a spare wheel and it no longer bothered her as it once had. She pulled out her pencil before her thoughts became too disconsolate. She began to write as the room settled into a comfortable calm. The chatter of the card game mingled with the crackling fire and the flipping of Lady Montgomery's fan. As was wont to happen, Evelyn soon became immersed in her writing and was startled by the sudden appearance of Oliver at her elbow. He peered over at her words and she shifted her body to try to block her writing.

"Am I in the company of the next Miss Radcliffe?" he drawled as she slid her papers underneath her reticule.

She hated that her heart pounded and the dreaded flush crept back up her neck. As much as she loved to write, the thought of strangers reading her writing filled her with dread. She managed a dismissive laugh, "Certainly not, sir. I write for my own pleasure, nothing more. I keep a diary, correspond with several friends and family members, and occasionally make observations about society, but I would not dream of writing as a profession."

She forced herself to stop fiddling with her pages and instead placed her hands in her lap and looked up to meet his eyes. She preferred him to think she had nothing to hide.

He shrugged and moved to sit in the seat opposite her at the small table. "I admire writers, as I am loathe to admit that I cannot count it among my own talents." He looked across the room and Evelyn thought she saw a look of pain, but it was quickly replaced with his apathetic visage as he turned back to her. "And what *do* you dream of, Miss Berkeley?"

Caught off guard by the question, Evelyn paused and cocked her head to the side considering her answer carefully. "A partner."

"A husband." he stated with a nod.

"Yes, and no," she responded haltingly. "I want a husband and children, of course; I long for a family of my own. But I wish my marriage to be a partnership, one built on love, respect, and support, to the mutual benefit of one another." Despite her calm words and calculated response, she knew her cheeks were still pink, but she did not shy away from her words, and instead met his eyes, challenging him to question her.

He rose to her challenge. "That is rather unconventional. What support do you have to offer a gentleman?"

"What do I have? What could a woman possibly know that her husband does not already, is that what you mean?" Her flush turned to one of anger as she sat straighter and moved to the edge of her chair. "Are you, sir, so arrogant that you could not acknowledge how a simple woman might have ideas, skills, or abilities that you do not? Can you not envision a world in which you might come down from your place in the clouds and lean on those around you, those who love you, for support? I do not speak of physical labor or dream that my husband might need my help balancing ledgers, but rather that I might be a sounding board when he is worried…or…a…a friendly face amongst a crowd of strangers." She stood, towering over him in his chair so closely that he could not stand as convention dictated.

"It was a pleasure to see you again, and I wish you luck on your family research." She dropped the smallest of curtsies and moved to the door making her excuses to Charlotte and Sophia on her way out.

Oliver sat silently for a moment, reflecting on where he had gone wrong with Miss Berkeley over the course of the evening. He had never prided himself on the small talk required of social settings and knew he had overstepped his bounds with his accusations at dinner, yet he seemed unable to *not* irritate her when they interacted. He did not care about her writing, yet he pushed her on the subject, and then essentially ridiculed her. True, he did not believe in such unrealistic dreams, but hers was not so different than many other young women. He glanced out the window, feeling remorse over his words, but unsure why her feelings mattered to him. As he looked away from the window, he noticed her notebook lying on the table under her reticule. He glanced at the other occupants of the room, but no one was paying him any attention. He stared again at the stack, knowing that the words were not his to read.

Her flushed, angry, yet beautiful, face came to mind and he could only imagine how much more livid she would be if she learned he had read her private musings. He looked away, then stared again at the small stack of pages. Finally, after what felt like days of indecision but was likely only a minute, he snatched the pages off the table and read the first words.

"A Love Story"
By Lady Cordelia Fitzgerald

"You only keep a diary and write letters, do you?" he muttered under his breath. He read a few sentences and saw that despite her protestations to the opposite, she was the heroine of her love story and William was the hero. He felt a pang of something at this realization but did not devote any time to considering what it meant.

He flipped a few pages and continued to read. Despite the circumstances of his surroundings and the forbidden nature of the words, he was entranced by her story. He read for several minutes and found himself alternately laughing and sympathizing with the characters of her story.

"Are you alright, Evelyn?" Charlotte's sweet voice cut through the room and pierced his concentration. He looked up and locked eyes with Evelyn, who stood frozen in the doorway.

He looked down at the papers in his hands and back up at her, guilt written across his face. He made a move to stand. "Miss Berkeley, I-"

She shook her head, managed a small smile towards Charlotte, and said, "I am fine, I simply came back for my reticule." Head up, but refusing to meet Oliver's eyes, she marched across the room, took her reticule from the chair where she had sat, and excused herself once more.

Oliver shut his eyes against the rising feeling of guilt. He should never have intruded on her privacy like that. Her pale face was seared into his mind. She had looked angry, yes, but more so she had appeared terrified. He gathered the pages and tucked them into his pocket, knowing that no one else had noticed their exchange. He rose to leave. He said his goodbyes to Lord and Lady Montgomery and made plans to meet Adam and William in the coming days.

As he stood in the foyer waiting for the groom to bring his carriage around, he devised a plan. They could help each other if he could convince her of the merits of his proposal.

Chapter 5

"A Mr. Oliver Marten is calling on Miss Evelyn," a footman relayed from the open doorway of the drawing room. "Are you at home, Miss?" He squinted slightly at the bright afternoon sun streaming through the room's large windows.

"Is she at home? Well of course she is at home for a gentleman caller," retorted Lady Berkeley in a piercing tone. The matron quickly set aside the fashion plates she had been perusing, and sat up in her chair, patting her coiffure to ensure it was neatly tucked in place. She did not even glance in Evelyn's direction and therefore missed the look of sheer terror that passed quickly over her face.

"Mama, I do not wish to see Mr. Marten," Evelyn began, but she got no further.

"Nonsense, child, of course, you do. You no longer have the luxury of patience, my dear. You know what they say about beggars." She looked at Evelyn imperiously and nodded as if to emphasize that she knew best for her daughter. "Who is he anyway?" she asked, almost as an afterthought.

Evelyn should not have been shocked to hear such demeaning platitudes from her mother, but her lack of subtlety was still surprising. She fought the desire to shrink back into her seat and wallow in embarrassment and instead sat forward, took a deep breath, and awaited the inevitable. "He is a friend of William Montgomery, Mama, and he is not at all agreeable."

"What an uncharitable thing to say about a young man you have only just met!" She lowered her voice to a whisper as she heard footsteps in the hall. "Are you not glad that I asked Marie to put you in such a lovely gown today?"

Evelyn just managed to not groan at the thought of how ill her pale skin had looked next to the pale yellow of the gown when she checked her reflection in the mirror that morning. She repressed a sigh. There was nothing to be done about it now.

Oliver entered and hesitated just inside the door to note the occupants of the room.

While custom dictated that he should greet her mother first, Evelyn realized that he had not yet been introduced. For a second she considered making him suffer in the awkwardness of the moment, but her years of practiced decorum forbid it.

"Mother, allow me to introduce a dear friend of William Montgomery, Mr. Oliver Marten. Mr. Marten, this is my mother, Lady Margaret Berkeley."

Without even a look in Evelyn's direction, Oliver moved to Lady Berkeley and offered a small bow in greeting. "How do you do? I am most grateful to you for allowing me to call so soon after meeting your daughter. I hope it is not too forward, but I would very much like to invite her for a ride through Hyde Park in my phaeton."

"I am so sorry to disappoint you, sir, but I am afraid that we have plans this evening and must rest beforehand. Perhaps another time." Despite her neutral words, Evelyn's tone said she hoped there would be no other time.

"Of course, you must ride in Hyde Park," contradicted Lady Berkeley. "It is a lovely day, and you do so *love* phaetons! We have plenty of time before dinner, my dear. Of course, you may ride. Enjoy yourselves!" She oozed sweetness as she looked back and forth between Evelyn and Oliver.

Evelyn remained silent for a moment, contemplating her options.

She did not want to speak with him, but she also had to admit to a bit of curiosity over what he had to say to her. Would he try to justify reading her writing? Would he reveal to William what she had written? Part of her would prefer to never find out and avoid all contact with him. Forever. But all she could do for now would be to claim a headache, and this was only a short-term solution, and also clearly a lie. Her mother would never let her avoid him twice, and she had a feeling Oliver would not be put off so easily.

As if sensing her hesitation, Oliver finally looked her way. A green jacket replaced the blue of the day before, but otherwise, he looked much the same as he had before. His brow was furrowed as if he could see no reason why she might not want to join him. Such arrogance! And would he continue to be this serious every time they met?

"Are you well, Miss Berkeley? You look pale."

Evelyn almost laughed at this confirmation of her own thoughts regarding her reflection, but instead smiled and assured him she was fine. "I am feeling quite well sir, but perhaps the fresh air will still do me good." She accepted the inevitable and stood. "I will just get my pelisse before we depart."

Oliver nodded and she stood to leave, glancing back to find him engaging her mother in casual conversation. As she walked up the stairs to her room, she thought back to the previous night and the sight of him reading her silly story. She groaned aloud in the hallway thinking of the romantic notions she had attributed to both herself and William as they fell in love in her story. What could he possibly want with her today?

She entered her room and took a bonnet from the wardrobe along with a white pelisse. She stopped and adjusted both in the mirror, pleased that she somehow looked less pale next to the white than next to the yellow shade of her dress. She did not care whether he found her attractive, of course, but she wanted anything that might bolster her own confidence for this outing. She would have an easier time handling his laughter, criticism, or anything else he might lob at her if she felt more sure of herself. With a pinch of her cheeks, she returned downstairs.

He rose from the seat next to her mother when she entered, and offered a small, approving nod. "You look lovely, Miss Berkeley." Was that a note of surprise she heard in his voice?

Her mother beamed as he moved to join her at the door and escort her to his awaiting phaeton. "Have a wonderful time, my dears," she crowed as they left the room.

They walked beside each other silently through the house and out the door held open by the butler. He offered her a hand to help her onto the high seat. She appreciated the strength of his hand and the steadiness it offered as she climbed into her seat. She pulled away from him as soon as she was settled, unnerved by the sudden flutters she felt at their contact. She glanced down at the street below and wished that she had not. He climbed into the seat beside her, rocking the carriage, and causing her to grab the edge for stability.

"My apologies, Miss Berkeley. I assure you that it will be a smooth ride once we begin moving."

Embarrassed, Evelyn pulled her hands into her lap and smiled tightly at him in response before staring straight ahead. He was not wrong, and the ride did become smoother as they moved along the crowded streets of London, but it did not settle her nerves. As he urged his matched pair into the first turn towards Hyde Park, the shifting motion again prompted her to grip the sides of the conveyance. He glanced her way, but said nothing, focusing instead on directing his phaeton through the traffic. At each shift, turn, or sway, Evelyn's breath caught and she held tighter to the vehicle. She tried to hide her reactions, but Oliver's sideways glances and silence led her to assume he had noticed but studiously chose not to comment.

She looked over at him as he drove and admired his confident bearing. Years of etiquette had taught her to carry herself with an easy lightness of manner as if unperturbed by the ebbs and flows of life. Yet she knew it was a façade and a thin one at that. Oliver's stoic demeanor conveyed a genuine unflappability. It was as if the tides of the London streets flowed around him. She was tossed about by the forces around her, but he seemed steady, like a rock. Between society's constraints and her mother's dictates, Evelyn never felt that level of confidence about her own life. Here she sat wearing a dress she hated, riding next to a man she barely knew and did not altogether like to whom she had inadvertently revealed her innermost desires. She wrote stories in which she alone controlled the outcomes because she had so little control in reality. Even as she watched the people pass by below, she nearly laughed at the thought that she could not even control her own stomach.

To her relief, she soon spotted the entrance to the promenade at Hyde Park. Rather than pull into the turn as expected, Oliver pulled the reins and came to a stop at the edge of the road some twenty yards shy of the entrance. He turned and looked directly at her for the first time since they left her home.

"Miss Berkeley, are you afraid of heights?" he asked.

Evelyn's eyes widened. She looked down at her hand, which was grasping the side of the phaeton as if it was a lifeline over a cliff's edge. She loosened her grip and placed her hand back into her lap properly before laughing. "I should like to deny the charge, but what would be the point in trying to save pride now?" She looked up and met his eyes, her face so pale, it matched her bonnet. "I do not like heights though I cannot explain to you why. My response to being even slightly elevated is irrational and verges on the ridiculous at times, yet I cannot seem to calm myself." She raised her chin at her admission as if daring him to laugh at her.

He tipped his head to the side. "Does your mother not know of this affliction?"

"Not know," she repeated with an unladylike scoff. "Of course, she knows. It is one of many deficiencies she sees in me on a regular basis." At this uncharitable mention of her mother, Evelyn's challenging air seemed to deflate.

"She knows, yet still encouraged you to ride with me today?" he pressed.

"Mama just wants to see me settled advantageously. All decisions are centered on that goal and something as trivial as fear will not stand in her way." Evelyn spoke with a laugh to dispel her own embarrassment over such a bold admission.

"I do not wish to make you uncomfortable, Miss Berkeley."

Evelyn laughed again, with a hint of sarcasm in her voice as she replied, "In what way do you not wish to make me uncomfortable, Mr. Marten? Do you mean by the phaeton ride? Or by invading my privacy? Or by questioning my feelings and thoughts on marriage?"

Oliver's dark eyebrows rose at her vehement response. "I did not realize that I had made so many mistakes in, what is it, just under three days?" The smirk appeared making him both attractive and infuriating at once. "I was referring to the discomfort of the phaeton, but believe me when I say that I have no desire to dissuade you from your goal of attaining a love match, as naïve as I believe that goal to be. I don't believe they exist, Miss Berkeley, but for your sake, I sincerely hope that I am wrong."

He glanced away and Evelyn detected a slight hesitation before he spoke. The smile was gone when he turned back to her.

"I am sorry for reading your writing. I should not have invaded your privacy like that, and I truly ask for your forgiveness." He looked directly at her as he spoke and Evelyn could sense his sincerity. She blushed, thinking of what she had poured onto the page about a fictional marriage with the very real William.

"Why did you do it?" she asked in a quiet voice. It was a question that had nagged at her all night.

He reached up and ran his hand along the back of his neck. He looked into the distance as if searching for an answer. Streams of carriages, hackneys, and pedestrians flowed by his phaeton as the two of them sat in silence.

"It is difficult to explain," he began. "My mother died when I was young, only twelve years old." Evelyn's brow furrowed in confusion at the odd direction of his answer, but she murmured her condolences as he continued his story.

"Before she died, we spent every summer with my grandfather at his estate, Longwood. I loved my grandfather. He was more of a father to me than my own. After my mother died, my father remarried within a year. With two older brothers, and half siblings on the way, I faded to the background of my father and stepmother's lives, but never my grandfather's. When I was sent away for school, I spent my holidays at his estate. He would tell me tales about his life in the King's service and how he fought in the Colonies. His son, my Uncle Jack, had followed in his footsteps and would entertain me with stories of his own. I could listen to them both for hours. At one point, I wrote to my father requesting my own commission to follow their lead, but he refused, pushing me instead towards the church."

Evelyn turned in her seat to face Oliver more directly, even though he looked away from her into the crowds while he spoke.

"I continued my studies at Cambridge, but I was directionless. I studied theology, history, Latin, philosophy...anything to keep me occupied. Then last year, my grandfather fell ill. I made it to Longwood before he passed and listened again as he told all of his old stories. I was reminded of how much I loved them. I tried to write them all down, in his words, as he told them for the last time, but he soon grew too ill to even speak."

Though she had only known him a short time, Evelyn somehow knew instinctively that Oliver was sharing more about himself than most people would learn from him in a lifetime. She had no idea where his narrative was going, but the storyteller in her was hooked.

"After his funeral, I returned to Cambridge and began seeking out other former soldiers, many of whom were friends of my uncle and grandfather. I filled pages of notes detailing their experiences, their injuries, and their fights for assistance when they returned. I have seen some who are still struggling with adjustments to civilian life and some who transitioned easily. Unfortunately, I see more of the former. I decided long ago to help these men who have given so much of themselves to our country, yet are often overlooked or tossed aside by society. I am gathering supporters to help fund a home that would provide a place to live and resources to help find work for these men as they transition."

Evelyn interjected, "That is brilliant! If it is needed, surely many in high society would love to contribute to be able to publicly demonstrate their virtue." She smiled as she thought of several ladies she knew who loved opportunities to show off their wealth and extol each other's goodness at the same time.

"I thought the same thing." The dejection in Oliver's voice surprised Evelyn. "I have struggled to find many who want to contribute. I am praised for my efforts by all, but the support ends with a handshake, not a donation."

Evelyn and Oliver sat in silence as she absorbed this information. After a moment she realized he was no longer gazing into the distance. He was staring at her with a look of expectation. "What does this have to do with why you read my notebook?" she asked again, this time with less hostility and more curiosity.

"I need your help," he declared by way of an answer. "I cannot write."

Evelyn's gaze fell for just a moment to Oliver's hands, still lightly clutching the reigns of his matching gray pair. She looked up at him with a questioning gaze. Oliver laughed humorlessly, and said, "My hands work just fine, Miss Berkeley; I meant it in a figurative sense." Evelyn's cheeks flushed at being caught with her initial assumption, but she laughed quietly.

"What do you mean you cannot write? And what does that have to do with me?" Evelyn asked again, to relieve her embarrassment.

"I have the notes, the stories, the knowledge, and the desire…I can interview people and learn their life's most intimate details. I can hear their words, even their voices, in my head, but when I try to put it all on paper, well, I can't. My writing is boring, flat, and completely without feeling. The only readers who would benefit from my writing are those suffering from bouts of sleeplessness." He tried to pull a half smile to deflect his despair, but it was clear from his tone that he was nearly disconsolate.

Evelyn looked at Oliver in shock. She was surprised at his revelation certainly, but more importantly, she was saddened at the level of despair she heard in his voice. He had only been serious and stoic before, yet now he had shown such surprising vulnerability, proving himself to be more sympathetic than she was currently comfortable with.

"Surely it is not as bad as all that," Evelyn said, attempting to deflect his criticisms. "Often I am harder on myself than anyone else, whether it is in relation to my writing, painting, or even playing of the pianoforte." She gave a rueful smile and added, "Especially my writing, though, since usually the only audience for that is me." She almost reached out and touched his arm in consolation, but clutched her reticule instead, and sufficed with an encouraging smile.

"You are right; I am my toughest critic, but I am not alone in my assessment. I have spent months approaching publishers, authors, and even friends to help me explore ways to bring these stories, and my ideas, to the public. All of them, including your dear William, have told me in varying degrees of politeness that I need to rewrite my essays, find another author, or just move on from my plans."

"He is not my William, dear or otherwise," Evelyn stated in a much less charitable tone than before. "Also, I still do not see what this has to do with me," she reminded him.

"Do you not?" Oliver asked. The expression he gave her was both regretful and contrite. "You are a writer."

Evelyn's look changed first to one of understanding followed immediately by one of incredulity. "You cannot be serious?" she cried. "You want me to write for you? I do not even know where to begin with the many reasons why that is not a good idea, but I assure you that it is not a good idea! I do not know the information, I have not met the people -"

"Wait!" Oliver put his hands up in front of her and she paused mid-sentence. "I had hoped to parade through Hyde Park and win you over, but clearly the first part of my plan did not work. Let us instead stroll through Hyde Park so that we might talk about this more thoroughly."

"I do not know what a walk will do to convince me of such a hare-brained idea, but I also find it hard to refuse with you if it means I can get down from this mountain of a vehicle."

His face broke into a grin at her honest admission, and he waved over a young boy selling flowers at the park's entrance. After negotiating to pay him half now and half upon his return, Oliver instructed the boy to hold onto his vehicle until he returned. Oliver made sure the amount was enough of an enticement to keep him there before offering Evelyn his arm as they moved through the entrance to the park.

The lanes and walkways were crowded with the members of society, emerging from their houses to enjoy fresh air, fine company and to see and be seen. Evelyn and Oliver moved along the pathways in silence for some time before Oliver spoke. "Miss Berkeley, while I should not have read your story, you must know that I found it delightful. You truly have a way with words, and that is saying something given that what I was reading was so frivolous."

"Frivolous?" she repeated. She looked at him aghast. "You are asking for my help and yet you call my writing frivolous? I will have you know that I was planning to submit that particular piece to the Royal Academy to be considered for academic publication."

Oliver grinned at her and visibly relaxed.

"Yes, frivolous. Anyone who would drone on about love and marriage in such detail is frivolous."

She sent him a scolding look. "We appear destined to disagree on the merits of marriage, Mr. Marten."

"Oh marriage has merits, Miss Berkeley, they are simply not those that you outlined in your prose. A wife and children are indeed advantageous to one's circumstances, particularly if a man can marry a woman of good standing. But a partnership and doe-eyed devotion like the one you described only belong in fairy tales. Marriage forces one to reveal their true motives, not those put on for society's sake. When pressed, everyone will reveal their self-serving desires regardless of how much they professed to love one another in courtship."

Evelyn cast her eyes sidelong at Oliver and shook her head. "You are rather cynical, sir. Perhaps you have not yet seen enough of love to truly recognize it."

"Perhaps not," he admitted, though his tone sounded unconvinced. "Regardless of my own views on the subject, I am not here to try to sway you from your heart's desires. In fact, quite the opposite." He drew her off the path and indicated a bench. "Shall we sit a moment?"

"And how do you know my heart's desires?" Evelyn asked as she sat down.

"I read them," he reminded her. "As I said, your tale was captivating. Even with a quick read at the Montgomery's, I could see your talent, but the more I read later, the more convinced I was."

"You read all of it?" she cried, raising her voice again in a combination of anger and embarrassment.

To his credit, he flushed, and looked down to avoid meeting her eye as he responded. "I couldn't help it! Reading your story transported me into some alternate place where I nearly forgot I knew the real characters. I wanted to know them better and learn their fate. I did not want to stop reading, even though I knew I should." He paused a moment, then asked, "Why did you sign as 'Lady Cordelia Fitzgerald?'"

She covered her mouth to smother a laugh. "It is such an elegant name that I decided to use it in place of my own. Besides, it is not as though ladies of society can publish under their own names."

She stood from the bench and took a few steps away to put distance between them as she processed her conflicting emotions. She was angry at him for picking up the pages and reading them, embarrassed at what he had read, and yet pleased to know he enjoyed it.

Without turning around, she asked, "Are you going to tell William?"

Oliver got up and walked until he was standing in front of her. She did not look up, but she could feel how close he was standing. "Miss Berkeley, I know you do not know me well, but please believe me when I say that I would never violate a confidence like that. It was not you who did wrong, but I." He reached out a gloved hand and tilted her face to meet his eye. "I will not tell William. I would not do anything to cause you embarrassment or scandal."

He did not remove his hand and Evelyn's breath caught at the frisson she felt at his touch. She drew a deep breath and felt her anger fade. She did not doubt his sincerity and was relieved she no longer needed to fear William learning of her plan.

A movement on the path near them broke the spell, and Oliver dropped his hand. She turned away from him and began to examine the blossoms on a nearby tree. He cleared his throat and approached the same tree, equally fascinated by its annual foliage. After a moment, Evelyn looked at him and asked, "How do you think I can help you?"

"I think we can help each other," he replied. "Forgive the very straightforward nature of my question, but am I right that you are in love with William, and hope to marry him?" He softened his tone and volume as if to soften the blow of such a blunt question.

"I am not in love with him, no, though I do hope that we might one day love each another." She could not meet his eyes as she answered. "I'm in my fifth year out, Mr. Marten. My parents despair of my ever marrying, and I must admit that I am beginning to understand their woe. Rather than trust fate again, I spent time this last year considering my options and decided that William is a fine choice. My only problem is that he sees me as more of a friend at best, and a sister at worst, not as a potential wife." She looked up at Oliver and smiled weakly to hide the tears she felt behind her eyes. "It seems that is how most men of my acquaintance see me, as I am able to count many men among my friends, but I have neither a husband nor a betrothed."

"Perhaps one day you will count me among those friends. I have known William for a long time, and think he is a good man. I intend to remain in Town for the duration of the Season, and while I cannot promise success, I will try everything in my power to make William see you as a potential wife."

"Why would you do such a thing?" Evelyn asked.

"Because William is a good man, and he deserves a good wife. And, perhaps, you might even find the love you seek."

"That does not sound like the self-serving interest you believe drives everyone," she retorted sarcastically.

Oliver chuckled and shook his head. "On the contrary, you would be helping me by writing, so it is still in my best interest." He hastened to keep talking as she attempted to interject. "I will give you all my notes, tell you all about my ideas and organization, and even take you to meet some of the people whose stories you'll be telling if you wish it. I could give you a portion of any profits I might make down the road, and of course, I would give you thanks in the preface." He finally paused and looked at her expectantly to gauge her reaction. "Well?"

"I think it is an awful idea, as you well know! I know nothing of the subjects on which you wish me to write. I write love stories and tales of adventures among forest creatures. I fear I cannot do justice to such an important topic," she exclaimed.

"Believe me that there is no way that your writing will not be an infinite improvement over mine!" He ran his hand through his hair. "What if we agree to a trial first? I will share information on a portion I have already written, and you will write your version. Once you are finished, I will show you my writing to compare it with yours. If yours is better, we can continue. If you feel it is not up to a high enough standard, we may part as friends, and go our separate ways."

She strolled around the area looking at the trees, the bench, the clouds, and the passersby as she considered his proposition. Evelyn had never allowed herself to dream of publishing her work as it was nearly unheard of for women. Even those who managed to overcome the social and gender barriers were often met with scorn and derision, particularly within High Society. Writing professionally was just not done. Yet this could give her a chance to see her writing in print. Granted, he would be credited as the author, but she imagined it would still be quite a thrill to see her words in a book. And then there was her own plan to consider. Oliver's encouragement may be just what she needed to get William to see her as a marriage prospect.

She turned back to face him. "I will agree to a trial phase for both of us. First, you must agree to give me back my pages the next time we meet." She paused expectantly until he nodded. "Secondly, I will attempt to write for you and you will attempt to convince William of my merits. If either of us wishes to end our agreement, we are free to walk away at any point. If, however, I do finish the book for you, I want a copy when it is published."

"And if I secure a marriage between you and William, what will I receive?" Oliver asked.

"An invitation to our wedding breakfast, I suppose," Evelyn answered with a smile.

"You have yourself a deal," Oliver said. His face broke into a full smile, and Evelyn briefly wondered how rare of a sight that was. He stuck out his hand and Evelyn reached to shake before she could change her mind. She felt the same jolt at his touch, and this time she quickly withdrew her hand.

Chapter 6

Evelyn and Oliver made plans to meet two days later at the British Museum. Oliver suggested it as a public spot where two people could bump into one another and talk briefly without attracting attention. Places like Hyde Park were certainly public, but their presence together would no doubt be remarked upon the more often they were observed together. It was the same for places like Gunter's. As Oliver pointed out, his efforts to assist Evelyn in a match would be thwarted if they were linked together in the gossip rags.

Oliver walked through the doors of the museum long before their scheduled meeting time. He had been awake since before dawn, anxious to give his notes to Miss Berkeley and see if she was the answer he hoped she would be. He was one of the first visitors through the door that morning, and he slowed his pace as he approached the top of the stairs to the second-floor galleries. He had spent hours in the Reading Room, but it had been years since he had taken the time to peruse the many cases and cabinets that filled the museum galleries.

He moved through the spaces filled with towering shelves of volumes comprising the original documents in the collection of the

British Museum. Rather than peruse the spines and get lost in the hundreds of volumes on such topics as the topography of Sussex or the history of Cambridge, he headed towards the next room and its cases of minerals and gems. It took him several minutes to make his way across the room, as he gazed upon diamonds from Brazil, meteors from Bohemia, and cobalt from Sweden. He pulled out some of the lower drawers from a few of the cases, examining the smaller collections of stones within.

The mineral displays were followed by what had been his favorite collections since his youth. He gazed up at a huge set of antlers once belonging to a species of deer attributed to Ireland, that was far larger than those he had seen on his own families' estates. He moved through the zoology displays, admiring brightly colored birds from around the world that had fascinated him for years. He had long considered the wide variety of species to be evidence of God's sense of humor.

Evelyn had not arrived yet as he made his way into the Department of Antiquities rooms. He stopped in front of a statue believed to be a muse. As he admired the figure, he heard her approach from behind. He felt rather than saw her move to stand next to him and turned to greet her.

She swept into a deep curtsy. "Good afternoon Mr. Marten." She gestured to the display before them. "What is your impression of the muse?" she asked.

He took her hand and bowed over it, but kept his eyes locked on her as he responded with a grin, "I am impressed by her loveliness as always, Miss Berkeley."

He enjoyed watching her flush at his teasing tone. He wasn't sure where the flirtation had come from, given his agreement to help secure William's hand. He pulled her hand through his arm, and they turned together to admire the marbles. Marie hung back, her quiet presence providing the chaperone society required.

They observed several statues in silence, stopping near two different depictions of Medusa. "That was never my favorite of the Greek myths," he commented. She tipped her head as if considering both his words and the figure before them.

"I appreciated the cleverness of Perseus in using her reflection, but I would expect nothing less of the son of Zeus," Evelyn responded.

They moved again, stopping in front of two more statues of the muses, one missing her hands and one missing her head. Oliver considered one of the female figures with her arm on writing tablets and thought of his own situation. There was a certain irony to having found Evelyn, his own muse of sorts, here inside the museum.

With that thought, he turned to face her and dropped her arm. He pulled a sheaf of papers from the bag he carried and held it out to her. "While I could peruse the galleries with you all day, Miss Berkeley, you must get home before anyone questions a casual trip to the museum. Here are your pages and a small selection of my notes to get you started."

She reached out for the stack, but he held on to his side of the bundle when she tried to pull it from him.

"I must have the papers to be able to write, Mr. Marten," she said with a teasing smile.

He did not return the smile but instead frowned. "It is hard to part with, Miss Berkeley. I am not sure I can convey how much these papers and these people mean to me. I long to be able to do them justice, and it is difficult to admit my inability to do so."

Evelyn tugged on the papers again, and this time he released them. She held them tightly to her chest and met his eyes. "I will do my best writing yet," she promised. She bobbed a quick curtsy to him and turned, handing the pages to Marie who tucked them safely into a satchel she carried. Oliver remained standing, watching the two women as they moved across the gallery and out of sight.

Three long days later, Oliver sat at his desk staring into the distance yet again. "How long is long enough?" he mused aloud to himself. He had no idea how much time she could devote to writing, nor how much time she would need to work. As a young unattached woman, it would be completely inappropriate to send her a note, but he had not seen her since their meeting at the museum, and he was growing impatient.

He had attempted to keep up his end of the bargain as much as he could over the last few days without appearing out of character. He had seen William at their club two nights ago and had tried to be nonchalant in mentioning that he had enjoyed meeting Evelyn. He had later brought up Sophia and Charlotte's efforts to find a husband to try to weasel out of William his own intentions in finding a wife. He casually mentioned that he thought red hair was particularly becoming on women, and asked William's opinion, but his response was disappointingly noncommittal on the subject. In desperation, he outright asked William his views on marriage and received a twenty-minute slightly drunken oration on how he was still far too young and had no intention of settling down anytime soon.

He had paid a casual visit to the Montgomerys' the day before hoping to run into Evelyn, but had found only Sophia and Charlotte taking callers. He had tried his luck with them at determining William's intentions but was met only by the teasing of his sisters. They held little hope for him making a sound match anytime soon. Oliver made sure to stay the requisite time and drop a few nice compliments about Evelyn before leaving, but he left feeling sorely discouraged. He had no idea how much Evelyn had completed but felt he himself had made no progress towards his part of the bargain, either. In frustration, he locked himself in his study and re-read what he had tried to write about his grandfather's experience in the colonies to remind himself to be patient.

He was pulled from his misery by the arrival of a note. His butler brought it to him as he stared out the window of his townhouse into the busy street below. His papers had lain forgotten on the desk as he instead imagined the scenes of his grandfather's life. It was an endless source of frustration to him that his imagination could be so vivid but his narrative so lifeless.

"A message arrived for you a moment ago, sir, and the boy awaits a response." Jennings held out the note to him and stepped back to allow him privacy to read the message. A quick perusal of the words brought an immediate change to his demeanor. He stepped across the room, dipped his pen in ink, and scribbled a quick response across the bottom of the note. He waved it dry and sealed it with a small bit of wax and brought it back to the butler.

"Thank you, Jennings. Please be sure to offer the boy something to eat and a bit of coin before he leaves." The older gentleman nodded and stepped from the room.

Oliver followed and ran lightly up the steps to his room, ringing for his valet as soon as he entered. He had removed his waistcoat and begun unbuttoning his sleeves when he arrived.

"Ah, Parker, slight change of plans for the evening. I will be attending a ball at the Montgomery residence. Please see to it that water is brought up for a quick bath. Also, have the carriage brought around in an hour." The older man acknowledged the requests and left to do as requested, returning shortly to lay out clean attire for the evening. Within the hour, Oliver was bathed, clean-shaven, and outfitted in brown breeches with a deep blue jacket. The valet finished tying his cravat before Oliver surveyed the final product with approval. "Very good, Parker. Enjoy your evening as I shall be more than able to take care of myself when I return tonight."

"Thank you, sir," he responded with a smile and nod. "Enjoy yourself as well, sir."

Oliver was soon on his way downstairs and out the door to climb into the awaiting vehicle. He settled himself into the carriage and peered out the window, wondering if Evelyn would have the same reaction to a carriage as she had to the phaeton. He arrived at the Montgomery's House within fifteen minutes and stepped down from the conveyance. He stood on the walkway observing the lines of people streaming into the front entrance and grimaced. He did not typically enjoy crowds, or balls, or dancing for that matter. But the note had said that William desired his attendance, and where he was, Sophia and Charlotte were sure to be also.

He straightened his jacket and moved up the stairs, waiting with the masses for his turn to enter. He greeted Lord and Lady Montgomery as well as William, Sophia, and Charlotte at the entrance, then made his way into the milieu that filled their lavish home. He moved along the walls observing the people and decorations evoking a Grecian theme. He made his way to a refreshment table, where he picked up a glass of wine, and continued to circle the room, hoping to spot William. Just as he had decided to give up on the ballroom and find the card room, he heard his name being called. He turned to see Sophia and Charlotte approaching from behind.

He bowed over both their hands as they dipped into a quick curtsy. "Misses Montgomery, I cannot thank your family enough for my invitation. It is a pleasure to see you both, and I hope I can find each of you again later and beg a dance." He smiled at the two ladies, wondering if he could identify which one was which if he was put on the spot.

The one in a lavender gown with grey accents spoke first, "It was our pleasure to invite you, Mr. Marten. I am sorry that you had not already received an invitation," she began.

"But William did not give Mama your address until today," finished the twin in grey with lavender trim. "She sent a message as soon as she could, and we are so pleased you could make it."

"Ah, why am I not surprised that William is to blame?" he joked. "And where is he hiding this evening? Surely, he did not extend an invitation to me without planning to attend himself, did he?" He paused before adding, "And what about your friend? Miss Berkeley, I believe. Is she here this evening?"

The second twin smirked at Oliver and asked, "Which would you prefer to find, sir, William or Evelyn?"

"Oh, do not tease, Sophia," remarked Charlotte. "William has promised Mama that he will not hide away in the card room; so he should be around, though he likely also arrived late."

"We must continue to make our rounds, Mr. Marten, but it was a pleasure to see you."

He bowed again as they moved past him. He continued his circle around the ballroom, noticing that the musicians were beginning to call for the first set, a quadrille, and much of the crowd was moving to the outsides of the room to make space for the dancers.

As he began his second full round of the room, he finally spotted Miss Berkeley. It appeared that she had recently entered and made a beeline for her best friends. The three had their heads together and were all smiles next to the refreshment table. Since he was too far away to hear their words, and too late to request she dance with him for this set, he observed the ladies for a moment.

Charlotte and Sophia's soft blonde curls matched perfectly and appeared neat and tidy with not a hair out of place. Their gowns were coordinated as always, and their arms were linked together as they chatted with their friend. They looked as though they had just stepped off of a fashion plate. In comparison to their outward perfection, Evelyn looked nearly wild. Her bold red hair threatened to break out of all the clips Marie had used with stray wisps surrounding her almost like a halo. The pink and white of her gown topped by her coiffure, brought to mind a sweet confection of some sort. Though he certainly could not claim to be an expert in ladies' fashion, it seemed as though something was odd in her choice of colors. The gown itself and her hairstyle were fashionable, but the overall effect was somehow...off. Despite his inability to enunciate the issue, he could not help but smile at the sight of her.

After watching for a few moments, he slowly picked his way through the crowd surrounding the dancers and drew closer and closer to the table. Just as he drew up to the trio, the song ended and the room was filled with laughter and applause for the musicians and dance partners.

Oliver moved next to the ladies and bowed. "Misses Montgomery, we meet again. Miss Berkeley, it is a pleasure to see you this evening."

All three dipped a curtsy. "Mr. Marten, I did not know you would be here this evening," Evelyn said, sounding surprised.

"I did not know it myself until earlier today," he responded. "Your friends thought I merited an invitation, but William could not be troubled to provide an address until today, so the invitation came at the eleventh hour."

Evelyn glanced around at the mention of William, but he was still nowhere to be found.

"I am sure he will be here soon," spoke Oliver. "I hope to have a few words with him myself," he added with a grin. "In the meantime, might I have the favor of the next dance, Miss Berkeley?"

"I would be delighted," she responded with a smile. She placed her hand in his and he led her out onto the floor amidst the couples gathering for a reel. As he took his place and looked across at his partner he saw she was still scanning the room, hoping for a sign of William no doubt. While he understood her desire to see him, he could not wait any longer to find out her progress.

"Well?" he asked as they began the movements of the dance.

She looked up at him as they met, and asked, "Well what?"

He waited until they were close and lowered his voice. "How is the writing coming?"

She glanced around as if checking to see if anyone was paying attention, but it did not appear to be the case. She stopped scanning the crowds and focused on him as she answered. "While you are the final judge, I am very pleased with how it is coming together," she said with a smile. "The first day, I struggled with where to start, what words to use, and what tone to capture. By the second afternoon, it was flowing nicely and I find I am enjoying the process a great deal," she flushed and added, "Having only written love stories and animal adventures, this is new territory for me, but the stories are exciting. I enjoy writing something that seems worthwhile."

They parted and then came back together again, flowing smoothly in time with the beat. She was glad that he was a good dancer, and she could talk without worrying that he would step on her feet. "I hope you are pleased."

He looked down at her as he twirled them across the floor, and answered, "I have great faith in you and your skill. I cannot wait to read what you have written." And he meant it. He could not wait to see what she had done. He knew he had been right in asking for her help.

She raised an eyebrow and grinned. "And what of you? Shall I expect a proposal anytime soon?"

He chuckled, unconsciously holding her tighter as he did so. "If your words are flowing as well as you say they are, I am afraid I may have gotten the better end of the bargain. My intentions are good, but I find the delivery of casual romantic encouragement more difficult than I expected. It seemed as though I was either expressing an interest in you for myself or attempting to determine his level of romantic interest in me as a partner...and certainly neither of those is my goal," he said with a grin.

Evelyn laughed at his jokes, as he intended, and he liked being the cause of her amusement.

As the song drew to a close, he asked, "Shall I call on you tomorrow to pick up the pages?"

"Oh no," she answered quickly. "My mother knows nothing of our deal and it is better to leave it that way. I will take Marie for a shopping excursion and meet you at the museum again in the afternoon."

"Wonderful. I will bring more notes and you can show me what you have written." As the music faded and the dancers cleared the floor to make room for the next set, he escorted her back to Sophia and Charlotte.

"Ladies, please excuse me while I hunt for your brother. Misses Montgomery. Miss Berkeley." He bowed again and then disappeared into the crowd.

"I thought he wanted to dance with us too," Sophia said with a pout.

"Apparently, he only has eyes for Evie," Charlotte teased with a small smile.

"No, no, nothing like that," Evelyn said quickly, but she felt a blush rise on her cheeks. "We simply share a love of the British Museum," she said.

"Even I would visit the museum with him," Sophia crooned with a fake dreamy smile, clasping her hands to her heart.

Evelyn grinned and shook her head at her friend. "So, a visit to the galleries holds no appeal for you unless it offers the chance to spend time with a handsome gentleman?" she asked with mock sincerity.

They all smothered their laughter for the sake of propriety and shifted the conversation to various acquaintances as they watched the crowds.

The twins were pleased when Oliver returned later with William for his promised dances with each of them. William approached Evelyn as Oliver led Charlotte onto the floor.

He smiled down into her eyes as he bowed over her hand and greeted her formally as befitting the setting. "Miss Berkeley, you look lovely this evening as always."

Evelyn flushed under his attention and was happy to bow her head low as she dipped in response, taking a moment to calm her nerves. "Mr. Montgomery, you are too kind. Surely your sisters have put you up to it!"

William laughed and released his light hold on her gloved hand, moving to stand next to her with his hands behind his back as they stood shoulder to shoulder and surveyed the room of dancers. "My sisters insist that I keep an eye on you, but I assure you that I develop all my flattery myself." He grinned down at her and she laughed at his teasing tone.

He nodded at Oliver and Charlotte on the floor as their set passed nearby. "I feel as though Oliver has set his cap on marriage, though I must say I am a bit surprised. They would make a handsome pair, would they not? As her brother, I must ensure Charlotte finds a good match and I could not find a better man than Marten, but I did not think he was ready to settle until these last few days."

Evelyn's heart did strange things as she watched the pair dance together, suddenly struck by just how beautiful they were together. She tried not to sigh as she noted the contrast of Charlotte's pale skin and hair next to his dark tones and dark hair. They were laughing together as if they shared a joke and Evelyn found herself dying to be laughing with them. She pulled her eyes away and continued her conversation with William.

"What makes you think he has decided to marry?" she asked.

"It is all he can speak of this last week. He has asked about my intentions, your intentions, my sisters' intentions, my views on beauty, and my perspective on marriage as an institution in general. I must say I had thought my reluctance to enter into such a contract any time soon was clearly understood but apparently, I was mistaken." He laughed at his own joke, oblivious to Evelyn's inner turmoil.

She blushed, then laughed at herself for being embarrassed about something he knew nothing about. She had been so sure of her plan to marry him and had thought Oliver's help would be just the push he needed, but perhaps she had misjudged his views, not just about her, but about marriage in general.

"To what do you attribute your reluctance? Surely you intend to marry at some point?" She asked innocently enough, keeping her eyes on the dance floor to avoid eye contact and the increasing embarrassment she knew it would elicit.

Having no idea of her mental dilemma, he laughed before answering, "Not if I can help it! Adam is set to inherit and no doubt the twins will make fine matches one day, but I have no desire to be tied to one place or one person forever. When last we spoke in our school days, Oliver and I agreed on this, but perhaps his views have changed."

Evelyn attempted to process this new information and figure out how to adjust her plans to overcome this new obstacle. "And what if you fell in love?" Her voice came out weaker than she intended and she did not think she could blush any more than she already was. Though her friendship with William stretched far back into their childhood, such conversations were generally considered taboo between unattached men and women.

"Love?" He laughed again and shook his head. "Love is fine in novels and fairy tales, but I see no evidence to convince me that it is a real, let alone lasting, sentiment. On this, I am quite confident that Oliver and I agree. He may be considering marriage, but it will be for his own convenience, not sentimental feelings, of that I can assure you."

Having spent the first part of the evening wishing for William's company, Evelyn now wished she could go back to before this conversation so that it might never have happened. William's words left her with more questions than answers. Could she ever convince William that they were a match worth changing his perspective for? Would she be content to marry for convenience without love? Did Oliver want to marry Charlotte? She knew he had visited the twins several times lately. Why did the idea of them together upset her so much?

Her years of social training served her well as she continued her conversation with William moving on to topics of the weather and the latest plays in town, despite her inner turmoil. She greeted a smiling Charlotte as Oliver led her off the dance floor and watched both partners carefully for any signs of affection. Oliver turned to Sophia and bowed to her, leading her onto the floor while Charlotte caught her breath.

William turned to Evelyn and held out his hand. "Will you join me for a turn, Miss Berkeley?"

Evelyn smiled brightly and placed her hand in his to be led onto the floor. As they began the opening steps of the dance, she considered her options. The Season was far from over and Oliver had promised to help her in her quest to convince William that she was a quality match. She knew that his mother wished him to marry, as she desired to see all of her children to marry. Her mind went through all the arguments she had mulled over for months before and found that she still saw William as her last chance at marriage before society put her on the shelf for good.

She looked over at her partner as they moved through the steps, and found him as charming as she always had. His hair was neatly swept back, framing a face that was often full of laughter and warmth. He was kind to his family and had many friends, and his hobbies leaned more towards intellectual pursuits than many of the vices that others of his age found so tempting. She imagined a lifetime of breakfasts and dinners across the table from him and found she had no objection to the image. She spared a quick glance at his lips and tried to imagine what it would be like to be kissed by them, but her only frame of reference was the novels she had read, so she felt unsure on that account.

She took a deep breath and squared her shoulders as they continued through the motions of the dance and she reminded herself of the strength of her plan. He was a solid, reliable choice with financial stability, a good reputation, and the sweetest sisters who already happened to be her best friends. He was safe and comfortable. What more could she ask for? It was well and good for characters in stories to have excitement, passion, and love, but she did not need such things to be content. Did she?

The musicians drew out the final notes of the song as the dancers bowed to their partners. Evelyn saw the crowds head towards the dining room and realized that she had shared the dinner dance with William, and would have the opportunity to spend more time with him during the evening meal. As the pair moved together into the dining room, her eyes searched the crowd for Charlotte and Sophia, finally finding them not too far away, each on either side of Oliver. He caught her eye and winked. She sucked in a sharp breath and looked away quickly, but not before noticing his grin at her shocked response. She tightened her grip on William's arm and avoided looking his way again so as to not encourage such inappropriate behavior. She focused on William's talk of an upcoming trip and ignored the way her pulse had quickened at Oliver's wink.

Chapter 7

Oliver looked across and down the table where Evelyn sat next to William, sipping her glass of wine. Her hazel eyes were fixed on William with a slightly bemused look on her face as his friend recounted a recent escapade with great animation. He was glad for her being seated where she was given her marriage goals, though he thought it likely had more to do with her long friendship with William's sisters than anything else. William's relative lack of attention to her during the meal reflected the easy companionship of old friends, not the devotion of a besotted suitor.

Oliver raised his glass of claret and surveyed his own table. Many of the guests were strangers to him given his recent arrival in town. He was intrigued by the presence of Lady Berkeley to his right and leaned closer to hear her conversation with another elderly matron seated on her opposite side.

"The modiste assured me the style was of the latest fashion. And the color is just perfect for such a young lady as herself," she intoned. "Evelyn was concerned she was too old for such soft colors, but I assured her that she had just the figure and complexion to wear it with ease." Her neighbor nodded in agreement as they both paused in their conversation to chew on the duck being served.

Oliver made a subtle glance back at Evelyn remembering his earlier observations about her dress. There was definitely something off with the color palette regardless of what her mother thought. The woman across from him, who could not have been any younger than Miss Berkeley was dressed in a lovely shade of blue and her conversation partner was wearing green and white. True, the style of their dresses looked very similar to Evelyn's, but there still seemed to be something different about her overall look that he could not explain.

The raised voice of Lady Berkeley to his right again commanded his attention as she exclaimed, "Oh Mrs. White, my Evelyn would just love that, would she not, Mr. Marten?"

He was glad he had tuned in just in time to hear the question aimed at him, but sadly not early enough to know what was being referenced. "I am afraid I am not privy to who would love what, Lady Berkeley," he responded with a small smile. "Would you kindly fill me in?"

"Mrs. White was just telling me of her recent visit to the Tower of London and what beautiful views it offers of Town. I am quite sure my Evelyn would love it, would she not?"

Oliver frowned remembering Evelyn's response to the height of a phaeton and felt confident she would not, in fact, love it. Luckily for him, Lady Berkeley had not actually sought a response. She turned back to the agreeable Mrs. White, who seemed content simply to smile and nod along to her friend's chatter while she enjoyed her meal.

His eyes drifted down the table to Evelyn again. Her smile seemed slightly more forced, but William's storytelling was in full swing as he held both hands up in front of his face mimicking his squint as he looked through the sight of his imaginary hunting rifle. Oliver smiled at the scene, thinking it was not that different from many married couples he had seen in one another's company. His smile faded as he thought back to his conversations with William at the club compared to his conversations with Evelyn at their first dinner. Even if William decided to marry, which seemed unlikely in the near future, would he be the type of partner Evelyn longed for?

Oliver had no time to dwell on the question as the gentleman on his left turned to him just then to ask his opinion on the best line of horses for carriages, and he was drawn into conversation. By the time they had addressed not only horses, but also dogs, sheep, and the pros and cons of converting pastures to orchards, Oliver saw that the guests were rising throughout the dining room to seek after-dinner entertainment. He saw William help Miss Berkeley from her seat and was surprised at his own thought of how her slight hand felt in his. He turned away from the sight quickly and headed back into the ballroom. Tomorrow's meeting to exchange the notes could not come soon enough.

The next afternoon, Oliver made his way to the British Museum more than an hour before their meeting time and again perused the galleries. He stopped and stared at a terracotta statue, wondering just how one might go about creating such a thing. The small label said it was another depiction of one of the muses found in a well during excavations near Porta Latina outside Rome. Art had never been his strength, but his recent failed attempts at writing made him question all of his creative abilities. The idea that someone could sculpt with such detail and passion impressed him. Even though this particular piece was missing the head and a hand, it still caught his attention. He had enjoyed the medium of watercolor as a boy, but his finished products always made him feel as though something was missing. His teacher had said his works lacked texture, and he always felt they lacked passion.

He was still admiring the antiquities when Evelyn approached him quietly from behind. "Have you ever felt you were inspired by a muse?" she asked quietly.

Without looking her way, he shifted to the side slightly allowing her to stand directly in front of the piece. "No," he answered simply. "You?"

She glanced his way from under her eyelashes, deliberating how to respond. She looked from him to the statue, then cast her eyes down at the floor and responded, "I thought I was...a few times, but

I was...mistaken. I have since chosen to look for inspiration in reality rather than trust in the inspiration of mythology." She looked back up at the sculpture then turned away, walking towards a larger statuary across the room.

Oliver moved up behind Evelyn and noted the way the top of her head came to just under his chin. He could smell a touch of lavender he was so close to her. Wondering at himself for even thinking about such things, he moved to stand beside her and asked, "Do you have the writing?"

At the question, Marie stepped up from behind her and produced a sheaf of papers bound in a ribbon. Evelyn took them from her and held them to her chest in front of her as if she did not want to lose them.

She looked up into his face, her cheeks flushed a becoming shade of pink that made her look even more like a flame with her red hair. "You should know that no one has ever read my writing as you are about to, Mr. Marten. My stories have entertained children and servants, but I have never tackled such topics as these. It was exciting. It was both stressful and exhilarating at the same time. It was terrifying." She laughed nervously at her intensity level, taking a deep breath before holding the papers out to him.

He bowed over them just slightly, and she grinned. She held on to them for a moment before releasing them as if she questioned her decision to share the pages. Once she let go, she clasped her hands together in front of her and looked up at Oliver. "Be kind, but be honest, too," she entreated.

"Believe me when I say that they cannot be any worse than what I have done," he responded with a rueful smile.

Several days later, Oliver arrived late to the musicale and slipped unnoticed into the back of the room. He could see a young woman perched in front of a pianoforte delicately moving her fingers across the keys as if they might break with too much pressure. Her blonde coiffure wrapped around her head coupled with her soft notes created an almost angelic appearance. He watched her for a moment, impressed as always at those blessed with such talents. Within moments of his arrival, her song drew to a close and she stood as the applause broke the spell she had placed on the room.

Oliver scanned the room as he clapped, noticing William seated towards the front on the left side of the room. The performer moved from her position at the front to the seat beside him, and William's attention fixated on the young woman. He took her hand and turned towards her, flattering her, no doubt, if her blush and downcast eyes said anything. Trying not to roll his eyes at William's behavior, Oliver continued to scan the room stopping only when he saw the red hair of his new co-conspirator.

She was seated with her friends, but Evelyn's attention was focused on the next musician to take a seat at the pianoforte and begin to play. Evelyn's hands were clasped in her lap and her feet tucked under the chair. Not a part of her demeanor, coiffure, or style of dress could be considered improper or out of place, yet as he continued to study her in the opportunity of the moment, he again had the feeling that she was different. Her red hair was obviously unusual and stood out in stark contrast to both the white of her gown and the more muted tones of the other attendees, but Oliver felt it went beyond her dress. She had a maturity of bearing and a sense of sincerity that Oliver found distinctly lacking in London society. While he thought her desire for a love match to be a flight of fancy, he recognized that she truly believed in it, and he found he respected her for it.

His attention was distracted as the audience burst into applause at the conclusion of the piece. He tried to focus on the young woman's next piece, but instead examined the audience members. He saw several of the individuals he had met in his research and fundraising efforts, and even one elderly veteran of his grandfather's generation. He met his eye and nodded, making a mental note to visit with him before the evening concluded. William's attentions still seemed focused on the young woman seated next to him. It appeared that their chairs were closer than they had been a moment earlier and there was a distinct flush to her cheeks. He glanced at Evelyn sitting a few rows behind them, and it seemed she had noticed the interaction as well. Her back was straight as a board and her gaze was locked on the performer, but her previous easy enjoyment of the music had been replaced with a strained smile.

Why now, William? he groaned to himself. *You write off women, belittle the idea of marriage, and laugh at my hints not one week ago, and now you are smitten?* His gaze moved between Evelyn and William as the former studiously pretended to ignore the other while the latter truly knew nothing of the heartbreak he was causing. Was she heartbroken? Did she already love William, or had she only convinced herself she one day could? Either way, she could not be pleased with his current attention.

Finally, the music ended and the hostess, Mrs. Staunton stood in the front of the room. "Thank you, thank you to our performers today, our lovely daughters Misses Sarah and Jane Staunton." She beamed with pride as the audience enthusiastically cheered the musicians once again. Both young women stood and curtsied deeply to the gathered crowd. The first woman who had caught William's attention was dressed in a modest gown of pale blue tied with a deep navy bow at the waist, flowers embellishing her hair. Her blonde curls were pulled back into an intricate design made to look natural with a few wisps around her face. Her blue eyes contrasted with her sister's darker brown, but both boasted the same lustrous golden hair. The second sister's dress of pale green had a white lace overlay and a matching green ribbon adorned her coiffure.

Oliver could not deny the loveliness of either lady, but he could not say that he was attracted to one of them. It had been some time since he had felt any desire to devote himself to the effort of courting a woman. Only once had he allowed himself to be dedicated to such pursuits and it had ended with his beloved - well, the object of his affections, at least - accepting the proposal of a titled and wealthy gentleman. When she professed her love even as she ended their courtship, he did not believe her words. She had done as anyone would and made the decision that was in her own best interest to secure her future. He knew now love was fleeting.

He shook his head to clear his thoughts from such negativity. With his focus on his writing project, he was not inclined to love again, particularly not now. Well, not *his* writing exactly. He looked around to find Evelyn in the crowd and smiled when he saw she was again relaxed and laughing with the Montgomery twins. He thought back to the words he had read and re-read over the last few days. They were everything his were not. Engaging. Powerful. Inspiring.

He moved across the room towards her, stopping to greet acquaintances as he went. He bowed low to Colonel Benjamin Kilpatrick when their paths crossed, though he hated to delay his conversation with Evelyn. "How did you find the music tonight, Colonel?" he asked.

"I liked what I heard well enough, I suppose, but it's nothing to a lively night around a fire with my men!" He slapped Oliver on the shoulder laughing. His daughter next to him shook her head at his statement looking both embarrassed and amused. Oliver laughed politely. He had heard the man tell rather impolite tales of his years leading Scottish troops and knew to not necessarily expect propriety from him.

"I think this concert is much better suited to mixed company, Colonel, though I agree with your sentiment," Oliver remarked.

"Bah! Mixed company is overrated," he said with a wink and another hearty laugh.

"Papa," his daughter chastised, though her laughter belied any real annoyance. "Forgive him, Mr. Marten; at times I think he left his manners behind in Scotland."

"No apology is necessary, Mrs. Fitzhugh. I find your father's sincerity a pleasure and would prefer an afternoon in his company to the poshest parlors of London," Oliver assured her.

"If that is true, you must accept an invitation to our home two days from now. We are hosting several of Papa's friends for dinner, and I'm sure you understand when I say I don't know what to expect, but it's sure to be entertaining. Please say you will join us, as they love to tell their stories to new audiences." She took one of his gloved hands in her own.

As he started to speak, he caught sight of Evelyn across the room. "I'd be honored to accept your invitation, Mrs. Fitzhugh, but might I be so bold as to bring a guest with me?"

"Is there a lucky lady now, Mr. Marten? I wondered why you weren't married when you visited us five years ago. Surely someone must have caught you by now," she simpered.

"Oh no, nothing of the sort, I assure you," Oliver hastened to dispel the notion, as he felt heat creeping up his collar at such a thought. "She is simply an acquaintance with an interest in similar stories. I think meeting your father, and others like him, may serve as an inspiration of sorts for a…project."

"By all means, you may bring your *acquaintance,* and I am certain Father will be delighted to regale her, too. Come now, Papa, we must make our way to some refreshments."

Oliver bowed as Mrs. Fitzhugh and her father moved away arm in arm slowly making their way towards a punch bowl set opposite the pianoforte. He was watching them walk as Evelyn turned and caught his eye. She smiled when she saw him looking her way and moved in his direction. Oliver thought again about why she seemed to be so different than the other young women around her but still did not have an answer.

He bowed as she approached and she dipped into a perfunctory curtsy but spoke softly before she had even fully stood.

"So?" She asked.

"I thought the music was lovely," he responded, glancing towards the pianoforte where the two sisters still stood among admirers as if in a receiving line. "What did you think?"

"The music was fine, as you well know," she said, sounding exasperated. "I meant...what did you think of my writing?" she hissed in a loud whisper. He looked down at her as she stood in front of him with her hands clasped together, eyes wide.

"Ahhh...the writing." He frowned and looked off into the distance, drawing the moment out just to see her squirm. "It is...how should I put it?" He looked away, savoring her discomfort. He met her eyes. "It is perfect."

He watched her eyes light up as she smiled. She bounced onto her tiptoes then down again and squeezed her hands together as if trying to contain her excitement.

"Oh Mr. Marten, I am so delighted to hear you say that! I have been so worried. I barely slept a wink...Oh, I am so happy!"

"What are you so happy about, child?"

Both Evelyn and Oliver started as Lady Berkeley appeared from the direction of the refreshment table.

"Oh, Mama! I was simply telling Mr. Marten that I was happy about...the new exhibit at the British Museum. I read that it is to be quite spectacular."

Mr. Marten bowed over Lady Berkeley's hand in greeting and she preened under his attentions.

"Really? Why would you bore Mr. Marten with such tedious information? He might think you are a bluestocking!" She laughed, but it sounded forced. "Besides, you don't even like that stuffy old place." She laughed again as if embarrassed by her daughter's conversation skills.

"I am quite a devotee of our cultural institutions, ma'am, and I was fascinated to hear of the new installations. Perhaps I might persuade your daughter to accompany me one day, even though she does not enjoy it." He bowed again slightly to Lady Berkeley as if asking permission but caught Evelyn's eye and smiled. He could see she was uncomfortable with the exchange as her cheeks were nearly the color of her hair.

"Accompany you to the museum? Why, I'm sure she would much prefer a visit for tea or a ride in the park to such a dull afternoon. And so tiring, walking around such large halls." Lady Berkeley looked sympathetically at her daughter and touched her arm, assuming they were in agreement on the subject.

"Of course, Mama. I'd be happy to take a ride with Mr. Marten," Evelyn said, though she spoke to her mother and did not meet Oliver's eyes.

Surprised by her acquiescence and subdued response, Oliver cocked his head to the side, studying her for only a moment.

"It is settled then," Oliver stated after only a moment's hesitation. "Shall I come for tea tomorrow afternoon?"

Lady Berkeley beamed, "Of course you will," she tittered, but Oliver's attention was focused on Evelyn. She met his gaze squarely, as if daring him to question her response, but he simply winked, bowed, and moved away from the ladies as Lady Berkeley led her daughter off for more chatter.

Oliver immediately sought out Mrs. Fitzhugh to make a simple request before departing to read through Evelyn's writing for the hundredth time.

Evelyn stared out the window as her sewing sat neglected in her lap. The mid-morning sun streamed through the drawing room windows, casting the room in a soft glow. The warmth of the setting suited Evelyn's mood, as her mind wandered more to the previous evening than to the embroidery in her lap.

Perfect. She hadn't stopped thinking of the word since Mr. Marten had said it last evening. She had hoped for more time to discuss, but she did not know when next they might have such a chance. Mama was certain to be present at tea, but she was struggling to find a reason to leave the house.

She sighed at the memory of her mother's statements regarding the British Museum. What must he think of her? She could only hope he knew that she meant what she said about the museum and was not pretending for his sake. But did he think she was a bluestocking? Did it matter if he did?

She set her work to the side and stood to take a turn about the room. She paused in front of the small mirror on the fireplace mantle and studied her reflection. Sarah Staunton's performance and appearance last night was nearly angelic. Could she blame William for his attentions to her? Yet Oliver had said that William was uninterested in marriage, so perhaps she had misread the situation. She sighed again.

"I really must stop sighing. It is most unbecoming!" She spoke out loud to the empty room, then laughed at herself for such behavior. She moved towards the window but kept her distance, preferring to look out rather than down. She stared into the back gardens without really seeing the hedges. What did Oliver think of her? What did she think of Oliver? She remembered hearing his hearty laugh the evening before and could not help but smile at the memory. He always seemed so serious when they spoke that his genuine laughter had surprised her, even from across the room. She wished she knew him better. Only because they were to be working together, she told herself.

The door opened, startling her from her thoughts. A footman entered. He held out a silver tray bearing a small card addressed to her. She took the card, thanking the man before he bowed and left. She did not recognize the seal and thought for a moment it might be from Oliver.

Dear Miss Berkeley,

I hope you will forgive this untoward introduction and note, but I would like to extend an invitation to you for dinner tomorrow night. A dear friend of mine, Mr. Oliver Marten, has informed me that you would be interested in meeting former members of His Majesty's service and hearing tales of their campaigns. My father and several of his friends will be 'holding court' tomorrow for dinner at our home, and Mr. Marten and I would be honored by your presence. Rest assured, there will be several ladies in attendance including myself, my sister, and my nieces, Sarah and Jane Staunton. I know you attended their performance last night and I am sure their presence will dispel any misgivings regarding your invitation and attendance at

our small party.
Please send your response at your convenience.
Mrs. Elizabeth Fitzhugh

Evelyn drifted back to the window to process the invitation. The mention of Oliver's name had made her stomach flutter, but she was less excited by the mention of the Staunton sisters. And what did she mean by "Mr. Marten and I" would be honored by her presence? Were they romantically connected?

"Mrs. Fitzhugh." Evelyn spoke her name aloud and recalled what she knew of the woman. She had known her nieces Sarah and Jane for some time through her friendship with the Montgomerys, but the girls had only just recently returned to town from their country estate. Mrs. Fitzhugh was Scottish and had married a Scotsman and settled in London during his time in the service. He had passed away several years earlier and she kept a home for her father, if Evelyn remembered correctly. She had seen the woman plenty of times, but had simply never crossed paths socially. She was glad now to have the connection of the nieces to allow her to accept the invitation.

She went to her writing desk and pulled out a note to send a reply. She hesitated for a moment, questioning whether her mother would approve, before dashing off the note regardless. While she was fairly certain that her mother would see this as appropriate, she did not concern herself with it either way. She was determined to go and hear more from Oliver about the writing. And perhaps learn more about him in the process.

She was ringing for a footman just as her mother entered. "I hope we shall have no more talk of museums today, child. Honestly, what will he think of you?" She lowered herself into her favorite wingback chair, fanning herself as she sat.

"Mama, he thinks nothing but that I enjoy art and history. A museum is perfectly acceptable for a young lady." Evelyn shook her head as she handed her note to a footman. "Please send tea when our guest arrives," she requested. She turned back to her mother with a smile on her face.

Her mother frowned at her. "It might be acceptable for some, but you can't afford such oddities at this point in your life."

"Oddities?" exclaimed Evelyn with a laugh. "You make it sound as if I'm trying to take up acting on Drury Lane."

"Heavens, girl, I should hope not. Even still, you should focus on your accomplishments and charms, not your drawbacks."

Evelyn took a deep breath to avoid arguing again over her mother's belief that a young woman who enjoyed natural history would never find a husband. She was saved from further debate by the entry of the footman.

"Mr. Oliver Marten to see you Lady Berkeley, Miss Evelyn." Oliver entered and bowed deeply towards Lady Berkeley as the footman retreated and closed the door behind him.

Her mother snapped her fan shut. "It is such a pleasure to see you, Mr. Marten. I was just telling Evelyn how becoming she looks in pink. Does she not look lovely, Mr. Marten?"

Evelyn could feel her face heat as Oliver turned to look at her. "Mama, I -"

"Indeed, she does," he interrupted, smiling as he took a seat across from her. "Is pink your favorite color then, Miss Evelyn?"

"Goodness no," she answered. "I much prefer darker colors like burgundy or deep blues, but -"

"Darker colors?" her mother cried. "Darker colors do nothing for your beautiful complexion, dear. Does she not have a beautiful complexion, Mr. Marten?" She did not wait for an answer but pushed on despite the pained look on her daughter's face. "She is quite accomplished too. Her skills at the pianoforte are quite something if I do say so myself. She is so shy that I do not often ask her to play in front of others, but oh, what a delight it is when she does play."

"I should very much like to hear you play one day, Miss Evelyn, if you would do me the honor." Oliver nodded in her direction as he said the words. "I cannot play a note myself but do appreciate the skill in others."

Lady Berkeley whipped open her fan again, moving it slowly near her face. "It is Evelyn's favorite pastime, Mr. Marten. She enjoys it above all things. And do you play picquet or whist? We must have you for dinner one night so that you might partner with Evelyn. She does love to play, do you not dear?"

"I, well...I," Evelyn hesitated, unsure of how not to appear uncharitable to her mother while still disagreeing thoroughly with her statement. She was saved from responding, however, as her mother pushed on extolling her virtues almost as though she were an object on an auction block.

"And her watercolors! Have you seen her watercolors, Mr. Marten? They could hang in those stuffy museums, they could. Not that I should like it if they did, but they are certainly as good as any I've ever seen."

Oliver nodded and looked as if he was about to speak, but Lady Berkeley continued on.

"Will you be taking Evelyn out for a ride today? I know she loved your last ride together in your phaeton. She spoke of little else for days."

It took every ounce of control that Evelyn had not to contradict her mother at this statement.

Oliver glanced in her direction and raised an eyebrow. His lip twitched. "Unfortunately, no, I will not be taking Miss Evelyn for a ride today. Perhaps she will allow me to call again one day soon and we can ride...or walk through Hyde Park."

Feeling almost superfluous to the conversation about her, Evelyn interjected before her mother could commandeer the conversation further. "Mr. Marten, how long will you be in London? Will you be returning to Cambridge soon?"

"Of course not!" Lady Berkeley cried. "You must stay for the whole Season, Mr. Marten, or we should be most put out. Surely there could be no need for you to return at this time of year."

Was it her imagination or did Oliver look uncomfortable at this question? It seemed his stoic demeanor had slipped and exposed a flash of nervousness before his unflappability returned.

"Rest assured I will not be going anywhere before the end of the Season," he responded. He looked from Lady Berkeley to Evelyn. "I am attending to business in town at the moment and will remain until it is completed."

Evelyn nodded in understanding at his reference to their project.

"And after that, sir? Where do you go next?" she asked.

He hesitated and looked out the far window. "My uncle has offered me a place at Grandfather's estate if I should like to make my home there. It is a generous offer, but I am not yet sure of my plans. I have always wanted to travel and may yet try to do so before deciding where to settle." He looked back at Evelyn, and she smiled at his response.

"You are braver than I am, Mr. Marten," she said. "I may love the displays at the British Museum, but I plan to keep my feet firmly planted on land. I have no intention to travel anywhere that cannot be reached by carriage." She laughed and added. "I feel much the same about ships as I do about phaetons."

"Nonsense, child," chided Lady Berkeley. "You would *love* being on a ship for the right reasons. I have heard that it is lovely to see the stars at night from the deck of a ship. Perhaps one day you might make a visit to the continent as part of a honeymoon tour."

Evelyn felt her face flush at the implications of her mother's statement and refused to look at Oliver. She was excited when the door opened and a footman entered and set a tea tray on the table next to her mother.

"Ah, excellent, thank you," her mother said as the young man turned and left. "You must try Cook's apple tarts, they are delicious," she crowed to Mr. Marten as she poured a cup of tea and passed it to Oliver. "We stole her away from a Duke's household, you know. She was taught by a French cook at the Duke of Waverly's before we hired her on here." She looked very pleased with herself as she bit into one of the tarts.

Evelyn poured herself a cup of tea and added far too much milk and sugar, much to her mother's obvious displeasure. Evelyn knew it was a little much even for her sweet taste, but she felt the need to exert herself even in some small way. She cast a look at her as if daring her to say something, before grabbing not one but two apple tarts and returning to her seat.

Evelyn felt Oliver's eyes on her and cast an imperious glance his way as well, but found his look was more approving than disparaging. He raised a tart in her direction as if in salute before taking a bite and turning back to her mother's prattle.

"Speaking of Waverly, have you heard about his daughter? I heard it on good authority that she has been writing stories for the newspapers. A *lady* publishing articles, can you imagine? Evelyn, dear, are you alright?"

Evelyn tried desperately to control the coughing fit that had erupted upon her mother's declaration, but her nerves and the overly sweet tea did not seem to be helping.

Oliver moved to her side, taking the plate and cup of tea from her hands and setting them down beside her. He knelt in front of her, took her hand in his, and echoed her mother's question. "Are you alright?" he asked.

Evelyn drew a deep breath as the coughing subsided and the embarrassment began to set in. But when she met his eyes, she was surprised to see he was smiling. With his back to her mother, he winked at her and squeezed her hand. Her face flushed at his nearness. She returned the smile, enjoying their shared secret. He rose and returned to his seat.

"I suppose that's what I get for taking two tarts, right Mama?" Evelyn asked with a laugh.

Lady Berkeley frowned at her daughter's jest and turned again to Oliver. "Mr. Marten, did I hear correctly that your mother has recently had another child?"

"My stepmother bore my father another son about six years ago now. David is a sweet boy, though perhaps a bit spoiled. Blackwood Hall is certainly livelier since his arrival," Oliver answered. There was no rancor in his voice about his new mother, though he spoke of them almost as if they were acquaintances rather than family. "My own mother died when I was 12, and my father remarried shortly thereafter. It is my mother's brother who has offered me a home at Longwood if I desire."

"Ah, I remember your father well from our younger days. We moved in the same social circles during the Season for years until he began to spend more time at Blackwood. Please pass along my greetings next time you see him, will you?" she asked.

"Indeed I will, whenever that might be," Oliver promised. He stood and glanced at the clock on the mantle. Taking his hint, Evelyn also rose.

"Thank you for joining us today, Mr. Marten," she said.

He bowed lightly towards Lady Berkeley and replied, "The pleasure was all mine, ladies. I hope I might visit again one day."

"You are welcome anytime," Lady Berkeley crowed, fanning herself once again. "You must bring that phaeton back for a ride," she suggested.

Evelyn turned towards the door and no longer refrained from shaking her head at her mother's comment. Catching Oliver's eye, she grinned apologetically, but he seemed unfazed by her mother's request. They moved out of the room together and Evelyn escorted him down the hall and to the staircase. A footman stood at the bottom with his hat and gloves.

He leaned in close and whispered, "I brought new notes and gave them to a footman when I entered. I explained that it was to be sent to your lady's maid immediately."

"It really was a pleasure," Oliver repeated, now at normal volume. "But if it is all the same to you, I would just as soon take a walk on my next visit." He grinned at her, then moved down the stairs and took his items from the footman.

Evelyn chuckled from the top of the stairs. "Don't let Mama hear you say such things!" she called behind him.

He raised his hand to her before making his exit, back into the bustle of the London streets.

She watched him go from the window on the second floor. Within minutes it seemed he had disappeared in the distance, but still Evelyn stared after him, lost in thought. Despite their rocky start, she found she enjoyed his company more each time their paths crossed. She was glad he had thought to bring more notes, but she hoped they would return to their clandestine museum meetings soon. He was still a bit of a riddle to her, and she wanted to solve the puzzle. In the meantime, she looked forward to Mrs. Fitzhugh's dinner party.

Chapter 8

Oliver tugged down on his waistcoat as he climbed the steps at the Kilpatrick's townhouse. A butler opened the door before he could even knock and within moments he was ushered through the door into the drawing room and the mingling guests within. He stood for a moment and got his bearings before spotting the colonel, and moving in his direction.

A boisterous voice came from his left. "Mr. Marten, it has been an age!" A white-haired gentleman leaning on an elegantly carved cane made his way towards him quite quickly for his age. "Where have you been hiding, young man?" he asked.

Turning with a smile on his face, Oliver held out a hand to greet the man. "Captain Baker, what a pleasure it is to see you. It must be two or three years at least since you entertained me with your tales of the high seas."

"Luckily for you, I've got more where those came from! What brings you here tonight? Still raising money for that idea of yours?" he asked.

"Not tonight, sir, I'm just here for the company. My idea needs more substance before I solicit funding again."

"Well, I hope you succeed one day, Marten. There's a lot of men out there in need of help, just like what you're offering. A small push in the right direction is all it would take," he encouraged.

Oliver nodded. "You're right, of course, and I assure you that it is my dream as much as ever, I just want to have a solid case next time I start asking peers to fund the endeavor."

The elderly captain shook his hand as Oliver continued towards Kilpatrick, surprised that Baker had remembered his plans for a veterans' home. He was both pleased that he saw such potential in the project and saddened that he didn't have more progress to report to the man. It renewed his conviction to finish a book as soon as possible to gain the support he needed. He glanced around the room but saw no sign yet of Evelyn.

He approached the colonel and stood listening as he spoke to several friends in a small semi-circle around his chair. His daughter had described it as 'holding court,' and there was no more apt description. The older man leaned forward in his chair holding tight to a glass of port in one hand while the other illustrated his adventures in the air with wide gestures when needed.

"My men snuck right past the American positions and raided their stores of rum...granted they did not have much, but they had even less after we were through!"

Oliver laughed along with the rest of the colonel's audience.

He glanced towards the door again just as Evelyn entered on William's arm. His stomach clenched at the sight of them together, but almost as quickly as the feeling came, he chided himself.

That is the point, you fool, he thought with a small shake of his head. *You promised to help make her a match with William.* He watched as Evelyn looked up at William and smiled, leaning in closer to share something with him. William bent down to hear and laughed at her comment. As he watched the two of them move further into the room, Oliver could tell the moment that both saw Miss Sarah Staunton approaching. Evelyn stiffened while William's smile grew even larger. Oliver cringed inwardly as he saw William pull away from Evelyn even as she attempted to keep her place at his side. Both ladies dropped into curtsies as they greeted one another while William bowed over Sarah's hand for what Oliver thought was an unnecessarily long time. Having watched long enough, Oliver moved towards them with no real plan other than to try to uphold his part of the deal and bring a smile to Evelyn's face.

"Mr. Montgomery and Miss Evelyn, what a fine pair you make this evening," exclaimed Oliver with no subtlety. I had no idea that you would both be here tonight, but I am happy for the opportunity for all of us to spend more time together."

"Mr. Marten, it is always a pleasure to see you my friend," William responded clapping his old schoolmate on the shoulder. He turned to Sarah and asked, "Miss Staunton, have you met Mr. Marten?"

"No, I have not had the honor," she replied in a soft voice.

"Miss Sarah Staunton, this is Mr. Oliver Marten, a friend from my school days. Mr. Marten, this is Miss Sarah Staunton who graced us with her astounding pianoforte skills two days ago. William beamed at Sarah as the two acknowledged one another with a bow and curtsy. Just as introductions were done, Oliver heard Mrs. Fitzhugh's voice over the gathering.

"Friends, thank you for joining us tonight. It seems that everyone who is going to be here is here, so let us move into the dining room for dinner. We shall not stand on formality tonight, so please feel free to seat yourself where you choose." She smiled and moved at the head of the crowd through the doors on the far side of the room and into the dining room. Oliver watched as she sat to the right of her father who took his place at the head of the table.

Oliver turned back to his friends in time to see William offer his arm to Sarah, who blushed before lightly resting her hand on his arm. William smiled broadly as they moved into the dining room together and found a place at the large table. Oliver looked at Evelyn and his heart sank at the look on her face. The sadness was only there for a moment before she remembered herself and met his gaze with a small smile.

"Miss Evelyn," Oliver said, extending his arm. "Might I have the pleasure of your company this evening?"

Her smile grew more sincere at his words, and she drew close to him as they moved together into the next room. "You sir, are not fulfilling your side of our bargain," she quietly teased.

"On the contrary, Miss Berkeley, I will shower you with praise and compliments tonight to such a degree that William will be overcome with jealousy at my attentions and will rectify the situation with an offer within days." Oliver smiled down at Evelyn as he spoke, pulling a small laugh from her. He knew as he said the words that it would not be difficult. The more time he spent with her, the more he discovered about her that he liked.

He squeezed her hand on his arm before seeing her into her seat and settling into the chair next to hers. He was happy to see he was only one seat down from Colonel Kilpatrick and Captain Baker was next to him. Kilpatrick's daughter Mrs. Fitzhugh was across from the captain and two other veterans, Benjamin Edwards and Richard Clayton, were directly across from him and Evelyn. William was two seats further down on the far side of the table from where they sat, too far for easy conversation.

As the first course was still being served, Captain Baker had already drawn Oliver into the conversation.

"How is your grandfather these days, Marten?" the elderly man asked.

Oliver frowned. "I'm sorry you have not heard, Captain, but my grandfather passed away several months ago. My uncle has inherited his estate."

"I'm sorry to hear that, son. He was a good man." The captain raised his glass in a small tribute before downing the liquid.

"He was the greatest man I knew," Oliver echoed. "What of you, sir? How is your family? Your grandson is also a sailor, is he not?"

The man's face lit up. "He was given his own crew just last month. He's a fine sailor. His mother misses him of course, and he misses his lovely wife, but he has it in his blood just like I did." He paused to take a bite then continued. "He lost his last ship to a fire off the coast of France."

The elderly man settled into story-telling mode and Oliver contentedly listened while enjoying his meal. Within a few moments,

Edwards and Clayton had joined in and were competing for who had the worst near-death experience during their years of service.

Oliver glanced down the table and saw William and Sarah deep in conversation. William had turned towards her and their heads were close, insulating them from much of the other conversation around the table. Oliver wondered why William was there in the first place, but felt bad for his somewhat uncharitable thoughts. Certainly, his friend had known some of these families for years, just as he himself had. He looked around at the others and caught the eye of Mrs. Fitzhugh. She nodded in the direction of Sarah and William and smiled warmly, obviously pleased with what she saw. *That explains the invitation,* he thought with a sigh.

He looked at Evelyn and could see immediately that she too had noticed the conversation between the pair. Her posture was tense, and she was far more focused on her food than on the conversation around her. She studiously avoided turning to her left while she ate.

Oliver frowned again. He couldn't do anything to break up the conversation from so far away. He would visit William tomorrow and deal with him directly. For now, he would ensure Miss Evelyn enjoyed the evening. He glanced down at her again. Her red hair was arranged neatly at the back of her crown with loose curls falling in the front and back to frame her face. As always, it gave the impression that it could break free from its pins at any point. Her dress was one he had not seen before in a shade somewhere between pink and orange. While it could be said that it nearly matched her hair, he wasn't sure that was a good thing. The sight of her brought a small smile to his lips.

She intrigued him. Her personality matched the fiery color of her hair when they spoke alone, but she was different in the company of her mother. Her logical approach to selecting William as her intended did not match her impassioned talk of love matches. Her writing was passionate and intense, just like her personality, and yet no one knew what she currently wrote except for him. He enjoyed knowing that secret side of her. It occurred to him that it was the type of knowledge he might have of his future wife one day. That is, if he chose to marry.

Evelyn took another bite of her bread as she considered her options. Her selection of William as her chosen husband relied on his remaining otherwise unattached. The addition of Sarah Staunton to the equation was a complication she had not anticipated, and one she felt unprepared to handle. She glanced down the table again in time to see Sarah blush and laugh softly at something William said to her. William beamed under her attention and Evelyn looked away with a small frown. Her gaze fell to the veterans, and she watched them instead.

She had never spent much time in such company, and she found she rather liked the older men so far. Their banter was easy as if they were all family. She laughed as the men shared tales of their experiences to determine who was the best with the ladies or who could hold their drink better. She knew she should be appalled by their conversation and topics, but found it impossible not to laugh at their antics.

It was obvious to her that Oliver felt much the same. He was engrossed in conversation with the man to his right. It seemed to Evelyn that he could listen all night. His face wore the smile that was so rare for him in most social settings. He was normally so serious, but his demeanor felt different here. She leaned in closer to better hear the conversation just as one of the two men across from her spoke.

"Clayton has the best escape story of all of us. Tell them about your night at Monmouth," the man directly across from her said. "Marten, have you heard this one? You won't want to miss it, that's for sure."

Oliver turned towards the man and smiled encouragingly. "I'm not sure if I've heard it or not, but I know my friend here has not." Oliver gestured towards Evelyn and nodded. "Mr. Clayton, Mr. Edwards, this is Miss Evelyn Berkeley, and she has a growing interest in the service of our men at arms." He turned his smile on her and she warmed as she returned his gaze.

Evelyn smiled at the two men. "It is lovely to meet you and I would so love to hear your story, Mr. Clayton," she encouraged.

"Well, I was injured in the conflict at Monmouth, but that's another story I'll save for later," he said in an aside towards Edwards with a grin. "I laid where I fell until nightfall when I managed to crawl my way into a nearby barn. No weapon. No food. Only a small amount of water in my canteen." He speared a bite of cheese and chewed while everyone waited for him to continue his story.

"Once inside, I found a small bag of old apples and some rags to tie up my leg wound. I felt restored and went in search of my men. That's when I learned I was surrounded. Everywhere I looked I saw blue coats on colonists lounging around their campsites. Defeated-looking men, I might add. Skin and bones, the most of them." He took a sip of his claret. "Upon my honor, I even saw Washington himself walk through the camp," he said, pausing for dramatic effect.

Edwards nodded enthusiastically, clearly having heard the story before. "George Washington," he said excitedly. "The General himself."

Evelyn smiled and had to admit a bit of awe herself. Men like Washington or Wellington seemed larger than life to her as if they were only legends, not real flesh and blood.

"I crept back into the barn, afraid I would never make it back to my unit. I slumped onto the floor in the corner and laid my head back. I propped my leg up on a bucket to relieve the pain a bit and stared up to the loft of the barn. And there it was. My salvation." Clayton grinned and took another bite.

Evelyn looked over at Oliver again and saw the smile on his face as he waited for the conclusion.

Captain Baker made a guess to fill the space. "A rifle?"

"Better!" exclaimed Clayton with a laugh. "A dress! A right pretty frilly number of pink and white. And a bonnet."

Everyone around the table laughed as the realization of what he had done dawned on them.

"A clothesline spanned the loft of the barn. Some lovely local colonist gave me my escape. I slipped off my red coat and drew the dress on right over my drawers. Lucky for me, she was not a small woman." He winked across the table at Evelyn, who laughed, despite his impropriety.

"I nearly balked at the bonnet, but I knew my mug would give me away if spotted so I tied it under my chin, real low on my face. I grabbed the bucket and stuffed my jacket inside and marched my way right out of the barn. It was dark, which helped, of course. After a few wrong turns, I made it to the road. I caught up with my men before dawn, and we made our way on to Sandy Hook," he concluded.

"You forgot the best part," cried Edwards.

At this, Evelyn was surprised to see Clayton's face turn a bit red, as he laughed and shook his head. "I have no idea what you're talking about, old man," he countered, though his laughter gave him away.

"One of his own friends propositioned him as he approached the lines," Edwards explained through his laughter.

Clayton tipped back a rather large gulp of his claret, with a face almost as red as his drink. "I can't help it if I cut a fine figure in a dress, Edwards."

His audience around the table roared with laughter, including Oliver. Evelyn could not help but look his way at the sound. She grinned at both the story and the change she saw in her new friend. He was different here somehow, and she liked the change.

She had an opportunity to see another side of him after dinner. The small number of women had gathered in the drawing room while the men retired to the study for port. She moved towards Mrs. Fitzhugh to thank her for the surprise invitation.

Evelyn smiled at the older woman as she approached. "Thank you so much for the kind invitation to join you this evening. It came as a most welcome surprise."

Mrs. Fitzhugh smiled and nodded at her words. "We were so pleased you could join us, especially as a particular friend of Oliver's."

Evelyn noticed the use of his Christian name and wondered again at the depth of their friendship. She seemed older than he was, but it would not be the first time an older woman had become attached to a younger man.

"He told me you were working on a project, but did not give me any details," Mrs. Fitzhugh explained, clearly fishing for more information.

Unsure of how much she should share, Evelyn guarded her response. "I am very interested in veteran stories as Mr. Marten stated. I feel that it is important for people to know of their sacrifices and contributions."

"Yes, I know that is how Oliver feels as well. He visited with Papa years ago to hear some of his tales. I only hope he is able to accomplish his goal. It is such an ambitious plan that he has; I know he faces an uphill battle," she added.

"It *is* ambitious to try to help with so many in need, and I will do what I can to try to further his plan," Evelyn pledged.

"Do you intend to visit his future facility in person?" Mrs. Fitzhugh asked.

Evelyn thought it was an unusual question, but answered nonetheless. "Of course, I would love to see the culmination of his efforts. I'm not sure I have much to offer, but at least I could bring small gifts and provide company on occasion."

Mrs. Fitzhugh looked confused by her response, but Evelyn had no chance to question her as the gentlemen moved into the room.

Colonel Kilpatrick spoke as he entered. "We spent years of our lives away from the fairer sex and in the company of men. I would much prefer to enjoy the company of women now when the opportunity arises." He moved towards his daughter and placed a light kiss on her cheek then turned to face the room again.

"I know this is an informal setting, but I have asked young Mr. Marten to say a few words about a plan he has. Some of you may know, but some may not, so please allow him just a moment to apprise you of his important work." He stepped aside and nodded at Oliver, who moved to take his place in the center of the room.

There was a bit of shuffling as everyone found a seat or space to make their own. Evelyn perched on a chair next to the fireplace where she could see most of the room but without being in the center of the group. She thought of how nervous she would be with everyone looking at her as they were looking at Oliver.

She need not have worried. Oliver turned in a small circle to survey everyone and to acknowledge those he had not yet spoken to directly. After everyone was settled, he began to speak.

"My grandfather told me stories of his service before I could even speak. I learned words like 'campaign' and 'drill' before I knew how to write." He looked around the room and paced slightly as he spoke. "It was not until I came into my majority that I began to hear more than just the fun stories. I heard of the deaths and the injuries. Of the mental toll of war, and the lasting burden many men bring home with them. I was saddened to hear of the limited help offered by our government."

Evelyn looked around the room and saw many nodding in agreement.

"I decided I wanted to learn more. I wanted to collect their experiences. I began to travel the country hearing from men about their experiences both during conflict and after they returned home. I met Colonel Kilpatrick and his daughter." He nodded in their direction, and Mrs. Fitzhugh beamed at him. "I met Edwards and Clayton, Captain Baker, and many more just like them. I also found younger veterans, newly returned from the fields of battle." He paused for a moment gathering his thoughts.

"The more I met, the more I saw their struggles. Injuries prevented work. Nightmares plagued their sleep. Pensions only go so far. The thanks and praise from the government does not put food on the tables of those now unable to work due to physical or mental limitations." Again, she noticed nods around the room.

"I slowly developed a new goal of creating a home for these men. A place for comradeship." He gestured around the room at the gathered friendly crowd to make his point. "A place for support and encouragement. And a place to help find work. Many of these men want to work, even if the work is in a different field than what they used to do. I want to create a place to facilitate new opportunities to work. To bring them out of economic strife and return their sense of confidence. When I took time earlier this year to be with my grandfather before he passed, I became more determined than ever to reach my goal."

Evelyn met his eyes as he looked her way, and she smiled back at him, encouraging his words. She was amazed by his small speech. It was more confidence, passion, and depth than she'd seen from him before. His seriousness was not gone but rather redirected. His stoicism was not a lack of emotion or feeling, but an expression of his dedication. She wondered if he hid other feelings behind that unflappable facade.

He hesitated as he looked at her as if debating his next words. Then he took a breath and spoke. "In fact, I feel as though I am making progress for the first time. My next step is to complete a pamphlet explaining the problem and my proposed solution." He smiled at her again and nodded, then looked away as he continued.

"Once published, I can use it as a tool to solicit funds to build and run my facility. I can offer a fresh start and the tools necessary to help these men and their families get back on their feet." He paused and looked down at his hands for a moment. When he looked back up, Evelyn saw his eyes shine with unshed tears.

"I could not have come this far without my grandfather and without each and every one of you." His gaze lingered on Evelyn for a moment as he looked around the room. "It is for all of you that I do this work. It is your stories that inspire me to continue, despite my own shortcomings. And it is each of you whose stories I hope will live on."

Despite the reasonably small audience, the applause was deafening as he made a small bow and moved back toward Colonel Kilpatrick. They shook hands and the colonel handed Oliver a glass of port as they spoke quietly. The guests moved to crowd around Oliver with pats on the back and friendly encouragement.

Evelyn sat rooted in her spot, attempting to process this different side of Oliver. She had already known what he hoped to do, but to hear him speak of it with such passion gave her a new perspective on both him and his project. She was more determined than ever to do justice to his plan, not for her own vanity, but for the men whose stories she told. She wanted to earn their approval, even if they did not know she was the author. Oliver would know it was her words, and that was enough. With a start, she realized how much his approval mattered to her.

She looked at him, now standing next to William, and appraised both of them side-by-side. She had been so intent for months that William was to be her husband, that no other gentleman had even merited consideration in that department. Yet Oliver was eligible, kind, and intelligent. True, he did not have two sisters who were her best friends, but Charlotte and Sophia's friendship did not rest on a marriage between her and their brother. She cocked her head to the side and considered the men from her current vantage point. Although the thought made her feel disloyal to her old friend, she found Oliver's dark hair and solid frame far more appealing than the sandy blond lankiness of William. As she watched, Sarah approached William, and he leaned in close to speak to her, a smile lighting up his face. Evelyn sighed at the sight and looked away.

She looked instead at Oliver just as he met her gaze from across the room. He tipped his head and raised his eyebrows as if to silently ask after her. She smiled back at him with a small incline of her head in acknowledgment of his thoughtfulness. He returned her smile and turned back to William and Sarah's conversation.

Perhaps she did not need to look far to find an alternative solution to her search for a husband. The thought brought a blush to her cheeks, and she quickly redirected her attention at the other guests around the room so as to not attract attention by staring.

She watched Mrs. Fitzhugh approach Oliver from across the room, hands outstretched as she moved towards him. He took both her hands in his and bestowed a full smile on his hostess. She leaned in close, speaking softly to him far out of range of Evelyn's hearing. He spoke back, staying close so they could carry on a private conversation. After a moment they moved apart, but stayed at one another's side. The older woman looked up at him with what could only be described as adoration, and Oliver looked content to tuck her arm into his and they moved about the room together, a seemingly perfect host and hostess.

Evelyn watched the interaction with a sense of sadness. Even as she knew with growing certainty that she was developing an attachment to Oliver, she realized with equal certainty that she may be too late.

Chapter 9

She was examining the Egyptian mummies when she felt him approach from behind.

"We must stop meeting this way, Mr. Marten," she said, turning to smile up at him.

"I have no idea what you mean, Miss Berkeley. I believe you are following me." He looked down at her with a serious look on his face, but she saw the twinkle in his eye before he turned to look at the Egyptian idols.

"Did you bring me more notes? I do hope they include your interviews with Mr. Clayton and Mr. Edwards. I would love to learn more about them and their service after having met them. And Captain Baker, too." She did not want to sound too eager, yet she could not deny how much she was enjoying the project. She had now penned several stories from his haphazard notes and she was excited at the prospect of telling the stories of the men she had now met.

"My most recent bunch does include Edwards, who will be thrilled to see his name in print, I assure you."

She smiled at the thought and moved on to the next room full of large Egyptian sarcophagi and statuary.

"What did you think of the company?" he asked from behind her.

She turned to look at him, but he was studying hieroglyphics on a stone tablet with great concentration.

"Well, there were improper jokes, an occasional lack of social decorum demonstrated by multiple guests, and a general informality pervaded the entire evening." Following his lead, she avoided looking at him as she spoke, but she could feel his eyes boring into her before she finished her statement.

"My apologies, Miss Berkeley," he began. His tone was so contrite she felt a pang of guilt and turned to meet his gaze with a smile.

"I loved it," she said, interrupting his apology.

The change that came over his face was instantaneous. His smile seemed to transform his seriousness into joy.

Her first thought was that he was far more handsome that way. Her second was that she liked being the cause of such joy.

"While it was certainly different than many high society dinners I have attended, I found the company infinitely preferable to stuffy matrons and insipid misses," she continued. "True, I occasionally felt out of my element, but at the same time, everyone was warm and welcoming despite my being an outsider." She looked up at him, meeting his eyes again. "I cannot think of a social event I have enjoyed more in any of my many years in Town."

He reached out as if he might take her hands, then thought better of it and interlaced his fingers behind his back.

"I am so glad to hear it. I had hoped it would help you to meet some of these men and put faces and voices to the words. Having a face with a name brings their stories to life for me, and I had so hoped that it might be the same for you." He unclasped his hands from behind his back and gestured as he spoke. "These men are so important to me, and therefore what I am doing - what *we* are doing - is also important." He glanced away as if debating his next words, then reached down and clasped one of her gloved hands in both of his. "Your words and your support are important to me. I do not know what I would have done if you had not come into my life when you did."

Although words seldom failed her, she now gazed back at him

unsure of how to respond, yet she longed to convey to him that she felt the same. Their meeting just weeks before in that very same building had brought about a great deal of change, but she was so grateful for the difference.

A sound of footsteps at the end of the hall broke the reverie before she could speak, and he dropped her hand as both took a step back.

Evelyn turned and moved towards a large figure of Isis, drawing a deep breath to regain her composure. "I am glad to be of service to you and to your friends," she finally said. She glanced at him and saw him smile briefly at her response, but it did not meet his eyes as his earlier smile had. She wanted to hear him laugh again.

"Will you be attending Ravenwood's ball on Thursday?" she asked.

"Yes," he responded, seemingly pleased to be on easy footing again. "I will look forward to a dance if it pleases you."

"Only if you promise to get me a dance with William as well," she said lightly.

She instantly regretted her words as the small smile on his face faded somewhat. He laughed and turned away again, admiring the Rosetta Stone. "I shall, of course, live up to my end of the bargain, Miss Berkeley. I will go out of my way to convince William of your many fine qualities and encourage a proposal. After all, we do have an agreement."

His smile still did not quite meet his eyes as he bowed and said goodbye before making his way towards the exit.

She watched as he walked away, cursing her choice of words with every step he took. He stopped and spoke with Marie before leaving the hall, but his kindness only served to make it worse.

"I simply do not understand why you refuse to see her as a possible match," Oliver began again. He was growing tired of the conversation with William but demanded of himself that he live up to his end of the agreement. The carriage ride to the ball had come to a halt as they waited in a long line of conveyances to be dropped at the steps of the stately townhome.

"And I simply do not understand why you insist that I do," William responded. "Evie has been like a sister to me for most of my life, and I cannot see her as anything else. Charlotte and Sophia would be thrilled if I did, I'm sure, but I would as soon propose to one of them," William said with a laugh. "Besides, I am not ready to make a match yet."

"You wouldn't know it the way you carry on with Sarah Staunton," Oliver grumbled.

"Ah yes, she is lovely, is she not?" William sat up straighter in the carriage, clearly happy with the change of subject. "She is beautiful and sweet, and calm and has such grace; she is everything feminine. She is a marked contrast to the intensity of Evelyn."

"She is lovely," Oliver agreed graciously. To himself, he added, *I for one, would prefer 'intensity' over triviality any day.*

"I tell you, old friend, Miss Staunton could make even me consider the bonds of matrimony," William said, with a shake of his head.

They lapsed into comfortable silence, each no doubt thinking of a very different woman until they finally disembarked at the well-lit home.

Oliver watched William move through the center of the throng in the crowded ballroom greeting people as he went. He chose instead a much slower and quieter move around the edges of the ballroom. He smiled at many familiar faces and even greeted a few acquaintances, but his attendance at such events was more perfunctory than preference. He knew his presence would be important when he earnestly began seeking financial backing for his veterans' home, so he made appearances and maintained friendships as much as possible.

He was debating with himself over how long he must stay to be proper when his gaze landed on a familiar trio of women. A pair of blonde-haired twins leaned in close with a red-haired companion, laughing at some shared joke or secret. Evelyn's orange dress made him smile, though he could not explain why. Charlotte and Sophia were the picture of current fashion in their coordinated gray and pink gowns, with lavishly styled curls framing their face and ribbons woven throughout their coiffures. Evelyn's tresses had already begun breaking free of their confines including one particularly unruly curl that was currently standing straight up at the crown of her head.

As Evelyn stifled a laugh at something Sophia had said, she looked up and caught Oliver watching her. Was it his imagination or did she smile bigger upon seeing him? He unwittingly matched her smile and moved towards her and her friends on the edge of the dance floor.

"Mr. Marten," Sophia exclaimed as he approached, "what a pleasure to see you this evening! Have you brought our brother with you tonight?"

Oliver bowed to each lady in greeting before responding. "We came together but he has already left me behind for more exciting company."

"Well, I for one am pleased with your company and would not wish for another," replied Charlotte sincerely. "Would you not agree, Evelyn?"

Evelyn blushed but smiled at Oliver as she replied. "Certainly not. Indeed, I believe I have been promised a dance, have I not?"

He returned her smile and offered his hand to her before guiding her to the line of couples gathering for the next dance. He was pleased when he realized it was to be a waltz, so they could talk uninterrupted for the set.

He smiled again at her unruly curl as he pulled her close and took her hand in preparation for the first notes. He thought for a moment what it might be like to reach up and brush it away with his hand, but refrained. He wasn't sure how she would respond, and he wasn't sure if he wanted it to lie flat. He liked her 'intensity' and somehow the wild lock fit with her unconventional personality.

"How is the writing progressing?" he asked quietly as they moved through the first turns along with the quartet's melody.

"I am so glad we have a chance to discuss it," she replied, excitement evident in her voice, despite her hushed tones. "Edward's interview was thrilling. Writing his experiences has been the most fun yet. I cannot wait for you to read it!"

He smiled down at her and tightened his grip at her waist. "Then I cannot wait to read it!" he replied. "When shall we meet for our next exchange?"

Her face fell as she considered her response. "My mother has become 'concerned' about my time spent alone lately. She cornered me yesterday and caught me writing, so I am not yet done. Do not worry; she does not know *what* I was writing," she assured him, "but she told me I was to stop writing and that it is not becoming of a young lady seeking to secure a husband."

Oliver frowned and looked over her head as he pondered this information. "Does she not know you love to write? That you are, in fact, a skilled writer?"

Evelyn laughed humorlessly. "She not only does not know, she would be horrified to know. She would see it as a shortcoming, not a talent." Her earlier excitement was nowhere to be seen as they moved among the couples on the floor in silence for several moments.

Oliver thought again of William's description of Evelyn. He was right that she was intense in all things. Whether it was loyalty to her friends, joy in her writing, or even despondency over her mother's overbearing dictates, she seemed to indeed feel deeply. Yet where William saw it as a fault, Oliver saw it as one of the many things he admired about her.

"What can I do?" Oliver asked. "How can I help?"

"Short of procuring a marriage proposal before the end of the Season, there is nothing you can do." She smiled up at him, though the smile no longer reached her eyes. "I shall write when I can get away from Mama's ever-watching eye; I just may take longer to finish my pages than before. I assure you, Mr. Marten, I will keep my promise."

Her words sparked an idea and he contemplated the ramifications only long enough to decide it was worth the risk. "What if I could solve both problems, Miss Berkeley? The proposal and the writing."

He nearly stumbled over his feet in his excitement to share his new idea.

"Is that not what we have already agreed upon, Mr. Marten?" she asked, confusion on her face.

"Yes, but perhaps our plan needs a slight adjustment. What if I call on you tomorrow, and the day after that, and the day after that? We can go for a drive, take walks through the gardens, or visit our museum."

She smiled at his reference to their many meetings at the museum. "While I like the idea of more trips to the museum, I'm not sure how this will help," she replied, clearly still confused.

"Your mother will be pleased that you are entertaining a gentleman caller, but you can use our time together to write rather than to entertain me." He paused and looked down before continuing with slightly less enthusiasm than before. "Perhaps my perceived attentions will also make William realize he would like to court or propose to you after all." He pasted a smile on his face, though with each passing day, he became less supportive of a marriage between William and Evelyn.

She looked away at the mention of William, biting her bottom lip. After several turns about the room, she looked up and her eyes held a bit more of their earlier enthusiasm. "That just might work, Mr. Marten."

"Please, call me Oliver," he said with a smile. "After all, if I am to court you, we may as well be more familiar with one another."

She laughed, making him smile even more. "As you wish, Oliver. And you may call me Evelyn."

The music came to an end and he released her, stepped back, and bowed. As he looked at her, he could feel his heart hammering in his chest, not from the activity of the dance, but from his own excitement at the idea of courting her.

Evelyn took his arm as they moved through the ballroom after their dance looking for Sophia and Charlotte. She tried to calm her nerves, but she could not stop smiling at the idea of Oliver's courtship. She reminded herself it was fake, but a small grin persisted nonetheless.

Her mood was broken by the shrill tones of her mother greeting Oliver.

"Mr. Marten, how good of you to honor our Evelyn with a dance this evening. She is a lovely dancer, is she not?" She smiled benignly at her daughter but gave Oliver no chance to respond before continuing. "She was just saying to me the other day that she prefers partnering with you above all others, did you not, dear?"

Evelyn flushed scarlet at this falsehood, but her mother either did not see or did not care about her discomfort and charged blithely onward.

"She longs for another ride in your phaeton, Mr. Marten. She could not stop saying for days how much she enjoyed the ride. Oh, do say you will take her out again soon!"

The older woman finally stopped for a breath and Oliver took the opportunity lest it not come again.

"My dear Lady Berkeley, your daughter hates heights and wants nothing more to do with my phaeton, which you would know if you paid the slightest attention to her instead of her prospects. And while I can say unequivocally that she is a lovely dancer, we have thus far only ever shared two dances making it difficult for either of us to accurately assess whether the other is preferable to 'all others.'" He paused here and glanced at Evelyn with a conspiratorial smile. Lady Berkeley seemed stunned into silence by his response and was possibly still trying to determine whether his words had been a slight when he continued.

"With that said, I should like to request permission to call upon Miss Berkeley tomorrow. I would very much like to hear her views on the latest exhibition at the British Museum."

Evelyn and Oliver both looked expectantly at Lady Berkeley, who was clearly torn in her response.

"Mr. Marten, surely you would prefer a ride through Hyde Park or a walk in the gardens. What would a proper young lady like my daughter know about the British Museum?" asked the matron with a forced laugh.

Stifling a smirk at the irony, Evelyn pleaded with her mother. "Oh, please Mama, you know I love the museum."

With a mischievous smile, Oliver added fuel to the fire. "I also have some recent political writings I have been working on that I would love to have your daughter look over. I am sure that someone of her intelligence could contribute much to my understanding."

At this, Lady Berkeley was truly rendered speechless. Evelyn almost felt sorry for her mother as she processed Oliver's words. She was clearly torn between her desire for the courtship and her disgust over the idea of Evelyn visiting a museum and discussing political pamphlets as a romantic afternoon.

As Evelyn knew it would, the prospect of a courtship won out over any other concerns and she gave her blessing. "Of course you may call, Mr. Marten, and Marie can accompany you both to the museum...if that is really what you wish." She said the last with a dismissive flick of her hand as if she could not imagine why that would be the case.

Evelyn gazed up at Oliver and realized he was schooling his features just as she was to avoid laughing out loud at her mother's reaction to their plans. They soon made their excuses and moved away from Lady Berkeley, looking again for the twins.

Once out of earshot, Evelyn pulled him to a stop and faced him, speaking softly. "Thank you. No one has ever spoken up for me like that." She gazed up at him, full of gratitude.

Oliver squeezed her hand and laughed, "It was fun to see the look on her face. Besides, no one should try to make you be something you are not." He bent down to look her in the eyes and continued in a gentler tone, "You are wonderful just as you are."

Evelyn gazed at him, swallowing past a lump in her throat, and praying she would not make a scene by bursting into tears in the midst of a crowded ballroom. "Thank you," she whispered again, smiling through watery eyes.

She saw Charlotte and Sophia approach from behind him and swallowed hard to calm herself. Oliver squeezed her hand once more then turned and disappeared into the crowd.

Chapter 10

Oliver tugged on the bottom of his waistcoat as a footman announced his arrival. He took in the room as he entered, noticing first Lady Berkeley seated in her favorite wingback chair directly in front of the window. Though she disguised it well, Oliver thought she seemed bored as she glanced towards the doorway, however, she schooled her features quickly and smiled at him as he moved to properly greet her.

He rose from a quick bow over her hand, and his gaze found Evelyn hovering behind her mother's chair. Her pale daffodil-colored dress stood in stark contrast to the boldness of her hair. Her fair skin looked nearly sickly next to the dress. Oliver thought he detected nervousness as well, which might also be contributing to her pale appearance. As he smiled and bowed to her, she returned his greeting with a sincere smile.

"Lady Berkeley, Miss Berkeley, it is a pleasure to see you both as always. Will we be joined by Lord Berkeley today?" he asked, as he sat down.

"He is squirreled away in the study with our steward at the moment, Mr. Marten. He loves the Season but hates to be away from the estate for so long," the older woman responded.

"I cannot say I blame him," Oliver offered. "My grandfather and my Uncle both prefer to be at their estates over anywhere else. Despite the pleasures of the Season in London, there is both comfort and responsibility to be found in one's country home." He looked from Lady Berkeley to Evelyn and found the latter to be listening intently.

"And what of you, Mr. Marten?" she asked. "Where would you prefer to spend your time?"

He wondered for a moment how she would respond if he spoke honestly of his desire to be in America, but decided instead to be more predictable.

"I can think of nowhere I would rather be right now than London." He nodded at Evelyn and was rewarded by a small smile and heightened color in her cheeks.

"If that is so, might I still convince you to take my dear girl on a ride through Hyde Park at the fashionable hour, Mr. Marten?" Lady Berkeley queried. "I am quite sure she would love it above all things," she cajoled.

From her position behind her mother, Evelyn widened her eyes and shook her head, and he grinned.

"I think we are both quite set on a leisurely stroll through the galleries of the British Museum this afternoon, but perhaps another time." Oliver stood as he made his statement and Evelyn stepped towards him.

Lady Berkeley fanned herself as they moved towards the door. "I do not pretend to understand how you find pleasure in such a dull activity, but do enjoy yourselves...if you can," she added.

Oliver and Evelyn smiled at one another as they made their way down the staircase to the entry hall where the butler stood. Oliver donned his gloves and hat while Marie entered and assisted Evelyn with securing her bonnet before their departure.

"I am quite sure Mama would prefer me to be caught in a scandal than to be forced to visit the British Museum herself," Evelyn said quietly with a laugh.

"She would certainly find one of those options to be more exciting than the other," Oliver agreed as they moved out the door together. "Since the weather is so agreeable, I had thought we would just walk to the museum, but we can call for my carriage if you prefer." Oliver paused on the walkway outside before choosing his next steps.

Evelyn began moving in the direction of the museum. "You forget our last phaeton experience, sir, if you think I might prefer a ride to a short walk," she reminded him.

He caught up to her in two long strides and placed her hand on his arm. Marie fell into step behind them, obviously having anticipated this particular choice. "I did not forget; I just did not want to assume," he explained.

"I love the walk, regardless of how I feel about your phaeton," Evelyn responded with a smile.

Oliver could not argue on that point, and they spoke for the duration of the walk about their favorite homes, shops, and flowers along the way. While he knew the walk was not far, he was still surprised at how quickly they arrived.

As they moved up the grand staircase to enter the Museum, Oliver realized how much he had missed having easy conversations with friends in the years since he had left school. Certainly, the company of his grandfather and his uncle in recent months had been priceless, but he enjoyed the easy banter of old friends.

He started at the realization that Evelyn was not, in fact, one of his school chums, yet he could not deny that he felt a level of comfort with her that he did not share with many others.

He held the door open for her and she moved in ahead of him.

Oliver spoke with the guard at the door, confirming the appointment he had made the day before. With a nod, the older man pointed him in the direction of the Reading Room, though Oliver needed no assistance. He eased the door open and peered about before breathing a sigh of relief. It was empty. Evelyn and Marie moved in behind him and quickly found a table where Marie brought out writing materials.

Oliver moved through a doorway into one of several adjoining rooms and returned with a rather large tome. "Manuscripts related to the history of Sussex by Sir William Burrell," he read from the spine.

Carrying the heavy book over to Evelyn, he addressed the women, his voice echoing in the large empty room. "I shall not go far, but if someone comes in, you can explain your presence with this book. Your family resides in Sussex and such research would appear eccentric perhaps, but reasonable."

"We will be fine," Evelyn responded. "Marie and I know our plan." She glanced at her maid who smiled back at her, despite a somewhat nervous look on her face.

"Are you sure you would not like me to stay here?" Oliver asked, clasping his hands.

"And have you staring at me while I write?" Evelyn asked. "Absolutely not. I wouldn't get three words written." She made dismissive motions with her hands towards the door. "Go! We will be fine." She smiled at him with what he assumed was meant to be reassurance, and he moved towards the door. His last view of Evelyn was her pulling pages towards her as she tapped the pencil against her bottom lip.

"I hope this works," he whispered to himself. He was so pleased with her writing that he was not sure what he would do if they could not finish. They were so close.

He moved out to the modern art gallery and positioned himself where he could move throughout the room but stay within sight of the doors. For nearly an hour he paced the hall attempting to move enough but not too much, so that his presence would not attract any undue attention.

Just as he thought he might have to fetch Evelyn from a writing reverie as their agreed-upon time approached, he heard footsteps behind him and a familiar voice.

"Mr. Marten, what a pleasure it is to see you here."

He turned to see Elizabeth Fitzhugh approaching, with Miss Sarah Staunton on her arm.

Groaning inwardly, he greeted them with a warm smile, bowing to each woman in turn.

"Mrs. Fitzhugh, Miss Staunton, what a lovely surprise this is," he murmured as he straightened. He tried not to glance at the doors to the reading room, but his mind raced at how he might handle the situation if Evelyn appeared.

He had no time to formulate a plan before Elizabeth forced the issue.

"And where is Miss Berkeley?" she asked, glancing around.

Oliver hesitated, unsure how to respond.

Miss Staunton spoke in a soft pleasant voice. "We called on her and learned she was here with you." She, too, glanced around as if Evelyn was hiding somewhere in the woodwork.

"We hoped to get to know her better," Elizabeth explained. "She and my niece have been acquaintances for years, but I only just met her at Papa's dinner party; I thought she was a lovely girl."

Something about the way she said "girl," made Oliver think she meant it as a slight.

Put on the spot, Oliver thought it best to go with at least a partial truth. "She is in the Reading Room," he said gesturing towards the closed doors down the hall.

Both women followed the gesture, then turned back to Oliver, confusion written on their faces.

He was glad they had discussed an alternative explanation and fell back on that now. "She has recently learned that her lineage dates back quite far in Sussex and wanted to learn more about the area. Rather than create any impression of impropriety, I decided to continue my perusal here while she explores within the library." He adopted a nonchalant stance as if a woman wanting to conduct historical research while on an outing with a gentleman was a daily occurrence.

"How is your father, Mrs. Fitzhugh?" Oliver asked, changing the subject.

Though clearly still confused and glancing towards the door of the Reading Room, Elizabeth responded to Oliver's question as social graces dictated. "He is quite well, thank you." Looking more intently at Oliver, she continued. "In fact, it is quite fortuitous that we saw you today as he hoped I would extend an invitation to you. He has reserved our box for the opera in two days and would very much like you to join us."

Oliver stifled a yawn at the idea of the opera and scrambled to think of an excuse. If he wanted to appear to be courting Evelyn, he could not be seen out with Elizabeth. And yet, her father held a great deal of influence as well as contacts within the veteran community; he could not afford to lose his good favor.

He smiled and bowed slightly before responding, "I would be honored to join your father. Please pass along my acceptance and appreciation."

Elizabeth smiled brightly as she gushed over how pleased she was that he would be joining her and how much she loved the opera, *The Devil to Pay.*

Oliver smiled at her enthusiasm but was soon distracted by the doors to the Reading Room opening at the end of the gallery.

He could see Evelyn's steps falter just slightly upon seeing Sarah and Elizabeth, but she recovered and approached the group as if nothing was amiss.

"Mrs. Fitzhugh and Miss Staunton, what a nice surprise," she exclaimed in greeting upon reaching the ladies.

Oliver knew she could not be excited at the sight of Sarah, but to her credit, her demeanor revealed no such turmoil.

Before either lady could respond, Oliver turned to Evelyn. "Did you find the information about Sussex you were looking for?" he asked.

"Yes, thank you so much for giving me a few minutes to look. Sir Burrell's research was quite extensive and I was lucky enough to find a reference to 'Berkeley's' in one of the church records that he transcribed."

"Well, we will not keep you from your perusal of the galleries," Mrs. Fitzhugh stated, glancing towards the door. "I look forward to spending the evening with you soon, Mr. Marten," she said with a smile in his direction.

Oliver could not help but notice the brief look of confusion that crossed Evelyn's face before she hid it with a society smile.

"Perhaps you can cajole Papa into donating funds to that project of yours," Elizabeth continued, reaching out to touch his arm. "I know how much it means to you," she said sweetly. "I could be persuaded to put in a good word for you," she added with a laugh.

If Oliver did not know better, he would think she was being flirtatious, and he did not find the notion appealing. She was certainly beautiful, despite being a few years older. He loved her father, and had spent many evenings in pleasant conversation with both of them. He could think of far worse fates than a life with Elizabeth, but that was not a future he was seeking at the moment.

Setting aside his contemplations, he smiled back at Elizabeth's beaming face and bowed over her hand and that of Miss Staunton.

"Goodbye Miss Berkeley, Mr. Marten," Sarah spoke softly as she moved away with Elizabeth.

Looking at Evelyn, Elizabeth smiled brightly and promised to call again soon.

Evelyn and Oliver stood in silence as the women moved away down the gallery hall. Finally, Oliver turned to Evelyn and asked, "Were you able to finish?"

As if his voice broke some kind of spell, Evelyn jumped slightly and took a step away from him. "Yes, I was able to finish what I set out to do today, so you will get your pages, Mr. Marten," she stated bluntly. "Shall we depart since my work is complete?" she asked.

Though conversation continued off and on for the whole walk, Oliver could feel that something had changed. The camaraderie he had felt on the walk over was gone. The comfortable chatter was replaced with polite small talk, and he couldn't help but wonder what had happened.

Evelyn sighed again as she lifted her teacup to her lips and sipped. She had tuned out the din of conversations in the drawing room some time ago and had fallen into a morose mood. Not typically one for self-pity, she had tried to push aside her melancholy in the three days since she had accompanied Oliver to the museum, but she was fighting a losing battle.

He had called on her yesterday, keeping up appearances of a tentative courtship, but it had been an awkward and painful meeting. She nearly groaned remembering the stilted conversation and her mother's blatant comments about how old she was, how she was not getting any younger, and how much she enjoyed card games. They had eventually escaped to the gardens for a walk, but even then their conversation was shallow and brief. She had been pleased to hear that he was happy with her most recent writing, and he had left his remaining notes with Marie before he departed, so she had that to look forward to at least.

She glanced at the clock again, willing it to strike faster, but still, it ticked on at the same reliably consistent speed, forcing her to face another ten minutes or more of her mother's callers.

Sarah and Jane Staunton sat across the room with their mother, who was dominating the conversation. The young ladies were the epitome of social grace, sitting up straight, sipping their tea, and never smiling too much at any joke. Evelyn had the immature and reckless impulse to stick her tongue out from across the room just to see if she could elicit a slip in their demeanor and perfection, but she had a feeling her mother would not approve.

Lady Berkeley's particular friend Harriet Pinckney sat between the young women and Evelyn and seemed to be enjoying herself immensely. She was not one to dominate a conversation, but enjoyed the presence and conversation of others, contributing her own thoughts now and again but generally happy to listen quietly.

The same could not be said for Lady Staunton whose rather large turquoise turban seemed in danger of falling off her head from the seemingly constant gesticulating that accompanied her steady stream of gossip about nearly every member of their acquaintance.

"Did you hear the latest about Lady Jane Anderson?" the garrulous woman asked. "She and her daughters have removed to the country early this Season. My neighbor says that she heard one of her girls was caught in a compromising situation." She shook her head as her daughters looked properly aghast. She continued, "Not surprising really. I remember her Season ended in a hasty marriage. Like mother, like daughter, I suppose."

Lady Berkeley and Lady Pinckney nodded at her words sagely.

"I am so grateful I have no fears on that account with my Evelyn," her mother offered, smiling benignly in her direction.

Evelyn's attention focused on the conversation more fully lest she miss some veiled instruction or hint on her mother's part. She found she preferred to know how her mother thought of her rather than be perpetually surprised at the things she attributed to her daughter in public settings that could not have been further from the truth.

Lady Berkeley continued, eager to contribute her own morsels of social rumors. "In fact, I believe we shall have our own happy occasion before too long."

Controlling her urge to groan, Evelyn instead smiled and attempted to control the flush she felt spreading up from her neck.

Lady Staunton leaned forward, asking, "Who might the lucky gentleman be?" Without waiting for an answer, she offered her own unwanted words of wisdom. "Be sure to secure an understanding quickly, if you know what's best for you." Shaking a closed fan in her direction, the elderly matron continued her advice. "You don't want to let another Season pass you by as he finds himself another bride, like those past suitors."

It was becoming increasingly difficult for Evelyn to either stifle the groan or control the redness spreading across her neck and cheeks.

Before she could come up with any type of retort, polite or otherwise, Lady Pinckney piped up. "Who *is* the lucky gentleman, Miss Evelyn?"

For a short second, Evelyn considered not answering, but she need not have bothered. Her mother answered for her, taking the decision out of her own hands.

"Mr. Oliver Marten," Lady Berkeley crowed, beaming at her daughter. "Such a handsome man he is, and so attentive to Evelyn.

He has called on her several times already and they make such lovely dance partners."

As the older ladies smiled and nodded in agreement at the pleasant news, Evelyn noticed that the Misses Staunton looked less staid at this news and in fact, appeared almost disconcerted. Evelyn did not have to wait long to discover the source of their concern as Sarah spoke up almost immediately.

"Do you not worry for her safety and future, Lady Berkeley?" she asked.

"Her safety?" her mother echoed. "He has been nothing but proper in his attachment, I assure you," Lady Berkeley responded in a shrill voice.

"Oh, I am quite sure he is," Miss Staunton clarified under the glare of Lady Berkeley. "Will- Mr. Montgomery speaks highly of Mr. Marten and I have no doubt of his character, I simply worry that if they marry you would miss your daughter when he moves her to America."

Evelyn froze with a calm look plastered on her face as she processed Sarah's statement. *America? What did she mean?*

While Evelyn preferred to keep her troubling thoughts to herself, her mother had no such compunctions.

"America?" she exclaimed in a voice far too loud for a drawing room.

Sarah looked taken aback by her surprise and looked to her mother for support.

"Did you not know?" Lady Staunton asked, pressing her hand to her chest. "According to Sarah, who heard it straight from his dearest friend, William Montgomery, Oliver Marten intends to move across the ocean and establish some sort of home for wounded soldiers." She waved her hand dismissively, obviously less concerned for the veteran part than the transatlantic move.

Lady Montgomery looked to her daughter, at a rare loss for words, but Evelyn could not yet formulate her own thoughts.

In all their conversations, throughout all of his notes, and through all their negotiations, he had never once said anything about America.

She wracked her brain thinking of their various meetings but she knew beyond a shadow of a doubt that he had never said he intended to go to America.

With a shock, she remembered the question Mrs. Fitzhugh had asked at the dinner party. Would she go and visit him? When Evelyn had said she saw no reason not to, Mrs. Fitzhugh had clearly been surprised and confused by her answer. She had known he hadn't planned for the home to be in England.

Taking a deep breath and speaking with a level of confidence she did not feel, Evelyn attempted a light laugh. "I know Mr. Marten has considered placing his veteran's home in America, but it is just one of his many ideas for how best to help the soldiers that are so dear to him." She picked up strength the longer she spoke and her words sounded less tremulous now. "I am sure that Mr. Marten would do so only after establishing a successful program here in his home country first." Evelyn met the eyes of each of the women around the room as if entreating them to agree with her.

Though she was loath to admit it at the time, Evelyn would be forever grateful for Sarah in that moment. She smiled brightly and chimed in with her support. "I am sure that is what Mr. Marten intends, Miss Berkeley. After all, we have so many men here who need our help, there is no need for him to travel across oceans to find veterans."

Lady Pinckney and Lady Staunton launched into a conversation about a handsome soldier who had broken the hearts of many women in their debut Season decades before, lightening the mood in the room considerably. Even Evelyn's mother shared her own story of a soldier who had caught her eye during a country dance in her youth. Evelyn smiled and laughed along with this pleasant turn of the conversation, but her heart ached.

He did not care enough to share this vital piece of information. His friends knew. Even his veteran comrades and their families knew. She was nothing but a means to an end in his eyes and did not merit such closeness or personal information. She drew in a deep breath as tears threatened at the back of her eyes.

She was relieved when the proper amount of time elapsed and the ladies rose to take their leave. She smiled, nodded, and promised future visits, even agreeing to call on Lady Pinckney soon to offer the older widow lively company. She followed her guests to the entry while her mother remained behind in the drawing room. As the door closed behind them, she turned and ran up the stairs to her room. She knew her mother expected her back below in case there were more callers, but she could not return.

She closed her door and moved to sit in the chair in front of her dressing table. She stared at her reflection, her face pale above an equally pale yellow dress, casting a sickly look over the entire ensemble. She felt sick to match her image. He had said it in their first meeting at Hyde Park. People would always act in their own self-interest, despite courtships or professions of love. Theirs was a fake courtship, yet Evelyn recognized now that her own feelings for him had become quite deep.

Did she love him? She enjoyed their friendly conversations. He was handsome and his attention to her likes and dislikes made her feel safe and appreciated in his presence. She wanted to support him in his plans and help him by continuing with the writing. The tears that had threatened earlier began to fall and she knew the answer.

But did he return those feelings? He valued her contributions to his project and even hoped to offer her something in return for her work, but he did not think her important enough to mention his plans. The tears fell faster as she faced the possibility of yet another failed courtship at the end of yet another failed Season. And this time, she was not sure she would be able to write herself a happy ending.

Chapter 11

Oliver relaxed as he sipped his tea and looked fondly at those gathered in the drawing room of the Montgomery's townhouse. A coincidental convergence had brought several friends to the house over an hour ago for what would normally be a brief social call, but a downpour had caused an impromptu luncheon with a celebratory feel despite the dreary weather. He looked out the second-floor window to the kitchen garden below as it soaked up the falling rain. He had always enjoyed watching the rain, and today was no different.

He looked away from the scene below and met Evelyn's eyes from across the room. He smiled at her and beckoned her to come join him. She leaned down from where she stood and spoke to the twins before moving across the room towards him.

He nodded out the window and spoke in a low voice as she drew near. "It seems I can offer no quiet walks in the garden for writing time today." He held out his hands as if in apology. "By the time this slows down, the time for social calls will be long over."

Evelyn stood up on her toes and peered out the window, trying to see outside from her position near the center of the room. "At least we have all had a fun time together," she replied with a smile.

Oliver made to move out of her way, but she rocked back on her heels and took a step back rather than closer to the window, so he kept his vantage point as they continued to talk.

Glancing behind her at William, he asked, "How are things on the marriage market?"

Evelyn blushed slightly and looked over her shoulder as if to ensure everyone was far enough away not to have heard anything. "Keep your voice down, Mr. Marten, or someone shall hear you."

Oliver would have felt more guilty if she hadn't laughed as she rebuked him, but she did not seem very concerned with his statement.

"Are you avoiding my question?" he teased with a small grin.

She cocked her head to the side and returned his playful smile. "What if it is going well?" she asked. What if I told you that not one, but two gentlemen have assured me that I shall have no shortage of dance partners at the Bennetts' ball in two days?"

Two? Oliver's smile faded as her response sunk in. He voiced the question he had asked himself to her. "Two? And who is this mystery dancer?" He attempted to keep his voice light but found himself far too interested in her answer.

Evelyn glanced over her shoulder again toward William, but this time her gaze lingered on the young man seated next to him. Oliver had known him for some time, but never well. Mr. Henry Holmes had arrived at school a year or two before he and William had left. They had moved in similar circles, but he was always better friends with William than he had been with Oliver. After their school days, Oliver had not seen much of him at all. According to William, he had become a vicar and traveled for a time serving in various parishes before taking a position just outside London. He was in town for several weeks and had chosen this dreary day to drop in on his old friend. Oliver had enjoyed visiting with him upon his arrival, but had quickly retreated to his spot by the window to allow William and Henry time to catch up.

Now, he examined the man again with a new perspective. He was certainly not unattractive by the standard conventions of his day. His hair was neat and trimmed to just above the collar and Oliver remembered from school that his blond curls could be quite unruly if left to grow much longer. He was tall and thin but more graceful than his height might suggest. Oliver had not yet seen him today without a smile on his face, a characteristic he remembered well from their school days.

Oliver started as he realized he had asked Evelyn a question and then promptly ignored her answer. He returned his focus in time to hear her say, "He was very kind to compliment my dress as I know very well I look like a confectionary's treat today, but I appreciate it nevertheless." Evelyn smoothed her hands over the front of her pastel pink dress, and Oliver had to acknowledge that the dress and hair combination was reminiscent of a sweet his mother used to bring home from the confectioners. Her cheeks were the same pink as her dress, and Oliver found the effect charming, despite the unusual combination of colors in her attire.

"Well, he was not wrong, Miss Berkeley," Oliver offered with a sincere smile. "I would ask you to dance even if I had not already made a deal to court you."

"*Pretend* to court me," Evelyn corrected with a light laugh. "I assure you, I will uphold my end of the bargain and cut you free, Mr. Marten." She looked down at her feet as she spoke and Oliver sensed she was hiding something, but when she looked back up at him, she gave nothing away.

Oliver nodded in acknowledgment and smiled, despite his conflicting feelings about the pretend courtship. "It sounds as though the original answer to my question then, is that the marriage mart is going quite well." He continued, "If my attentions were to help bring William to his senses, perhaps those of Henry as well will accomplish it even faster. Just remember to leave me my pages before you run off with a special license." He looked down at her with a grin, but she did not return the look.

Evelyn crossed her arms and her gaze turned intense. All evidence of banter or teasing was gone from her voice when she hissed, "I would never leave you empty handed, Oliver Marten. If you think I would run away from my part of the deal, you don't know me nearly as well as I thought you did."

"I did not mean..." he began.

"This may be a means to an end for you, but I gave you my word to finish and I intend to do just that," she exclaimed.

Unsure of what had just happened, Oliver watched as the redhead turned her back on him and rejoined the welcoming circle of the twins, William, and Henry. Oliver could not pretend to be an expert on women, Evelyn, or courting, but he was pretty sure had had just done something wrong. Try as he might, he could not figure out what it was. How could she be upset by the idea of marriage, either to Henry or William? That was what she had wanted the whole time. Right?

With a sigh, he leaned against the window frame and continued to watch the gray skies as the rain dragged on.

Evelyn watched in the mirror as Marie clasped the ruby necklace behind her. Once secured, she stepped back, giving Evelyn an unobstructed view of her mother's latest choice in fashion. The cream-colored gown was a far sight better than many other colors she had donned at Lady Berkeley's insistence, but she knew it made her look pale, almost sickly. She cast a resigned smile at her reflection and headed downstairs.

The carriage ride to the Bennett's was quiet as Evelyn and her mother watched the busy streets of London pass outside their windows, each apparently deep in thought. Evelyn pondered the conversation with Oliver two days ago. He had sent flowers yesterday with a note explaining he had family business to attend to, and he had not called on her. She did not try to deny that the news had disappointed her. She looked forward to his visits and their comfortable banter. She had hoped to apologize for getting angry at the Montgomerys', but now she would have to try to find him tonight to say she had overreacted.

She had never met someone who had such an extreme effect on her. She could be moved to tears at the depth of her feelings for him, then be angry at him for saying something unreasonable only seconds later. She often felt giddy when he arrived and struggled to make intelligent conversation for the first minutes, yet she had also never felt more herself around any suitor before. She shook her head to correct herself; he was not a suitor. And he was moving to America.

Her mother's voice broke into her silent conversation. "What are you thinking about, child?" Without waiting for an answer, she continued. "I hope Mr. Marten will be in attendance tonight. Of course, he shall ask you to dance." She fanned herself in the confines of the carriage. "Sit up straight, dear. Why do you look so forlorn?" She scowled at her daughter, who had not known she was looking forlorn at the moment. "No man wants to marry a woman who sulks." Her mother punctuated her statement with a snap of her fan.

"I am not sulking, Mama," Evelyn countered, sitting up straighter even as she said it. "I am... contemplating."

"What have you to contemplate? It is not your first ball. It is not even your first Season." Lady Berkeley looked at her as if she had three heads. "When a gentleman of good standing asks you to dance, you dance." She made a mock bow in the carriage to drive her point home. "You smile, you talk about the weather, and you secure a betrothal."

At this simplification, Evelyn snorted out an unbecoming laugh. "Mama! If it were that simple, I would have been married four years ago." She shook her head at the idea, unsure whether her mother was trying to make her laugh, or truly thought such an outcome was possible this evening. As quickly as she had been moved to laughter, her smile fell and she sighed. Though her mother did not - could not - know of her agreement with Oliver, Evelyn knew there would be no proposal from him tonight.

Not to be deterred, Lady Berkeley persisted. "It may happen," she argued. "Or perhaps you will make a new acquaintance and he shall be your future betrothed. I have no partiality for Mr. Marten." She swished her hand through the air as if she could dismiss Oliver and make a new husband appear at her command.

Would that she could.

"Mama, I shall be as I always am. I shall smile, but not too much. I shall dance, but not too much. I shall talk, but not too much." To herself, she added, *I shall be liked, but not too much.*

Evelyn attempted to take her mother's admonition about sulking to heart and donned a pleasant and content demeanor as she moved into the crowded ballroom at the Bennett home. Her mother preferred a fashionably late entrance, while the twins preferred to be early, so she perused the crowds looking for the dual blonde heads of her friends. She moved around the outskirts of the room admiring decorations paying homage to ancient Greece and Rome. Faux columns were placed around the room displaying statuettes, vases, and even trays of food adding to the ambiance. Two sets of doors were thrown open in the back of the room to offer fresh air and admission onto their terraced garden walk. Evelyn looked longingly out the doors but knew her mother would disapprove of escaping before she had even shared one dance with...well, with anyone.

She spotted Charlotte and Sophia and moved in their direction. As always, she admired the closeness of the two that was so evident in their interactions with one another. Sophia's fire and ice was the perfect foil to Charlotte's sweetness and calm. Evelyn could not imagine how they would deal with their own courtships and marriages. It was impossible to imagine them apart, but she knew they both dreamed of their own families, so the day must come at some point.

Evelyn was not surprised to see that both William and Henry were with the twins on the edge of the dance floor. She could not decide if she was happy or sad that Oliver was not with them, but she had no time to contemplate before William spotted her.

"Miss Berkeley," he crowed, "it is high time you arrived. The girls are beside themselves in your absence." The old friends greeted one another with a quick bow and curtsy extended among the group, as William continued. "I was just telling Henry here about all our fun as children. You three used to follow me around and beg for me to entertain you with boat rides or carriage rides about the village."

They all laughed at the pleasant memories, but Sophia did not have quite the same impression as William.

"Are you sure we followed you?" Sophia asked. "I think you followed us because we were such fun!"

"You are both wrong," Charlotte chimed in. "William followed the cook around looking for sweets!" The group laughed comfortably together. They all turned to the east end of the room as they heard the unmistakable sounds of the musicians preparing for the next dance.

William turned to Evelyn and bowed in acknowledgment once again. "Would you do me the pleasure of this dance, Miss Berkeley?" he asked. "I should dearly love to reminisce with you as we take a turn." He held out his hand with the optimistic and expectant look of a child used to receiving handouts.

How could she say no? And why would she? Evelyn smiled at the invitation and put her hand in his. She turned to walk with him towards the dance floor and bit back ironic laughter. Had it been only weeks ago that all she desired was this moment? She had focused all her efforts on her plan to get William to see her as a marriageable young woman. Now he held her hand in his and led her to the dance floor, bowing over her hand with impeccable grace and charm that could not help but elicit a sincere smile from Evelyn.

They began the reel and moved through the steps effortlessly, both well-versed in the twists and turns. Though William valiantly tried to keep up a steady conversation about youthful escapades, the maneuvers of the dance made it inconsistent at best. Their broken conversation allowed Evelyn the chance to observe him, both as her partner and as he spun with others. She could not deny how handsome he was. His height was above average but not so tall that he towered over others in the room. His hair was neat and trim, just above the shoulders with a perfect wave across his forehead. His blue eyes shone from a pleasant visage that was almost always smiling. His family's finances kept him in the finest of fabrics and the height of fashion. He was an unquestionable prize for any woman.

They came together again and Evelyn felt his hand envelop hers as he pulled her through the steps. She felt the pressure of his hand on her waist and waited to feel...something. She had never considered herself either to be too practical or too romantic. In fact, she developed her "plan" to marry William based on logic, not emotions. But shouldn't she feel *something* in his arms? She glanced up at his face again and imagined pushing back the curls or touching his cheek. Her gaze fell to his lips and she imagined what it might be like to kiss him. Given that she had no more experience in that arena than friendly touches on the cheek, she really couldn't speak to it. She felt her neck flush with her unabashed perusal of him in such an intimate fashion, and she quickly looked away.

He glanced down at her as they moved across the floor and attempted to engage her in conversation again. "You look lovely this evening, Miss Berkeley. Your necklace matches your hair beautifully." He smiled down at her just as they broke away again and Evelyn found herself passed to her next partner.

If she had not known the steps in her sleep, she might have stopped in her tracks. Even with her years of social training, she nearly burst out laughing at his statement. The humor of the situation was not lost on her. She looked like a torch with her pale dress and flaming hair, though the ruby necklace did, in fact, match her hair. Six weeks ago, she was longing to hear William speak such pleasantries yet now she did not know what she wanted. Would William finally consider her as a possible match? What of Miss Staunton? She had not seen her here tonight, but it was the first time in several weeks not to see the two in close proximity.

What about Oliver? The thought came to her mind unbidden but seemed to conjure him from the crowd. Just as she returned to William's strong arms and smiling face, she caught sight of Oliver at the edge of the crowd. He had not seen her yet and she watched as he engaged in conversation with several of the guests. She could not believe how she had once found him to be too serious. He was not frivolous, perhaps, but his eyes were kind and his smile lurked just below the surface and appeared often among friends.

The dance came to a close and William and Evelyn bowed to one another. As she rose and took William's hand to walk back to the edges of the room, she looked up and met Oliver's gaze directly in front of them. He raised his eyebrows in question, a teasing grin on his face, and she could not help but smile back.

"Oliver," exclaimed William when he spotted his friend. "Nice of you to grace us with your presence this evening," he joked.

"Someone needs to take your allowance at the card table. It might as well be me," Oliver retorted with a smirk.

"I look forward to taking you up on your challenge, but for now, please excuse me," William said with a glance towards a gathering of young men on the other side of the room. "Mr. Marten, Miss Berkeley." With a quick nod to each, William made his way towards his friends. They watched him go in comfortable silence for a moment before Oliver turned his attention more fully on Evelyn.

"Miss Berkeley," Oliver addressed Evelyn with a bow. "A pleasure to see you, as always."

She put out her hand and he bowed low over it. Even after he released her, she could still feel the warmth where he had touched her hand, even through their gloves.

"The pleasure is mine, Mr. Marten," she replied. "I hope your family is well?"

A look of concern passed over his face, but Oliver disguised it quickly. He nodded and explained, "My uncle sent a request that I end the Season early and join him at his estate. He was vague in his reasoning, but I am worried he is unwell."

"I am sorry to hear that," Evelyn responded. "I know how much you admire your uncle. I do hope it is simply that he misses your company," she finished with an encouraging smile.

"I will join you in hoping, but my fear will not subside until I see him myself to confirm." Oliver moved to take her hand, resting it on his arm as he steered her away from the dance floor and towards the refreshments closer to the doors. "Can I get you something? You are no doubt thirsty after your turn with William."

"Thank you," she agreed. "It is quite hot in here and it is only exacerbated by the dancing. I am parched."

They moved to the tables and Oliver fetched a lemonade for each of them. They stood for a moment watching the crowds and enjoying the slight breeze from outside.

"Speaking of William, have we succeeded in our mission yet?" Oliver asked in a stage whisper meant only for her.

Laughing, Evelyn tapped his arm in rebuke and shook her head. "I am as un-betrothed now as I ever have been. Clearly, you are failing in your duties, sir."

Taking a step back with his hand to his chest in disbelief, Oliver feigned offense. "Me? I have sung your praises, waxed nostalgic on the blessings of the matrimonial state, scolded on the importance of maturity and fulfilling one's obligations, and even attempted to elicit jealousy on your behalf." He looked at her in mock rebuke. "I think I can hardly be found guilty of negligence, my dear."

Laughing, Evelyn had to agree. "I supposed you are right, though it pains me to agree." She turned to look at the musicians who were just beginning the opening strains of the next number, then glanced back at him. "Though you have not yet fulfilled your promise of a dance." She felt herself flush at the boldness of her statement but was rewarded with a grin rather than disdain.

"May I never be accused of not fulfilling my promises," he said. Bowing dramatically over her hand, his eyes never leaving hers, he purred, "Will you do me the honor of this next dance, Miss Berkeley?"

Evelyn attempted to remain nonchalant in her reaction, but her response stuck in her throat, and she found she could only nod. He led her to the floor just as the opening notes began. It was a waltz. She felt his hand grasp hers lightly as his other rested firmly at her waist, drawing her close as they moved together into the first steps of the song.

Ever the observant writer, Evelyn could not help but take notice of the differences between her two dances. Her heart raced and her hand tingled from the pressure of Oliver's hand on hers. The feel of his arm on her waist had her stomach in knots. She gazed up at him, having nowhere else to look, and she felt herself flush under his observing eye. Was this then what the novels talked of as love?

Belatedly she realized he had asked her a question. She pulled herself back to the ballroom. Was she unwell? How to answer that honestly without giving herself away?

"I am quite well, thank you," she responded after only a brief hesitation. She knew her words sounded weak and continued, gaining more strength with each word. "Why do you ask?"

"You seem...distracted this evening," he replied. He cocked his head to the side and looked down at her. "However, you look quite lovely."

She chuckled at how he paid her the same compliment as William. "I do not mean to laugh at you, sir, but rather at your words. William said the same thing to me not fifteen minutes ago."

Oliver shook his head and laughed. "I cannot believe I am coming in second place to that fool."

Evelyn laughed. "At this point, I believe neither you nor William is in first place," she clarified. "I am the only one who has lived up to my end of the bargain." She paused for a moment. "Well, almost. I should have the last notes completed within the next few days."

"I have not given up on my part of our deal either," Oliver said squeezing her hand. "I promise on my honor as a gentleman that I will do everything I can to secure you a betrothal before the end of the Season." Whether conscious or not, Evelyn felt him hold her tighter and was at a loss for words. She debated whether now was an appropriate time to bring up his plans to sail across the Atlantic, but decided to put that off for a more private moment.

They danced, comfortably silent for several moments until Evelyn felt Oliver tense in his steps. She did not know what had caused the reaction until the steps of the dance turned her around and she spotted Elizabeth Fitzhugh at the edge of the crowd watching them dance. Evelyn looked up at Oliver with an unspoken question, but his only response was to smile at her in a way that was likely supposed to be reassuring before looking away.

As the song came to a close, far too soon for Evelyn, Oliver avoided meeting her eyes as they moved off the floor. If Evelyn did not know better, she would have suspected that he tried to avoid moving in the direction of Elizabeth, but she could think of no reason why he would do such a thing. In fact, the last time she'd seen them together, his feelings for her had seemed quite affectionate. Whether it was his intention to avoid her or not became irrelevant as Elizabeth moved straight towards them.

She greeted them as they drew near. "Miss Berkeley, what a pleasure to keep running into you." Elizabeth took her hands and dipped in greeting. "I am so glad we are getting to know one another better. Oliver's friends are my friends, " she proclaimed in a singsong voice.

"The pleasure is all mine, Mrs. Fitzhugh," Evelyn responded. Her exterior revealed nothing of her inner turmoil as she processed everything she had said. Oliver? When did they move to a first name basis? And why were they sharing friends?

Turning to Oliver, Mrs. Fitzhugh asked, "Did you tell her the exciting news, dear?" She placed a hand on Oliver's arm as she said this and did not remove it.

"I..." Oliver began. He looked at the floor and then at Elizabeth. "We are leaving next week for my uncle's estate." He looked around the room, seeming to look anywhere but at Evelyn. Elizabeth's hand still hadn't left his arm. "Colonel Kilpatrick will be joining us as well, and of course, my uncle is there." Evelyn wasn't sure why he needed to clarify that his uncle would be at his own estate. "The colonel would like to make the acquaintance of my uncle, so I invited him along for this visit."

Unsure what her response was *supposed* to be but knowing there should be some kind of response, Evelyn tentatively praised the news. "I am so glad to hear it. I hope you have safe travels and a safe visit with your uncle." Elizabeth still had not removed her hand and Evelyn found she was unnaturally interested in how long she would leave it there. "When will you be back?" She posed the question to Elizabeth, but then looked at Oliver for an answer as well.

"I hope to return as soon as I can assure myself that my uncle is in good health," Oliver replied quickly.

Elizabeth piped up and added, "I have always wanted to explore Longwood, so of course we will take some time for that as well, but it should not be longer than a few weeks, right dear?" Elizabeth moved closer and the hand shifted from lightly resting on the arm to covering his arm while she gazed up at him.

Oliver looked down at Elizabeth returning her gaze, but Evelyn thought he almost looked confused.

Deciding it was probably better to take her leave, Evelyn made her excuses. "I hope you find your uncle in good health. Enjoy your travels." She nodded at both and offered a quick smile before turning on her heel and moving away to find the twins.

She wandered with no direction for several minutes, scanning the ballroom without seeing anyone in it. She was not sure she had ever had a more emotionally draining evening in all her life. What she would not give for the normalcy of a conversation with Lord Allen right now, she thought with a laugh.

She paused in her search for Charlotte and Sophia and headed towards the doors, anxious for a quick breath of fresh air. The night was clear and warm, and a slight breeze provided a refreshing respite from the still, humid air of the day. She moved to the railing that overlooked four terraces stretching away from the main house. Paths wound through the gardens, but all the foliage was short so one could walk the paths for some time and remain in sight of the house.

Evelyn leaned over the railing and tried to make sense of the evening. She had danced with the man she had hoped to marry. He had said she was lovely, but she had felt nothing as they danced. No tingles, no butterflies, and she certainly did not forget to breathe. He was the perfect gentleman, reminding her why she had idealized him as a husband in the first place.

Then she had danced with her pretend suitor. She had felt tingles and felt slightly nauseated in a good way, but she was supposed to feel those things for William. Elizabeth had greeted him and spoke of their upcoming travels together as if there was an understanding between the two of them. Was there an understanding? She had no claim to him, and Mrs. Fitzhugh was a smart and independent woman. They would be lucky to have one another.

Somehow, she had gotten off course. She still wanted to marry, but she could no longer see herself with William. She thought of Oliver but she could not imagine him without seeing Elizabeth's hand on his arm. What other option did she have? She felt tears prick at the back of her eyes and a familiar sense of resignation came over her as she faced the possibility of another unsuccessful Season.

Her reverie was broken by a voice from behind her. "Miss Berkeley, I hope I am not too late to claim my promised dance."

She brushed lightly at her eyes and turned to find Henry Holmes standing a few feet behind her, his characteristic smile visible even in the dim light of the evening. Her heart lightened at the sight of him. She had only met him once, but she found him easy company and welcomed a distraction on this particular evening.

"Mr. Holmes, your timing could not be better," she replied.

If possible, he smiled even wider and put his arm out towards her to escort her back into the crowded ballroom. The sounds of a reel began as they moved into the room and he expertly maneuvered them among the couples to find a spot.

She found Henry to be an excellent dance partner. He was graceful and light on his feet and he seemed to enjoy the dance. She had yet to see anything that he did not enjoy, and his optimism and cheerfulness were contagious. His ongoing chatter about nothing brightened her mood considerably and the exertion of the lively dance forced aside her disconsolate thoughts of earlier.

She could not have known the sadness with which Oliver observed her bright, smiling face as they danced by him repeatedly just before he departed from the ball.

Chapter 12

Evelyn stretched her hand, working out the cramps gained from the last hour of writing. She leaned back to stretch and turned her face up to feel the sun for a moment. It had been weeks since she had written anything significant for pleasure, and she had enjoyed returning to her simple stories. The work she was doing for Oliver was important, and she was proud of her part in it, even if no one else knew what she had done. But her stories were an outlet and an escape from the realities and pressures of the real world. She had enjoyed losing herself in her pages again.

Oliver would scold if he knew she could have been writing for him, but instead had chosen to return to childhood animal stories for the afternoon. The last section seemed to be taking her longer than any other. She knew she was drawing it out because she didn't want it to end. Not the writing part, but her work with Oliver. She loved their meetings at the museum and secret conversations. She would miss their silent communication and trading of materials through Marie. She would miss him.

She sighed as she stood and began gathering her materials. Charlotte had sent a message yesterday inviting her to attend dinner with them this evening and it was time to prepare. Her friend had called it "an impromptu celebration among friends," but had not indicated what was being celebrated. She assumed it was in honor of William's recently arrived friend Henry, but she did not know for sure. Regardless, she had responded positively to the invitation and looked forward to a relaxing evening among friends.

Marie approached from the house and Evelyn scooped up her satchel and walked to meet her lady's maid across the lawn. The two walked arm in arm discussing the latest in her story then proceeded upstairs where Marie had prepared a bath for Evelyn. Evelyn enjoyed a brief soak in the warm lavender-scented water before she donned a green gown for the evening. She had to admit that this color was not one of the worst that her mother had chosen for her most recent fashions from the modiste. At the right time of year, it might look as though she was trying to blend in with the decorative greenery around the house, but she preferred holly comparisons to confectionery delights any day.

Due to a headache, her mother chose to stay home, so Evelyn proceeded alone to the Montgomery residence only several streets away. The footman showed her into the drawing room where she was pleased to see a gathering of some of her very favorite people in the world. The twins were seated in front of the fireplace, heads close as if conspiring about something. Henry and William were close by, though William was paying far more attention to the beautiful Miss Staunton than his old school pal. Evelyn was proud of herself for not frowning at the sight and continued her perusal of the room. Oliver, Elizabeth, and Colonel Kilpatrick gathered in front of the window on the far side of the room from the door. The colonel was seated with his daughter next to him while Oliver stood over them both, talking and glancing out the window on occasion. Lord and Lady Montgomery were speaking just inside the door to the Stauntons, who were all smiles.

She made her way across the room towards Sophia and Charlotte, who had looked up at her entrance and waved her over.

Sophia greeted her first, "I am so glad you could make it on such short notice!" She glanced knowingly at her sister and added, "I imagine it will be a night you will not soon forget."

Both girls giggled, but Evelyn did not know the cause of their laughter. She had no time to ask before a footman entered and announced that dinner was ready. Being such an informal gathering, Evelyn noticed that no one followed social order but rather deferred to the elder Colonel Kilpatrick in allowing him to enter first and take up a position of honor to the right of the host.

Evelyn followed the twins to the opposite end of the table where she found herself seated between Henry and Charlotte, directly across from William. Oliver was on one side of William and Miss Staunton on the other beside her parents. Evelyn steeled herself to limit her sighs during dinner. She had already stifled several aimed in the direction of the smitten William before the first course had even been cleared.

William was clearly besotted. And Evelyn had to admit that the feeling appeared to be mutual as Miss Staunton smiled happily throughout the meal, her eyes never straying from William for long. Though she spoke softly and Evelyn never heard their conversation, the two blond heads were close, and adoring glances were common for the duration of the four courses. The one part of the conversation at which Evelyn had to laugh was Oliver's vain attempts to intersperse himself into their circle, but he gave up halfway through the second course and instead spoke only to Elizabeth on his right.

Evelyn frowned at the woman and then immediately chided herself for her uncharitable thoughts. Elizabeth had done nothing wrong and deserved none of her ire, yet Evelyn felt nothing but annoyance at the very sight of her sitting next to Oliver, touching his hand when she spoke, and smiling up at him far too often. Evelyn was self-aware enough to know it was jealousy that drove her emotions, but that knowledge did not make it any easier to deal with the sight of Oliver refilling her wine glass after each course.

Given the options in front of her, Evelyn did her best to engage her two neighbors in conversation. While Charlotte was the quieter of the two twins, their years of friendship made the conversation flow easily to her right. She had known Henry for far less time, but she found him to be a very pleasant conversationalist throughout the meal. She was surprised to discover that she hadn't sighed once during the fourth course after starting a conversation with the gentleman.

"You cannot be serious," Evelyn said in shock.

"I do not understand why it is so hard to believe that I am a country vicar," Henry said with mock seriousness in his tone. The laughter in his eyes belied his tone, and Evelyn grinned.

"You do not seem like a vicar, sir," she explained trying not to laugh so as to not cause offense.

He sat up straighter in his chair and looked down his nose at her. "And what, pray tell, is a vicar supposed to seem like, my dear woman?" He could not hold the stern look for long and soon relaxed into a smile. "Perhaps you must give me longer, for I have only held the living for a short time," he posited.

"I am sure you are a fine vicar," Evelyn rushed to say, hoping not to hurt any feelings. "I'd wager your flock loves you," she continued. "I just have rarely seen one so...young in the role full time." Evelyn caught herself just before saying 'jovial,' and instead referenced his age. She knew it wasn't fair, but most of the vicars she knew were much more staid at best and morose at worst. She had the distinct impression that she would enjoy his sermons more than most she had heard in recent memory.

Their conversation lagged for a moment as he paused to enjoy his candied fruits and Evelyn couldn't help but notice that the smile never left his face. His blond curls bobbed as he looked up and down the table catching snippets of conversations here and there and engaging when he could, always adding a pleasant word or encouraging phrase. His contrast with Evelyn's initial impression of Oliver could not have been more different and she stifled a laugh. She glanced again at Oliver, who seemed entranced in what Elizabeth was talking about - her endless sources of funds for his project no doubt, and she looked away in frustration.

She started when she realized Henry had spoken to her and she had not responded.

"Excuse me," she said, "I was wool gathering." She smiled up at him in apology.

He beamed back at her. "No apology needed, Miss Berkeley. I was asking if you have ever been to St. Paul's Cathedral?" he repeated.

"I have seen it from the outside but I have never attended a service there, if that is what you mean," she answered.

"If you would be interested, I will be visiting with an old friend of mine who can get access to the dome. Would you care to join me two days from now to see for yourself just how at home I am inside a church?" He grinned at her expectantly, like a child eagerly awaiting permission to play.

Evelyn took a sip of her wine to delay her response yet again, but she could not deny she was intrigued by the idea. St. Paul's magnificent silhouette dominated the views from nearly anywhere in London. Her father had once told her that it was the tallest building in England, and she had no doubt when she looked up at it from the base of its large and imposing steps. She swallowed down an encroaching sense of panic at the idea and thought instead of how exciting it would be.

She looked over at William, who would have been hard-pressed to be closer to Miss Staunton without violating all rules of propriety. She glanced at Oliver just as he unconsciously reached over and removed a small feather from Elizabeth's hat that had fallen to her shoulder. She looked up at Henry's handsome smiling face.

"I would love to join you," she replied, returning his smile with her own.

A moment later, Evelyn and Henry's conversation was interrupted by the sound of Lord Montgomery clearing his throat as he stood at the head of the table.

"Lady Montgomery and I would like to thank each of you for attending." He paused and nodded around the table. "You are all our particular friends and we would not wish to share this special night with anyone else."

Evelyn's mind raced at his mention of something special, echoing the statement of the twins earlier. What could it be that was both secret and exciting for the family? She scanned the faces around her, some looking as clueless as she felt, while others smiled at their secret knowledge. As her eyes fell on William and Miss Staunton, her stomach sank. The two looked at one another as if they were the only people in the room. All sense of shyness appeared to be gone from the young woman whose socially polite smile had been replaced by a smile that lit up her entire face.

Having been raised in Society, Evelyn knew to school her features into a smile for the happy couple as Lord Montgomery announced their betrothal. She clapped her hands in excitement as he explained that their wedding would be one month away and all were invited to their wedding breakfast. She returned the hug from Charlotte to her right and leaned across the table to voice her own congratulations to the pair. She was proud of herself for never, not even for an instant, losing her poise.

Until she met Oliver's eyes. His gaze pierced hers and she was dismayed to find pity there. She felt tears prick at the back of her eyes. She swallowed hard and looked away, blinking them back lest they start and not stop. How dare he pity her? She did not need his pity. She did not need him.

He had promised to help her and where had that gotten her? She was no better off now than she had been at the start of her Season. She would finish his last section and see him off to America and she would go back to living as she always had. She would visit with her friends and write her stories of happily ever after. She would not entertain the deals of gentlemen who did not deliver.

All at once, she wished to return home immediately and finish her notes for Oliver. Once they were done, she could wash her hands of their partnership and move on. He had not managed to elicit a proposal from William or anyone else. His attentions towards Elizabeth proved that any sentiment she may have thought he felt for her was purely for his own gain. How could she have thought that either of them - William or Oliver - would feel anything more than friendly affection for her?

Afraid that she would not be able to hold back the tears for long,

Evelyn moved away from the table to make her excuses to Lady Montgomery and slip out. She would congratulate the betrothed and claim she must get home to check on her mother.

The guests were all standing now as Lord Montgomery encouraged everyone to retire to the drawing room. Evelyn managed to catch Miss Staunton and congratulate the young woman.

"Oh Miss Berkeley, I am so happy." She looked up at William who was speaking with Lord Staunton. "I cannot wait to be his wife."

"You must call me Evelyn," she responded. "I am sure we shall be good friends." And she meant it. She squeezed her hands and let go as the other friends and family gathered around her to offer their blessings.

Evelyn made her excuses to Charlotte, Sophia, and Lady Montgomery on her way out of the dining room. She signaled a footman and requested that her carriage be made ready and Marie to be brought from below stairs so that they might leave.

He had watched the light leave her eyes even as her face lit up with a smile while she congratulated William. He knew she no longer had girlish dreams of a love match with William and had not for some time, but that did not make the reality any easier to accept.

Oliver followed her out of the dining room and found her donning her gloves in the entryway as she waited for her carriage.

"Evelyn." He said her name softly from the top of the short staircase leading from the formal rooms down to the foyer.

The light reflected off her tears as she looked up at him in surprise.

"No," she said. "Do not pity me, Oliver." She drew a shaky breath. "Just let me leave with some semblance of pride."

"Evelyn, please," he said, more quickly now. "I'm so sorry..."

"Stop," she interrupted, all trembling gone from her voice. "You owe me no apology. You may leave for America with a clean conscience knowing you tried, Mr. Marten, so do not trouble yourself over me."

Oliver started at her mention of America. How had she known?

She shook her head at his hesitation and spoke again. "Yes, I know your real goal." She looked away and Oliver's heart broke as he saw another tear glisten on her cheek. "I only wish you had thought enough of me to tell me yourself."

"Would it have made a difference?" he heard himself ask.

He could see her posture stiffen at his question and immediately regretted his words.

"No, Mr. Marten. It would have made no difference to our *deal*." She spat out the word as if it was a curse.

He felt his anger rise. "You agreed to the *deal*, Miss Berkeley," he countered echoing her tone.

A step sounded on the stair above them and both turned to see Henry. "Is everything alright, Oliver? Miss Berkeley?"

Oliver cringed at being seen with Evelyn in such an awkward position and was pleased to hear Marie's voice from the doorway next to Evelyn.

"Are you ready to go, Miss?"

Evelyn turned towards Marie with an overly bright smile on her face.

Oliver turned to Henry while Marie busied herself straightening Evelyn's bonnet. "I was just seeing Miss Berkeley off, Henry. What brings you away from the revelry?"

Henry moved down a few stairs. "I wanted to ensure that Miss Berkeley was not feeling ill. I saw her leave and hoped I could still call on her tomorrow."

Oliver noticed the way Henry was speaking to him, but looking right past him at Evelyn. She beamed up at Henry and nodded.

"I am quite well, I assure you," she said. "My mother was not feeling herself and I would like to get home to her, but I look forward to our outing tomorrow."

Oliver raised his eyebrows in a glance towards Henry, who caught his meaning.

"Miss Berkeley has agreed to join me on a visit to St. Paul's tomorrow." Henry smiled with his customary good humor and added, "I am very much looking forward to being amongst the birds after we climb to the bell tower."

Oliver cast a quick glance at Evelyn and thought he saw her pale a bit at his words.

"The Bell Tower?" Oliver asked, glancing her way. "But aren't you..."

She cut him off. "Excited? Yes, I am quite excited!" She smiled up at Henry through her lashes and continued. "I am looking forward to spending the afternoon with Mr. Holmes…and visiting the cathedral," she added. She and Marie took a step towards the door. "Good night Mr. Marten. Mr. Holmes."

She and Marie turned and left without another word. He watched through a small window as they climbed into their carriage and set off for home.

Henry called down from above. "I believe they were setting up for card games. Can I partner you in a game of piquet?"

Forcing a smile Oliver responded, "Certainly. I shall be right behind you."

He watched the young man walk off thinking of him taking Evelyn out tomorrow. He should not care. He knew Henry to be the best sort of person. Amiable, kind, and God-fearing, yet the thought made him unreasonably angry. Not at Henry, but at Evelyn. She was as fickle as any other woman. He had thought she might be different. But she had transitioned her affections from William to Henry without so much as batting an eye. He had thought she might have feelings for him, but he was mistaken. She had sought only her own gain with no thought for the feelings of others. He grew even angrier as he realized he might leave in two days without the last section of his notes.

"We had a deal," he muttered as he moved to follow Henry back into the drawing room.

Chapter 13

M r. Oliver Marten," the footman announced from the door. Evelyn looked up with surprise. After their conversation last night, she had not expected to see Oliver again any time soon.

He moved into the room and glanced around as if looking for something. She didn't know whether he found it or not, but he moved to her mother and bowed low over her hand in greeting.

"Mr. Marten!" she exclaimed, smiling at Evelyn over his shoulder, "a pleasure to see you as always."

"Lady Berkeley. The pleasure is mine." He smiled at her, and moved to sit across from her.

"Evelyn has told me that you are escaping to the country before the end of the Season," the older woman said. "Why would you go and leave all the young ladies bereft like that, Mr. Marten," she asked with a good-natured smile.

Oliver laughed, but it sounded forced to Evelyn.

"I am confident that Society will go on in my absence, Lady Berkeley," he said with a small smile. "My uncle has estate business and he has requested my presence." He looked down as he spoke, not meeting Evelyn's eyes.

"Your uncle?" she repeated. "Does he not have a steward? Surely he could allow your absence through the end of the Season." She pouted as if she herself was a Debutante sad to miss out on his company, and Evelyn forced herself not to groan.

Oliver again looked down at his feet and forced a laugh. "His last missive indicated something of a sensitive nature, Lady Berkeley, else I should not dream of depriving London of my charms."

Evelyn could not help but smile at his playful tone with her mother, though he still did not look at her.

Lady Berkeley swatted him on the arm with her fan and grinned before pushing herself to a standing position from her wingback chair.

Oliver jumped to his feet at her motion and offered his arm to escort her to her destination.

She patted his hand but did not take the offered arm. "Thank you, Mr. Marten, but I think I shall retire to my rooms." She moved towards the door. "The heat this year is brutal, and I need some rest before tonight's ball." She moved past where he stood and pulled the bell for Marie. Evelyn's lady's maid entered at the same time that Lady Berkeley made her exit. Marie moved to the seat in front of the window and took up a small basket of sewing as a distraction.

After her mother left, Evelyn remained silent and motionless on her settee, unsure of Oliver's intentions. Their interaction the night before had been awkward at best and antagonistic at worst. While her affection for him remained, she was unsure of his feelings for her given his behavior towards Elizabeth Fitzhugh. Would he talk to her as his partner, Miss Berkeley, or as his friend, Evelyn?

She saw his shoulders rise and fall as he took a deep breath and then turned to walk towards her. He sat on the edge of a small ottoman directly in front of her. For the first time that day, he looked right at her. She held her breath.

"Miss Berkeley," he began, but she interrupted.

"I am sorry, but I do not have the notes here for you." Out of the corner of her eye, she saw Marie raise her head at this statement, but she quickly went back to her needlework.

"I did not..." he began again.

"Is that not why you came?" Evelyn asked, interrupting him again.

"I did not...that is, I..." he paused.

Evelyn raised her eyebrows in question but remained silent this time.

He glanced away and then looked back at her, but did not speak. She sat still, looking down at him on his stool, feeling like a governess disciplining an unruly student.

Perhaps recognizing his disadvantaged position, he suddenly stood and began pacing the room in front of her. He ran his hands through his hair then stopped in front of her, dropping back down to his seat once more.

"Why are you riding out with Henry today?" he asked.

Evelyn was not sure what she was expecting, but this was not it.

"Why would I not?" she responded. "And more to the point, what is it to you, sir?"

"To me?" he began but paused again.

"You have no claim over me, Mr. Marten." Evelyn stood as she said the words, feeling anger swell within her. "We had a deal. I would write and you would try to elicit a proposal from William." She turned her back to him and moved towards the door. "Nowhere in it does that prevent me from accepting an invitation from any other gentleman." She turned back to face him, head held high. "I ask you again, what is it to you?"

He stood to face her, meeting her gaze. "You are afraid of heights," he said.

Evelyn felt her face flush, but countered, "That is not your concern. Perhaps this outing will help me conquer my fears."

He stepped towards her and grabbed her hands. "Please don't go, Evie" he begged.

Evelyn gasped in surprise and looked down at their hands, but did not move away.

Her emotions warred inside her. Her heart leapt at his touch, but her mind conjured images of Elizabeth. Evelyn loved him and had thought he might return the sentiment, but he had not trusted her enough to share his plans for America. His imminent departure with Elizabeth spoke more to where his heart lay than any perceived moments of affection in their recent friendship. Why must he leave with her?

Evelyn took a deep breath and felt tears prick at the back of her eyes. Meeting his gaze, she echoed him. "Please don't go, Oliver."

His face turned from a look of hopeful desperation to one of despair. He squeezed her hands. "I must go to my uncle, he has sent for me."

"And Elizabeth Fitzhugh?" Evelyn left the full question unasked, but her meaning was clear.

Oliver's face fell further. "It is critical at this juncture that Mrs. Fitzhugh and her father accompany me." He looked at the floor, unable to meet her eyes.

Evelyn dropped his hands and turned away from him. "If that is all you have to say to me, then I see no reason why you should have any say in my outing with Mr. Holmes."

"Evelyn, I am sorry that I did not tell you about my plans for America, but..."

"But what?" she interrupted, spinning to face him. "But all you cared about was my ability to write?" she spat out. "I was a means to an end for you, not a confidant, not a friend, and certainly not anything more." She hated that her voice broke on the last words, but she squared her shoulders and held his gaze.

"Anything more?" She heard the tone of anger now in his voice. "How could I contemplate anything more when your entire focus was on marriage to William? How was I to compete with that?" He turned his back to her and began to pace again. "Little did I know your affections were so fickle that they would change from William to Henry in a day's time."

Evelyn was grateful at least that with these words her tears dissipated, and she felt only anger.

"Fickle?" she responded, lowering her voice in direct contrast to her growing desire to scream. "You are one to speak of constancy as you depart in the morning with Mrs. Fitzhugh. Did you invite her before or after you promised a fake courtship with me?"

"Mrs. Fitzhugh has nothing to do with this," he countered. He reached out and lightly grabbed Evelyn's shoulders as he spoke, lowering his gaze to meet her eyes.

Evelyn reached out her hand and placed it on his chest. "If that is true, tell me you do not intend to leave with her tomorrow. Tell me you did not share your dreams of a home in America with her instead of me." She paused and spoke softer. "Tell me you will stay and I will not go with Henry."

His shoulders sagged and he dropped his hands, but he held her gaze. "I cannot."

Evelyn stepped back. "I think it is time for you to leave, Mr. Marten. Our partnership has run its course to its natural end. I appreciate the help you have offered, and I wish you the best in your endeavors." She was proud that there was no tremble to her words.

She held out her hand to him, head held high. He looked at her hand for what felt like ages. Just when she debated pulling it back, he took it between both of his. "I hope you find what you are looking for, Miss Berkeley."

He bowed formally over her hand, lightly touching his lips to her skin. He looked up and met her eyes, and Evelyn saw a resigned sadness there. Then he was gone.

For the better part of an hour, Evelyn debated begging off on her outing with Henry. She would later thank the Lord for her indecision.

She stood, startled when the footman announced his entry. She had lost track of time as her thoughts vacillated between her conversation with Oliver and her upcoming visit with Henry. She instinctively reached up to check her hair, fluffed her yellow dress, and pasted a smile on her face as he entered the room. She put her hands behind her back to prevent wringing them.

He smiled as he walked towards her, unaware of her inner turmoil. "Miss Berkeley, you are like a ray of sunshine in that color." He bowed low in front of her in greeting.

Unable to resist his sincerity, Evelyn felt herself relax in the face of his boyish smile and compliments. "Mr. Holmes, you are too kind. Surely my mother put you up to such a comment." She curtsied and signaled to Marie to prepare to leave.

"I am grateful to share your company today," he said as they moved together towards the door. "I have been in London now for several days and have longed to go, but such a visit is so much more enjoyable with company such as yourself."

Evelyn exited in front of him and moved down the stairs to the entry. "You flatter me with such praise, but I am no more uniquely fit for such a visit than any other," she countered.

"You do not give yourself enough credit," he corrected her, shaking his finger. "Anyone who can admire an incomplete figure of the muses is indeed "uniquely fit."

Evelyn stopped on the stairs and he nearly bumped into her from behind. She looked up at him in surprise. "Who said I admired the muses?" she asked, though she knew the answer.

"Oliver spoke of it the other night as we played cards. As a newcomer to London, I discussed the sights with him and William. I cannot see everything and wanted to be selective with my time." He gestured ahead to encourage their continued descent as he spoke. "According to Oliver, you have an unequaled appreciation for art."

When she didn't move, he walked down the stairs around her and waited for her at the bottom. "In fact, he suggested that I ask your opinion on the British Museum as he said you are quite the expert."

Her already troubled thoughts became more tangled. Such praise from Oliver shared unbidden and without ulterior motive, spoke to a true understanding of who she was.

She shook her head, dispelling her confused thoughts. He had left. She did not need to dwell on their past interactions any longer.

She continued down the stairs, joined momentarily by Marie who handed her a bonnet and gloves fetched from her room. As she donned the articles, she responded to Henry's words. "I do love the arts and would recommend a visit to the British Museum to anyone in London for more than a day or two."

"I see he was right," Henry beamed down at her. "I hope you are as enamored with St. Paul's as you are with the British Museum."

Evelyn's smile faded slightly at the thought of the towering dome, but she said nothing, and they moved out the door and into his waiting carriage.

She was not sure whether it was her nerves or the geography, but it seemed as though they arrived at the steps of the massive cathedral much faster than she had expected. Henry had regaled her with frivolous tales of the members of his country congregation and she barely noticed the passage of the city streets until the vehicle drew to a stop.

The footman opened the door and Henry stepped down, reaching back for Evelyn and Marie's hands. Both women stopped and looked up at the impressive sight in front of them. Evelyn barely kept her jaw from dropping as it seemed she nearly bent over backwards craning her neck to see the cross on its dome.

Henry had begun to move across the open court in front of the cathedral. The ladies hurried to keep up with him as he passed through a gate in a small stone wall and walked towards the west side and down the length of the church towards its double portico entrance.

He kept walking past the large stairs leading up to a set of doors bracketed on either side by tall spires almost resembling castle turrets. He moved around to the north side of the church where he found a door and knocked for admittance.

Evelyn was not sure whether the man who met him at the entrance was the friend he had mentioned or not, but he took several coins from Henry and moved to allow them entry. They made their way into the sacred space, their soft footsteps echoing through the cavernous interior.

She was surprised by the relatively austere interior decorations compared to the grandeur of its outward appearance. The simple black and white checkered marble floor led to an altar under the dome. An organ sat above in the gallery and the choir space was filled with ornately carved stalls for its members.

Each column, pew, and table was ornately carved revealing the unquestionable skill of the craftsmen responsible. Evelyn and Henry moved through the space slowly taking in the beauty around them while Marie followed behind.

Henry offered a mock salute at the grave of Lord Nelson while Evelyn paid homage to Dr. Samuel Johnson, many of whose belongings were located at the British Museum.

They moved through the library, and Evelyn stopped momentarily to admire two levels of books reaching from floor to ceiling. While the space was small and the collection nothing compared to the volumes of the British Museum, books had been her constant companions over the years and she loved to be in their company. She breathed deeply, inhaling the musty scent so common in older buildings, particularly those housing books. Though some found it repugnant, she had always loved the smell.

Henry drew up behind her as she surveyed the library. "What is your assessment, Miss Berkeley?"

"It is magnificent," she breathed. She looked up at him and found he was studying her. She did not look away but rather took the opportunity to do the same. His body language and persistent smile reflected a natural charm and confidence that many men lacked. He need not try to make friends; people seemed to be drawn to him.

She realized that she had not thought of Oliver once since she had entered the church. She was pleased by the distraction and she was enjoying Henry's company. She felt comfortable in his presence, much as she felt with one of her brothers.

"Shall we continue?" she asked.

He proffered his arm as he responded, "I am ready when you are."

They moved through the cathedral towards a staircase and began to climb. Evelyn appreciated the enclosed nature of the stairs and realized her fear of heights was more of a fear of high perspectives. She focused her eyes on the steadily climbing back of Henry moving ahead of her. This narrow focus and enclosed situation worked well until they arrived at the gallery located on top of the colonnade.

Henry exclaimed in delight at the views offered by the high vantage point. As he moved out of the darkness of the interior and into the sunlight of the day, he reminded Evelyn of a young boy who had been given a present. She laughed at his enthusiasm and followed behind him, but her laughter died quickly on her lips.

Evelyn began to tremble and she would have bet that her face was even paler than normal. She felt Marie try to guide her forward to the balustrade at the edge of the gallery but her feet were frozen in place. She was far enough out of the structure to see tiny people walking on the streets in the distance, but not close enough to touch the low wall surrounding the gallery walk.

Henry disappeared around the curve of the structure, and Evelyn felt her panic increase. She squeezed Marie's arm and did her best to take deep breaths to calm her racing heart.

Marie pulled lightly on her arm. "Would you like to go back inside, Miss?" she asked.

Her voice helped calm Evelyn for a moment and she shook her head. She offered Marie a wan smile and said simply, "I am fine."

Evelyn laughed weakly at the skeptical look on Marie's face, but she did not retreat. She focused on the sight of the Thames in the distance and took one step forward.

Marie patted her hand in encouragement. "Well done, Miss," she said softly.

Henry reappeared around the corner, clearly looking for the two women. His face revealed his surprise as he moved towards them quickly, hands outstretched.

"Miss Berkeley, what has happened? Are you well?" He looked her up and down. "Are you hurt?"

Marie moved back and Henry stepped where she had been, wrapping an arm around Evelyn and taking her hand to support her.

"I am fine," she assured him, though her voice sounded weak even to her own ears. She smiled up at him but knew she was unconvincing.

He remained quiet looking down at her and she knew in an instant that this was a tactic he used on his parishioners to get them to open up to him.

She looked up at his face, hovering over hers with concern written in every inch. She took a deep breath and forced out a light laugh.

"I am scared of heights, Mr. Holmes."

He did not respond immediately, but he looked out towards the city streets surrounding them in all directions.

Copying Marie's actions of moments earlier, he attempted to steer her back towards the stairs from which they had exited, but she resisted his efforts.

"I am fine," she repeated. "I just need a moment to compose myself," she continued in what she hoped was a nonchalant voice.

"You are not fine," he said in response moving to stand in front of her, blocking her view from the railing. He cocked his head to the side and asked, "Why did you want to come today?"

Evelyn looked at her feet, embarrassed to be called out so directly for her decision.

As Evelyn considered how to answer she shifted through the many explanations. She did not know how high it was. She thought she would be able to handle it. She enjoyed a good adventure. All were true and none were true at the same time. Her shoulders sagged with a sense of emotional exhaustion. She looked up at his expectant gaze and shrugged her shoulders in a most un-ladylike of gestures. "It is often easier to just be agreeable."

A change came over his face at this statement. His quiet confidence was gone, replaced by what Evelyn recognized as the same exhaustion she felt.

"Yes," he said. "Yes, it is."

They stood for a moment looking at one another, each finding comfort in the understanding of the other.

A bird flew overhead drawing Evelyn's attention. Henry tugged on her arm and smiled down at her, his easy charm returning.

"Come, Miss Berkeley. Let us talk."

They turned and went back inside, navigating the staircases and inner passageways until they returned to the library. He steered her into a cushioned wingback chair near the center of the room and pulled a matching chair to face her.

She smiled at him, feeling perhaps more relaxed than she had all day. "I see now why you are such a great vicar, Mr. Holmes."

He smiled back at her, but she saw sadness behind the look. "The great irony there, Miss Berkeley, is that I do not know if I want to be a vicar." He laughed. "As you said, sometimes it is easier to just be agreeable."

"Is that why you are here? In London, I mean?" she asked.

He nodded. "I have been steered towards the church since childhood, but I have never felt that it was really my decision." After an...incident earlier this year, I finally did what I should have done long ago and stepped away to chart my own course."

"Will you return to the church?" Evelyn asked.

He shrugged and looked at the floor. "I do not know yet."

She reached out and lightly touched his arm. "I choose to believe that you will find your way back there again, Mr. Holmes."

He smiled and placed his hand lightly atop hers. "Thank you, Miss Berkeley."

He pulled his hand back and leaned back in his chair with his arms crossed in front of him. He tilted his head and looked at her with a frown. "Enough about me. To whom do you need to say no?"

She could not help but laugh at his question.

He laughed too and leaned forward, his normal charm returned. "Let me be the first to hear you practice."

Evelyn laughed again and thought of the many times over the years when she should have spoken up. *I do not like this color, Mama. Thank you, but I would prefer not to play whist. I would like to write stories instead of painting watercolors.*

To him, she said, "Thank you for the invitation, Mr. Holmes, But I am afraid of heights and would prefer not to climb to the top of St. Paul's."

He laughed at her seriousness and she could not help but laugh at herself as well.

"I am so sorry to hear that, but perhaps we can visit the British Museum instead," he suggested.

"That sounds lovely, Mr. Holmes."

He crossed his arms again and asked, "Now was that so hard?"

She laughed, then sighed. "I wish it were that easy in the moment."

"If it were, neither of us would be where we are right now, Miss Berkeley." He looked down and Evelyn felt he was considering his next words carefully. "What did you not say to Mr. Marten that you wish you had?"

Evelyn felt her face flush.

"Forgive me for the bold question, but I wondered after your last conversation if there was an understanding between you."

"There was no understanding." She shook her head and thought about his question. "It was different with Mr. Marten. I never had to say no, he always knew without me having to say anything."

Henry remained quiet.

"He told me not to come today. That was the conversation that you walked into." She swallowed hard. "He saw me more clearly than I saw myself." Evelyn was embarrassed when her next words came out with a tremble. "In a matter of weeks, he knew me better than anyone ever has, but I guess what he learned wasn't enough to keep him here."

Evelyn swallowed again and took a deep breath, plastering on a smile. Her vision was only slightly blurred as she looked across at Henry.

His face was full of sympathy. "I will offer you no platitudes about what is 'meant to be,' Miss Berkeley, but I will say this. If God wills it, you may one day be married, but you must show the world who you are first."

She remained silent, unsure of what he meant.

"If you hide behind an agreeable countenance, no one will ever truly see you to know your worth." He continued, "As Shakespeare said, 'this above all; to thine own self be true.' Do not be so agreeable to others that you are disagreeable to yourself." He smiled, clearly happy with his own wit, and Evelyn could not help but echo his enthusiasm.

"You seem quite pleased with your wisdom, sir, but shall you take it to heart for yourself?"

His face fell, but only for a second. His eyes lit up with excitement. "I believe this meeting has been fortuitous, my dear, so I will make you a promise."

She sat forward, intrigued.

"In one year, give or take, I will find you and report to you on my progress of self-discovery. And you shall do the same."

She put her hand out in front of her and they shook, laughing at their own mock-seriousness.

After a moment he stood and held out his hand to help her up. She rose from the chair and he took both her hands in his. "I feel that this is the start of a fond friendship, Miss Berkeley. I did not know what the future held for us when I met you, but I knew I liked you enough to find out." She blushed and laughed at his bluntness, but he held up a finger to continue. "I see now that your heart is otherwise engaged, so I will instead be a friend and offer encouragement if you wish it."

Evelyn felt tears prick at the back of her eyes again, but this time they were tears of happiness. She struggled to find the right words. "I am so glad I am scared of heights," she blurted.

They both laughed loud enough to earn a look of displeasure from another visitor passing on the far side of the cathedral library.

Henry turned towards the door and they moved out into the sunshine of the courtyard once more. Both gave one last look back at the imposing structure before climbing into the carriage.

Evelyn spoke up as the conveyance jerked away from the curb. "I am sorry you didn't make it to the top."

He smiled, looking out the window as the church slowly faded into the distance. "I will come back to the church one day, just as you said."

Chapter 14

Oliver stared out the window of his carriage, avoiding conversation with his present company. It was not that he disliked Elizabeth, but he was in no mood for casual conversation. He knew she would make hints about a future together and it was getting increasingly difficult to find ways to avoid answering or to forestall the conversation.

He was not sure when this had gotten so out of hand. It seemed as though one minute she had offered to support his goals financially, and the next she was vying for the role of Mrs. Marten. He had thought her motives were simply a reflection of her love for her father; it seemed natural that she would support a home for veterans. He had not done anything to encourage a romantic attachment. Had he? He sighed.

Would it have mattered if he'd been more honest and open with Evelyn? He did not know when he had begun to love her, but the timing hardly seemed important now. All he knew was that he had lost his opportunity with her when he left with Elizabeth.

He glanced over at Elizabeth and saw she had fallen asleep. Her head rested on her father's shoulder, and they both snored softly. He glanced back out the window. What was Uncle Jack going to think?

He did not have to wait long to find out. His uncle's staff met the three of them at the door and ushered them to their respective rooms. He was sitting on the edge of his bed when a quick knock sounded at his door and his uncle pushed into the room. Despite the strain of his visit, he could not conceal his excitement at seeing the older man.

"Uncle!" he cried, rising to greet him. He grabbed his hand and shook while the gentleman clapped a hand on his shoulder.

"I could not wait to see you, young man," he beamed at his nephew. "Forgive me for barging in on you like this."

"It is your house," he countered. "You may barge in anywhere you would like." Oliver returned his smile, sincerely glad to see him.

Wasting no time, Jack got straight to the point. "What is this I hear of you bringing a woman with you?"

Oliver's face fell. "It is not what you think, Uncle. It is complicated."

"Women are always complicated, son, but that doesn't change the fact that you have brought her here." He looked pointedly at the younger man. "That must mean something."

Oliver looked at the floor, recognizing the truth in his words. "It is complicated," he repeated.

Moving to the chair in front of the fire, Jack sat down. "I am in no rush," he said. "Tell me what is so complicated."

Oliver looked out the window and considered where to begin. "A few years ago, I had an idea," he started. He told him of his plans and what he hoped to accomplish in America. His uncle interrupted a few times to ask questions, but for the most part, he let him speak. He explained that he had interviewed Colonel Kilpatrick and they had grown close, which brought him to know Elizabeth Fitzhugh. When she became interested in funding the project, he took her up on the possibility without realizing that she had deeper intentions than he did.

"Uncle, I do not know where I went wrong." He hung his head. "I did not mean to give her the wrong impression, but I do not have any romantic feelings for her. I feel no more strongly than any man would care for a friend or a sister."

His uncle considered his words for a moment. "Is she attractive?" he asked.

Surprised by the question, Oliver considered it for a moment. "Well, I suppose so, yes. She is a few years older than me but could pass for younger. She wears the latest fashions and is well-liked by all who know her."

"I must admit, I am confused, son." Jack frowned as he spoke. "I do not understand what the problem is. You have a woman who seems fond of you and wants to support your plans. By your own account, she seems lovely. What is so complicated?"

"I do not love her, Uncle." He responded. He knew his words sounded petulant, but they were true nonetheless. "I do not want to marry her."

Jack stood and walked to the window, admiring the estate below. He turned back around and faced Oliver. "Is there someone else?" he asked.

Oliver sighed. "Not anymore."

Jack moved closer and grinned. "Now, that sounds complicated."

Oliver could not help but laugh a little. "Really, Uncle, you're not helping."

The older man sat back down in his chair and leaned forward with his elbows on his knees. "Start over, and this time tell me everything."

After only a moment's hesitation, Oliver filled in the gaps. He admitted his difficulty writing and how he had negotiated with Evelyn for her help. He described their deal and how he had grown to look forward to their encounters. He also told him of their last conversations and her plans to go out with Henry.

This time his uncle did not interject a single word. When Oliver finished, he looked at the floor. Uncle Jack leaned back in his chair and crossed his arms.

"You're a fool," he said.

Oliver looked up, shocked at the man's words. "What did you say?" he asked.

"You heard me," the man repeated. "You are a fool. You had a girl who loved you and you left her. For what? A dream?"

Oliver felt his anger rise. "A dream? Uncle, this is what I have been working towards for years, it is not just a dream." He stood up and paced. "Besides, she broke her end of the deal and did not finish the writing. I was supposed to get it before I left and I did not." He walked to and fro in the small bed chamber. "She never said she loved me. She wanted to marry William. She agreed to go out with Henry."

He stopped pacing and faced Jack. "I am going to see this through, Uncle, and I hope you will stand by me."

Jack stood and walked to Oliver, placing a hand on his shoulder. "I will always stand by you, Oliver, but I hope you know what you're doing." He turned and walked to the door. "I look forward to meeting Mrs. Fitzhugh and the colonel at dinner."

Oliver nodded, appreciative of his uncle's effort. Maybe Jack was right and things did not need to be so complicated. He would focus on the future, not the past, and see where it led him.

Given the intimate nature of a dinner with only four attendees, Jack sat at the head of the table with the colonel to his right, Oliver to his left, and Elizabeth next to her father.

By any measure, the dinner was a success. The food was delicious with Uncle Jack's cook serving an array of roast beef and vegetables after a savory first course of soup. Oliver felt each course was better than the last. He made a note to thank Cook later for providing such a positive backdrop to their conversation and undoubtedly keeping everyone in good spirits. The wine and conversation flowed smoothly throughout the meal, for which Oliver was grateful. As would be expected, the conversation naturally turned to Oliver's plans.

It was Uncle Jack who brought it up first. "Tell me more about your plans, son," he said as he dug into his venison.

"Yes, yes," Colonel Fitzgerald echoed, "let's hear how your work progresses. Have you finished your pamphlet?"

Resisting the urge to dwell on his frustration with Evelyn's unfinished manuscript, Oliver focused on the positives. "It is nearly complete. I hope to have it sent to publishers within the month."

Elizabeth chimed in, "I am sure it will be fantastic. What will you do next?" she asked.

"I intend to plan a large event to bring together veterans and members of society who would have an interest in offering support," Oliver explained.

Elizabeth smiled conspiratorially, "You can certainly count on us for a rather large contribution, right Papa?"

Colonel Kilpatrick raised his glass in agreement but did not speak past the cake he was engaged with at the moment.

Uncle Jack took a sip before asking, "And what exactly is your plan? I understand your goal is a home, but did I hear correctly that you hope to build it in America?"

"Yes, Uncle," Oliver responded. "I blame it on you and Grandfather if you want to know!" he laughed.

At his uncle's look of confusion, he continued. "I used to love to listen to your stories and tales about America. I have dreamed of going there since I was a child."

"But must your home be there?" Uncle Jack asked.

"For some time now, America has been peaceful, and it offers much opportunity. It is hard to find work here and impossible to gain land. Both are available in abundance across the water and I plan to unite good, capable, hard-working men with those opportunities," he explained. "So, yes, Uncle, I believe my home must be there."

"I dread the idea of your being there alone, my boy," his uncle added then laughed. "I guess I dread the idea of my being alone here, too, if I'm being honest."

Elizabeth laughed, too, and sent a knowing look his way. "No one says you have to go alone, Oliver," she said as she sipped her wine.

Casting her a smile, but avoiding the implications of her words, Oliver continued with his ideas. "Once I have financial backing, I will recruit men who are interested to sail with me to find the land and settle. We will use veterans as the labor to create a residence of sorts while I establish contacts within the local communities." He paused and looked out the window. "I plan to start in New York, just as Grandfather did." He looked at the older man. "I would appreciate your blessing, sir."

His uncle held his gaze and Oliver held his breath. Elizabeth and her father were silent.

"My dear boy, you have always had my blessing." Oliver released his breath as his uncle continued. "Your mother used to say that I could deny you nothing." Oliver thought he heard a tremor in the man's voice. "I shall not start doing it now. But..." Oliver held his breath again. "...you must sit down with me and my steward to discuss the future of the estate before you leave."

Oliver felt a twinge of guilt. He knew his grandfather and uncle had both hoped he would eventually take over the running of the estate. He had never had an interest in living in the large home, but he owed it to them both to have the conversation. "Of course, Uncle. We can talk tomorrow if it pleases you."

His uncle nodded. "I'll send a message around to Wiley to meet us in the study tomorrow afternoon."

Elizabeth clapped her hands together. "Wonderful! The sooner your affairs are settled here, the sooner we can put your plans into motion." She smiled at Oliver from across the table and did not notice Jack's frown.

Oliver smiled across at Elizabeth and her father and gestured to both of them. "I hope you can both find something to occupy yourselves tomorrow while we meet."

The colonel waved a dismissive hand. "Think nothing of it. We shall enjoy this beautiful estate of yours before we head back to the confines of London. I see now why Elizabeth wanted to come see it so badly."

Why *Elizabeth* wanted to come see it? Oliver glanced at the woman and thought he saw a slight flush on her normally staid complexion. She sipped her wine and seemed to avoid his gaze, focusing instead on her father.

"Papa, I think it is time we retired for the evening. What do you think? I am a bit tired from our travel."

"Well, I suppose so," he answered after finishing his wine. He raised the empty glass in a mock toast. "My compliments to your staff, Moreland. This was as fine a meal as I've had in recent years."

Elizabeth moved to stand and a footman stepped forward to help her with her chair. Oliver mirrored her on the opposite side of the table.

"It was our pleasure to welcome both of you to our home this evening," Jack said, standing as well.

Oliver nodded to the older man as his daughter steered him out of the room, still avoiding his gaze. He frowned at their backs as they left the dining room. What was Elizabeth hiding?

He had put the thought from his mind the next morning when he awoke early. Being back in this house with his dream closer to reality had made it difficult to sleep. As the sun peaked in around the heavy drapes, he finally gave up and dressed himself for the day. His valet, Jennings, was surely still sleeping, but Oliver was more than capable of managing for the morning. He pulled his riding boots over a simple pair of trousers and a waistcoat and headed for the stables. He did not own a horse of his own, but his uncle had several. During his visit earlier in the year, Oliver had befriended Freya, a cinnamon-colored mare with white on three of her four hooves. She was docile but playful, and Oliver had come to look forward to their rides through the estate.

Though it was early, Oliver found a young stable hand to be up already. He looked up in surprise as Oliver entered, but greeted him fondly once he was over his shock.

"Good morning, Master Marten," he said with a crooked smile. Oliver was a bit sad to see he looked both taller and older than the last time he had seen him. The lad was only about twelve and had quite a mischievous look about him. Oliver found this rather endearing and was afraid that he would grow out of it.

"I have told you before, Jeremy, there is no need to call me Master. Mr. Marten is just fine by me." Oliver clapped the young man on the shoulder as he moved into the darkness of the stables.

"Yes, sir, Mr. Marten, sir," Jeremy grinned at him in a way that made Oliver assume he would still call him Master next time he saw him.

The young boy spoke up again. "Shall I ready Freya for you, Mas-Mr. Marten?" He tossed his head to push his shaggy sandy-colored hair out of his face and grinned again.

"Aye, lad, please bring her around for a short ride this morning." He headed out of the building and leaned against the fence, looking across the fields of his uncle's estate. What would Evelyn think of this, he wondered. He shook his head, unsure of where the thought came from. What did it matter what she thought of it? She was in London with Henry and whomever else caught her eye. Had she managed to crest St. Paul's? He sighed and pushed away from the fence, pacing the area in front of the stables as he waited on Jeremy.

He admired the view to clear his mind from the less welcome thoughts. He had always loved Longwood, even though he had a hard time imagining himself running the estate. The home itself was a massive symmetrical structure made of stone. The central portion dated back the farthest, but subsequent great-grandfathers had added two wings that stretched back from the main house adding a grand ballroom, a gallery, and an absurdly large dining room that they rarely used anymore. The master suite was on the second floor overlooking a beautifully manicured garden with low flowers and hedges laid out in geometric designs stretching away from the house between the two wings. Beyond the garden's end were rolling fields dotted with trees, and in the distance, he could just make out the edge of a small forest that marked the boundary of his uncle's lands to the east. That was his destination this morning.

Jeremy came into view, pulling Freya behind him. The horse whinnied a greeting and Oliver rubbed her affectionately on the nose before pulling himself into the saddle.

"Shall I ride with you today, Master Marten?" Jeremy asked.

"Thank you, but no. I just need to stretch my legs a bit and will not go far nor ride long," Oliver answered.

Jeremy released the reins and stepped back, clearing the way for Oliver to ride. Oliver glanced back at the house once, then rode away from it, aiming for the tree line in the distance. Once clear of the gardens, he gave Freya more rein and enjoyed the feeling of freedom that riding always gave him. He crested each small hill and reveled in the views, the wind in his face, and the sense of peace he felt. It did not take long for the pair of them to reach the distant forest, and Oliver set off down a well-marked path into the trees. He slowed his pace but continued to soak up the sights and sounds around him. He had spent countless hours playing in these woods in his youth. The trees were enemy soldiers that he bravely fought with swords made of branches and shields made of pots commandeered from Cook's kitchen. The memories made him smile but also brought sadness. He missed his grandfather. And his mother.

He pulled up as he reached his final destination. Under the canopy of the quiet forest sat a columned gazebo. It was ornately carved in a Grecian style and featured a ring of benches in the center. His grandfather had commissioned this to be made for his grandmother before he left on one of his many missions. Oliver had very few memories of his grandmother, but those that he did have were here. She would sit with his mother while he played in the woods. They would laugh and talk together. Sometimes they brought canvases and painted while he protected them from many imaginary threats.

He gazed at the beautiful structure, now overgrown with ivy and honeysuckle, and imagined Evelyn sitting on one of the benches, papers strewn about, tapping her pencil against her lips as she contemplated her next words. The image took him by surprise, but he did not dispel it. *She would like it here*, he thought.

He dismounted from Freya and looped her reins loosely around a column. He walked into the middle of the circle and sat on a bench. He could have a table added if she wanted.

He stood up. What was he thinking? Not only was Evelyn not here with him, she never would be; this was not his home. He would not be commissioning anything of the sort. He would be an ocean away achieving his goals, and she could write wherever she pleased in London.

He walked back out of the gazebo and mounted Freya with an easy movement. "Let's go," he urged as they moved away from the gazebo and back down the path. He resisted the urge to look back over his shoulder. When they broke from the trees, he slowed to a trot as he returned to the stables. He rode along the forest line admiring his uncle's fields and the row of cottages in the distance. He would make time tomorrow to visit with the tenants that he knew and leave messages with those he did not. His uncle's lands were prosperous. They had been steadily profitable for decades and Oliver was proud of his family's estate. He turned Freya back towards the house and let his mind wander down the familiar paths of his future plans without any more invasive thoughts of Evelyn. At least for now.

As he walked back inside after his ride, he saw the colonel moving slowly through the hall outside the library.

"Good morning, Colonel," Oliver called out to him.

"Good day, Mr. Marten," he returned. He held out a packet of papers to the younger man. "I found these in our belongings and assume they are yours. I can't imagine how they got in with Elizabeth's dresses."

Oliver saw the handwriting on the top paper and gasped. It was Evelyn's writing. He reached out for the paper. "My thanks, sir." He took the pages and rifled through them. "Where did you say you found them?"

"I was looking for a book that I thought Elizabeth had brought for me. I found this in one of our trunks and knew it was part of your pamphlet." The old man shook his head. "I never did find my book."

Oliver clasped the packet to his chest and drew a deep breath. "Thank you again, many times over." He turned to head up to his rooms, then paused. "Feel free to explore the library and read anything you find, Colonel." He gestured to the large paneled door to the left, then turned again to leave.

He took the stairs two at a time, holding the package as if it was a precious babe. He had so many questions. So many emotions warred inside him. Why did Elizabeth have it? When had Evelyn finished? He reached his rooms and sat in a chair by the window. He looked through the pages, not really seeing the words. They were done and he could move on with his plans now. He let the pages fall on his lap and stared out the window. He had always loved to imagine he was looking towards America when he gazed out his window at Longwood. But today he found himself captivated by the view right outside, not into the distance. He loved the gardens, the woods, and the fields. Evelyn would love the gardens, too, but maybe not the view from the second floor. He smiled at the memory of her fear from being in a simple raised curricle.

He shook his head again. She had made her choice and so had he. He needed to prepare for his meeting with his uncle. And he needed to talk to Elizabeth.

Oliver was surprised to find Elizabeth and her father in the study when he entered later that afternoon. His uncle sat behind his desk, frowning while his steward stood next to him, hands behind his back. Wiley had been his grandfather's steward and was a large part of the reason why their estate was successful. The man's appearance was immaculate, down to each of his black hairs in perfect place slicked to the side and cut just at the collar line of his tailored waistcoat. He never showed much emotion, but his steady guidance and mild temperament had thus far never steered the family wrong.

Oliver nodded in the direction of Colonel Kilpatrick and Elizabeth but moved closer to his uncle and Mr. Wiley. "Good afternoon, gentlemen. Shall I call for tea since our guests have joined us?" He smiled towards the two visitors, but his uncle's frown did not leave.

Elizabeth cleared her throat. "Oliver, your uncle discouraged us from joining you today for this meeting, but we feel our presence is important. We have such a...personal connection to your future that I think I - we - should be a part of the conversation." She gestured to her father as she spoke, but Oliver had the feeling that the older man had come along only to placate his headstrong daughter. The colonel shrugged and smiled at Oliver, sitting back comfortably in his chair with his cane between his knees.

"I am sure this is to be a boring conversation of numbers and costs, Mrs. Fitzhugh. I can bring you up to speed later if you like." Oliver offered.

She laughed, but it did not sound sincere. "I am quite familiar with numbers and would think that my own contribution of such numbers would merit myself a place at the table."

Oliver held up a hand. "I am grateful for your support of my endeavors, Mrs. Fitzhugh, but we have not yet agreed upon any terms for you and your father's investment, so we can settle that another time just as well after I speak privately with my uncle."

The woman pouted. "Oh, do be kind, Oliver and call me Elizabeth. There is no need to stand on ceremony when are such dear friends." She smiled at him. "I shall sit and listen and not say a word. You will not even know we are here. That way, I will learn more about your needs and will know how best to support your endeavors."

Oliver had not even realized he had switched to a more formal address, but he knew it was because of her father's discovery. He forced a smile that he knew did not reach his eyes and nodded. He signaled to a footman. "Please bring Mrs. Fitzhugh and Colonel Kilpatrick some tea." The man bowed and moved from the room as Oliver turned from the guests and took a seat in front of his uncle.

The man's face softened as he looked at Oliver fondly. "I would hate to see you leave, Nephew," he said. "When you are in London, I know we are on the same soil. I cannot imagine being separated from you by an ocean."

Oliver thought back to the hours spent following this man around and felt a pang of regret at hurting him. "I shall miss you too, Uncle." He leaned in conspiratorially. "You are not my only family, but you are my favorite." They both laughed and Oliver relaxed a bit.

Jack leaned forward and rested his elbows on the desk. "Let's not delay any longer. I had hoped to pass this estate to you, but you will no longer be in any position to run it once you have left England." He pulled some papers in front of him. "Wiley reviewed our ledgers and it looks like I can provide you with £5,000 to help you on your way."

Oliver raised his eyebrows, unable to hide his surprise. "That's a rather large sum, Uncle. I do not want to leave you in a difficult position." He felt a weight settle in the pit of his stomach. His uncle was offering him nearly half of what he had calculated was needed to put his plan into motion. He felt confident he could raise the rest, but it did not sit well to take so much from the man.

Elizabeth chimed in from her spot across the room. "What a generous offer for you, Oliver. You are so blessed to have such a loving relative looking out for you." She smiled at Jack, but he did not return the look. "I - my father and I, that is - would be pleased to contribute another £2,000."

Oliver's stomach felt even worse. He smiled at the woman but did not speak. What was wrong with him? Why was he not more pleased?

He looked up at his uncle. "What will happen to the estate? In the very distant future when we lose you, I mean."

Jack chuckled. "While I do not intend to go anytime soon, I will revise my will and leave it to your cousin. Your grandfather's brother's grandson is a good man. He lives in London and currently works as a barrister. It will be a nice step up for him in the world, but from what I know of him, he will care for the place." He nodded at Wiley and continued. "I will of course set aside a living for Wiley on the condition that my heir allow him to continue as the steward for as long as he wishes the position."

Wiley, who had not yet spoken a word, nodded in appreciation at the man and offered a small smile. "I would be honored."

Oliver's stomach churned. He looked past Elizabeth out the window. He had a hard time imagining this property in someone else's possession. He had known this would happen through the whole process, but hearing the words did not make it easier. He looked back at Jack. "I need to think, Uncle. Can we talk again later?"

Elizabeth coughed, but Oliver ignored her attempt at interruption.

His uncle nodded. "As I said last night, I want this question settled before you leave. My offer stands. You may walk out with £5,000, or you may inherit Longwood one day. The choice is yours."

He stood and bowed to the two men at the desk. He moved to leave the room, wanting to clear his head but Elizabeth stepped in front of him. "Oliver, I hope you see what a great offer this is for you. I'm so happy that you will be able to accomplish your dreams." She put her hand on his arm.

He looked down at her hand and it was all he could do not to physically remove it from him. He did not want to hurt her or embarrass her, but he knew in an instant he would also never take her money. He turned to face her properly, letting her hand fall from him as he turned. "Mrs. Fitzhugh, will you take a turn in the garden with me? We need to have a talk."

She beamed up at him. "Of course, Oliver. I am at your disposal."

He stepped aside and gestured her out the door in front of him. He looked back at his uncle, who was watching him closely. He tried to smile encouragingly, but he worried that it looked more like a grimace as he followed her out of the room.

They moved along the path in silence for a few minutes putting some distance between themselves and the house. Oliver kept his hands behind his back, avoiding even the politest contact with her. He was angry with her. He was also confused. What were her intentions? He laughed to himself. He knew her intentions. He had known for some time that she desired a union with him. He could not go so far as to say she had feelings for him, as he did not think she knew him well enough to develop feelings, but her goal of marriage had been clear. He had thought he needed her money so he had allowed their friendship to grow, but he had tried not to mislead her on his own feelings. Or lack thereof.

He drew to a stop and turned to face her. She stopped, too, and looked up expectantly. "Why did you have Evelyn's pages in your trunk?" He hated the harsh tone of his voice and cringed inwardly, but he couldn't take back the words now.

Her face fell for an instant but was replaced quickly with her same steady smile. "She asked me to deliver them to you. I simply forgot they were in my trunk. I am so glad you have them now and can get everything published." She gestured back to the path as if to encourage their walk to continue but he stood firm. She crossed her arms across her waist. "Are you not excited to have all the pieces falling into place?" she asked.

He lowered his voice and asked again, "Why did you have Evelyn's pages? I know she did not give them to you." Their partnership had been a secret and he knew she would not have violated his trust. She had too much to lose. He stared down at Elizabeth waiting for her answer.

She hesitated for an instant before her mask fell. Her normally placid smile was replaced with a look of disdain. "I found them lying on the table in your entry hall. It only took me a second to realize what they were. I hid them." She forced her smile back into place. "I hid them for you, Oliver. I did not want anyone to know that your words were not your own."

He stared into the distance considering her words, then gazed back at her. "Why are you here? You told me your father wanted to visit with Uncle, but now your father says it was your idea. What are you hiding, Elizabeth?"

Again, her smile slipped, but this time she did not try to hide her annoyance. Her snide tone revealed the depth of her frustrations. "Is it not obvious, Oliver? I want to go with you. I want to escape. I am tired of a life full of dinners with old men telling the same stories day in and day out."

Oliver pulled back from her, shocked by the vitriol behind her words. "I thought you loved-"

"My father? Of course, I love my father," she said, her face softening. "But I cannot do this forever, Oliver. I am young still. I married Sean Fitzhugh thinking we would travel the world together." Her eyes welled with tears. "When he died, my future died with him. I had nothing of my own and had to go to Father. When I heard your vision, I began to hope for a new future." She reached her hands out to him, but he kept his arms behind his back. She rested a hand on his chest. "Please, Oliver. We would get along well together, you and I."

Oliver stood still, attempting to make sense of Elizabeth's true motivations. He had known her for years and had never seen her this discontent. His heart went out to her, but he could not look past her deception. "What of your father? What would he do if you left?"

While he knew she would never get what she sought, he was curious to know the extent of her plans.

She looked back at the house and gestured. "I thought...if we...he could stay here." She looked down at her feet, looking remorseful for the first time. "He and your uncle are similar and have a lot in common. I thought they would be good company for one another."

He shook his head, amazed she had thought through so much and he had been so clueless. That was her reason for coming here. She needed them to meet and make sure they got along well enough to putter around in a big old house into their dotage.

He turned his back to her, processing all she had told him. Part of him was glad to know that it was not him she loved, but the idea of what he could offer her. He had no desire to hurt anyone else. His mind turned to Evelyn. She had referenced Elizabeth in their last conversation. She had known her intentions and had assumed he returned her affection because of this visit home. What else could she have thought after the way Elizabeth had behaved? He sighed. It was not just Elizabeth's behavior. He had been so determined to find the funds he needed to reach America that he had gone along with her plan. His silence could only have been taken as tacit agreement by both Elizabeth and Evelyn.

He took a deep breath and squared his shoulders. He did not know how to fix things with Evelyn yet, but he knew what needed to be done with Elizabeth.

He turned back around and faced her. "I am sorry, Elizabeth, but this is not going to work." She opened her mouth to speak but he held up his hand to forestall her. "I am sorry that you are unhappy, but I am not your ticket to a new life in a new world."

She crossed her arms over her chest. "I will not give you any of our money if you do not take me with you." Her smile and supportive demeanor were long gone by now.

"I do not want your money, Mrs. Fitzhugh," Oliver said firmly, mirroring her stance with his arms across his chest. "I will succeed or fail on my own."

"On your own?" Elizabeth scoffed. "You were willing to accept help from Miss Berkeley, were you not?"

Oliver stiffened. "Do not take your anger out on Evelyn," he said. "Your quarrel is with me, not her. She will be scorned by society if you reveal her role as the author." He reached his arms towards her and gripped her shoulders. "Please, Elizabeth, do not ruin her."

She looked away from him as he pleaded with her. "Since when did you start using her Christian name," she asked, instead of answering his question. She looked back at him, resignation in her eyes. "I did not know you returned her affections. I might have fought harder if I had."

Elizabeth stepped back, breaking his hold on her. She stood straight as if steeling herself. "I thank you for your hospitality, Mr. Marten, but I must beg leave of you now. My father and I would appreciate use of your carriage to return to London early."

"Mrs. Fitzhugh, please-"

"I hope we shall still be friends when our paths cross, Mr. Marten." She dropped into a quick curtsy and walked swiftly away towards the house.

He watched as she retreated, head held high the whole way. He filtered through her words. He still could not believe he had not seen her ulterior motives before now. But what had she said about Evelyn? *I did not know you returned her affections...* Did Evelyn still care for him? He stood rooted to the spot in the gardens replaying memories in his mind. Could there still be a chance? He stared at the house.

He did not know how long he stood there lost in thought. It was as if blinders were lifted from him. He had sought something so distant for so long, that he had failed to see what was right in front of him. He looked at the gardens, the trees, and the house. He focused on the house for a moment and felt as though he was truly seeing it for the first time. Not as a child or as a nephew, but as an outside observer. Suddenly, he set off for the house. His pace quickened as he moved and his excitement grew. The weight in his stomach lifted. For the first time in a long time, the disparate parts of his plan had coalesced into one vision. He knew what he needed to do and he didn't want to lose another moment's time.

"I do not know what has gotten into you, Evie," Lady Montgomery quipped. She looked down at her daughter with a tight-lipped frown. "You are being argumentative. And what on earth are you wearing?"

Evelyn sighed. "I am not being argumentative, Mama, I just do not want to go." She looked down at her lap and smoothed the gown she wore. "What is wrong with my dress?" she asked.

"What is wrong with it?" her mother echoed. "Where did you even get it?" she asked. "It is...dark."

Evelyn felt her mother wanted to say more than she did but could not overcome decades of social training even with her own daughter.

She smiled, again smoothing the folds of her gown in her lap. "Yes, it is dark, but I like it. Lady Montgomery recommended her modiste and you know she is always dressed so lovely."

Lady Berkeley's lips pursed again. She looked as if she had tasted something foul, but Evelyn knew she was warring inside between her respect for Lady Montgomery and her frustration at Evelyn's initiative.

"What will you do instead that is so much better than attending a musicale?" Lady Berkeley asked, her tone implying that nothing could be better than such an evening in her mind.

Evelyn smiled benignly at her mother and replied, "I believe I shall write for a bit."

"Write?" her mother repeated. She might as well have said she was staying home to kill small animals.

"Yes, Mama, write." She kept calm and kept her smile in place. "I enjoy writing short stories."

She almost laughed as her loquacious mother was actually struck speechless by this revelation.

"Do not worry that I will be ruined, Mama," she added. "I will not take to scandalous activities in dark corners or illicit meetings with rogues. I write silly love stories and playful pieces about animals." She gestured to her stack of papers on the table next to her. "Would you like to read any of it?" She held her breath hoping her answer would be no.

If possible, Lady Berkeley's look of horror increased with this question. "Read it?" she screeched. She took a deep breath, finally realizing she had lost her composure. "No, I do not wish to read it, thank you. I do not wish to encourage this habit and hope it will be only a passing fancy."

Evelyn remained silent and did not reveal that she had been writing for nearly 15 years now so it was not likely to be short-lived.

"No, certainly not," her mother repeated. She turned up her nose as if her daughter literally reeked of scandal. "I shall make excuses for you tonight, but this cannot become a habit, Evelyn. People will talk." The older woman made a clicking noise with her tongue and exited the room, no doubt to rest up for the evening after the stress of her daughter's behavior.

"Yes, Mama," she replied to her back as she left. She figured it was easier to fight one small battle at a time. She had ordered two dresses, a new bonnet, and a new pair of gloves with Charlotte and Sophia the day after her eventful visit to St. Paul's. She had only just received them yesterday, and their arrival had caused much shock to her mother. Though her father had sanctioned the purchase, it appeared he had not informed her mother, who had been dismayed at having been left out of the process.

She looked down at the deep green folds of fabric in her lap and ran her hands over it again as if to convince herself it was real. She took a deep breath to calm her stomach, which still seemed to rebel each time she took a stand on something.

She stood from her chair and called for Marie. She met her lady's maid at the door as both prepared to depart. She had made plans to meet Charlotte and Sophia at Gunter's this afternoon and looked forward to their reactions to her new look. The two women left the house and walked towards the shopping district, navigating the busier streets as they drew nearer to their destination.

As they moved through the crowds, her gaze landed on a familiar face. She could think of only two or three people that she would not want to run into and this was one of them. In fact, she was probably first on the list. Despite Evelyn's prayers to not be noticed, Elizabeth Fitzhugh had spotted her and Evelyn saw no way to politely avoid her without cutting her directly.

She drew closer and pasted a bright smile on her face as they greeted one another. "Mrs. Fitzhugh, what a pleasure to see you today."

The other woman smiled, though perhaps less brightly and replied. "The pleasure is all mine, Miss Berkeley."

There was a brief pause as Evelyn considered her next statement, but Elizabeth broke the silence first. "How is your family?"

"They are quite well, thank you. My mother looks forward to the end of the Season and a return to the country, but we are all well." She shifted her weight from one foot to the other. "And how is your father?"

"He is quite healthy, thank you," Elizabeth responded.

Silence stretched again and Evelyn looked past her, hoping to find something in the area to inspire a comment or question.

Before she could come up with something, Elizabeth spoke again. "How is Mr. Marten?"

Evelyn tried to hide her shock at the question. "Mr. Marten? I thought to ask you the same. Are you not..." she trailed off, the implication clear.

Elizabeth's smile looked rueful and she did not meet Evelyn's gaze. "Mr. Marten and I parted ways some time ago, Miss Berkeley. It appears we had different goals for the future after all."

Again, Evelyn schooled her features to disguise her surprise. "My apologies, Mrs. Fitzhugh, I had no idea. I have not seen him since your departure."

Suddenly she paled as a thought occurred to her. "Has he left?" she asked. "Has he already sailed for America?"

Elizabeth shrugged in an unladylike fashion. "I do not think so, but I am in no position to know his plans any longer. For my part, I do not care if he ever succeeds." She turned to go. "It was a pleasure,

Miss Berkeley." She nodded and moved away, continuing on her path and leaving Evelyn standing in the middle of the crowded street speechless.

She gathered herself and turned to face Marie. "Have you heard anything about his departure?" She knew that servants saw and heard much in their roles as silent observers.

Marie shook her head, "No, Miss, I haven't heard nothing of him in weeks."

Evelyn grabbed her arm, "Come, we must speak with William."

"But, Miss, what about Gunter's?" Evelyn stopped at Marie's words. She was right, she needed to keep her appointment with her friends first. Perhaps they knew where she could find their brother this afternoon.

She and Marie pushed through the crowds, arriving at Gunter's breathless just as Charlotte and Sophia approached from the opposite direction arm in arm. She felt the familiar pang at the sight as she longed to be that close with someone. She shook off the self-pity quickly and moved to meet the girls.

Though they had never known of her secret pact with Oliver, they did know of their friendship and had suspected she had feelings for him. In the way of good friends, they had not spoken of him since his departure with Elizabeth. She appreciated their silent support and had done her best to put him from her mind. Most days she did not succeed.

"Evelyn, you look like you have seen a ghost," Charlotte commented as they sat down.

A waiter approached and Evelyn could not answer right away. She ordered a lemon ice while Charlotte and Sophia both ordered raspberry. As he walked away, Evelyn leaned closer to her friends.

"I ran into Elizabeth Fitzhugh on the way here."

Sophia gasped. "Was Mr. Marten with her?" she asked.

"No!" Evelyn answered quickly. "That is what has caused such surprise." She leaned in even further. "According to Mrs. Fitzhugh, she has not been at Longwood in weeks. She has no knowledge of his whereabouts, or even if he is still in the country." Evelyn sat back and considered their conversation again. "She seemed angry," she said.

"Angry? At Mr. Marten?" Charlotte asked.

Evelyn shrugged. "I can only assume so. She said she did not care whether he was able to create his home or not."

"Perhaps he did not tell her that he intended to sail to America, either," suggested Sophia.

"Perhaps," Evelyn conceded, "but I think she knew." Evelyn recounted their conversation about whether or not she intended to visit his facility upon completion.

The waiter returned with three ices on a tray and the conversation paused for a moment as the women enjoyed the treat.

Sophia wiped her mouth with a napkin. "So, what are you going to do with this information?" she asked.

Evelyn did not respond right away. She did not know the answer for herself yet.

She knew she missed Oliver. With each event she attended, she had to force herself not to watch for him. She wanted him to read her stories as she finished new ones. She longed to know what he would think of her new dress. She knew she had developed feelings for him, but she did not know if those feelings were returned. His closeness with Elizabeth had made her think they had an understanding, but apparently not. She had been inspired by his dreams of helping veterans and she was proud to have contributed her small part to his goals. She knew that regardless of anything else, she wanted to see his dream come true.

"I need to speak with William," she finally said. "Do you know where he is today?"

Sophia shook her head, but Charlotte replied, "I heard him tell Mama yesterday that he would be at home today. We can pay him a visit."

The three women focused on their ices and observed the other patrons around them for the next half hour until they were finished and had paid for their treats. As they rose, the twins pointed out their carriage waiting around the corner and the three of them found Marie and departed.

It took no more than ten minutes to reach the Montgomery townhouse where Adam and William currently lived. Adam had decided to move with his bride to one of their country holdings after their fall wedding and William intended to remain in town with Miss Staunton after their nuptials. It was a beautiful home, as Evelyn observed when they were admitted by the butler. It had a masculine feel to it, but Evelyn was sure that a new bride could and would change that upon arrival.

The ladies were shown into the drawing room where Adam and William were both already seated. The two men had been in the middle of a game of piquet and looked up when the footman announced their entry. The brothers stood, both appearing sincerely happy to see the young ladies.

"Sisters!" William exclaimed, rising to greet them each with a kiss on the cheek. "To what do we owe the pleasure?"

"Can we not visit our brothers out of kindness?" Sophia asked with a grin. She flopped into one of the chairs as her brothers returned to their card table.

Charlotte laughed, "They know you better than that, Sophia," she replied before either of the brothers could.

Evelyn smiled at their banter as she perched on a settee. She was pleased with herself that she felt no sadness or awkwardness in the presence of William. She was glad she had never revealed her intentions to him and created any kind of barrier to their old camaraderie. She was happy for him as he entered into marriage and she sincerely wished him well.

"As it happens, we do have a question." Charlotte glanced at the other two girls and continued. "We were having ices at Gunter's-"

"Ohhh Gunter's," Adam broke in. "You did not invite your dear brothers?"

Charlotte laughed. "No, we did not. But while we were there, we saw Mrs. Fitzhugh."

Evelyn glanced up at Charlotte's slight misrepresentation of the facts, but she did not interrupt.

"We had thought that Mrs. Fitzhugh and your friend Mr. Marten had an understanding, but we learned today they did not."

Sophia picked up her story. "I was fascinated with his plans to start a home for veterans. We decided that you might know whether he had sailed for America yet so we came here to ask."

Evelyn tried to remain calm and appear disinterested but she was desperate to hear William's response.

William put his cards down and stood, moving over to a writing desk by the window. He picked up a piece of paper from the desk and glanced at Evelyn. "It is an amazing coincidence that you visited today because I had a letter from him just this morning."

He returned to the card table and sat back down, unfolding the letter. If she had been less cultured, Evelyn might have stood and snatched the paper from his hands, but she resisted the urge.

"According to his letters, he has not managed to secure the funding for his home yet. He is still hopeful to do so one day, but has decided to focus on things a little closer to home for the time being."

Evelyn gasped. "He can't give up," she exclaimed. She flushed in embarrassment at her outburst, but plunged ahead anyway. "It is such a worthy goal, and I know how much it means to him."

Adam nodded his agreement. "You're right Evelyn, and William has told him the same thing." He jerked his head towards the same writing desk. "There is a newspaper there with an article about his plans. He has not given up and is, in fact, starting the process of soliciting funds."

Evelyn stood and moved to find the article he mentioned. She tried to appear calm, but she knew she was not succeeding. Her eyes scanned the page until she found the short notice. Much to her embarrassment, her eyes teared up as she read. It was her words. The notice told the story of his childhood friend Stafford, though it did not use his name. It concluded simply with a message that anyone interested in supporting our nation's brave soldiers after their service to contact him. The address listed was Longwood. his family's estate outside London.

She read and re-read the words while she attempted to blink away her tears. She felt connected to him as she read and she was reminded again how she missed him. But more importantly, she was reminded how much she cared about his dreams. She remembered how passionate he had been as he told her of his plans and enlisted her help in writing. She wanted to see the project through to its completion, regardless of the fact that she had already fulfilled her obligation..

She glanced up and saw everyone's eyes on her. She straightened up and held out the newspaper. "May I keep this?" she asked.

"Of course," William answered.

Oliver had asked her to write for him, so she would write.

Chapter 15

"Do you have everything?" Evelyn asked.

Marie held out a small package. "Everything is ready, Miss." She smiled encouragingly at Evelyn. "I am excited, if I may say so."

Evelyn laughed. "Of course, you may say so, Marie." She took a deep breath. "I am excited too, but I am more nervous right now."

Marie pulled open the door and gestured for Evie to leave. They stepped out into the street and began to walk towards the shopping district. Evelyn clutched a small piece of paper with the name, "Louis Scott" written on it with an address. According to their inquiries, he was a newspaper editor who would hopefully publish her piece.

She took a deep breath and picked up her pace as the streets became more crowded with all walks of life. Young street urchins raced among the throngs soliciting change while merchants hawked their wares from the sidewalks. Evelyn spotted a beautiful cart of flowers and nearly detoured from her plan to stop for a moment, but decided to return only if she was successful in her endeavors.

Finally, they stopped across the street from the newspaper office. Evelyn looked at Marie, who looked nervous. " Are you ready?" she asked.

The young woman nodded and turned to cross the busy road. She pushed open the door, casting one more look over her shoulder, and stepped into the office.

Evelyn could not see or hear anything but she knew Marie was asking for Scott because that was their plan. He had published Oliver's piece so they hoped he was sympathetic to her cause. Evelyn began to pace as worry set in. She would have preferred to go in herself, but she knew that could harm her reputation if she were recognized. Instead, Marie would explain that she was representing someone else and simply leave the materials. After that, it was out of their hands.

Time dragged for what seemed like an hour, but Evelyn knew it was no more than ten minutes. Just when she began to contemplate storming in, she saw Marie emerge from the office. She froze, clutching her hands in front of her and watched as Marie approached through the busy crowds of the London street.

"Well?" she asked, as soon as Marie was in ear shot.

Marie drew near and Evelyn tried to read her expression. Was she confused or happy? It was hard to tell, despite having known the woman since she was young.

"What did he say?" she asked, as soon as she was close enough.

"You are never going to believe this, Miss," Marie said, a grin spreading across her face. "I can scarce believe it myself."

She held out something and Evelyn took it from her. She read the words in front of her three times before she released the breath she had not even realized she was holding.

"Honor, Duty, and Loyalty: Tales of His Majesty's Forces"

By Lady Cordelia Fitzgerald

"He published it, Miss. He published your words with your name." She laughed, "Well, with sort of your name."

He had published his pamphlet. She was so proud of him, she thought she might burst. She could not contain herself and hugged the document to her chest.

She looked down at it again. He had used her pen name. He had given her the credit even though that was not their deal. Her eyes blurred as they filled with tears, and she choked out a laugh as she hugged it to her again.

Her outburst was drawing unwanted attention, so Marie steered her just off the street into a doorway as Evelyn continued to gaze at the document. She had always imagined what it might be like to see her words in print. She had pictured it more as a children's story than a social pamphlet, but the difference hardly mattered now. They were her words.

As she calmed down, her mind raced. What did this mean? Was he still leaving? Had he already left? What about her letter?

She looked at Marie and grabbed her hand. "What happened? Did Scott take the letter? Is he going to print it?"

"One question at a time, Miss," Marie responded with a quiet laugh. "He was quite surprised when I said I was representing Lady Cordelia Fitzgerald. He recognized the name right away. This draft was sitting on his desk, it was." Marie gestured to the pamphlet clutched to Evelyn's chest. "I was caught off guard at first, but then pretended like I had already known about the document."

"Smart girl, Marie," Evelyn interjected.

Marie beamed at her praise. "I said that my client had *another* important piece to publish and would he be interested. He tried to act uninterested, but I knew he was curious. I made to leave, and he urged me to stay. Even offered me a biscuit."

Evelyn laughed at her sweet lady's maid's excitement over the experience. "I hope you took it," she said.

"Of course!" Marie exclaimed. "I sat back down and he brought me a small cup of tea with the biscuit. I nibbled while he read the letter."

Evelyn wrung her hands in front of her. "And what did he say? Did he like it? Will he print it?"

Marie leaned in close. "He said it will be on page two tomorrow, Miss. Page two!"

Evelyn was silent. This time she did not stop the tears as they fell, despite the crowded street around her and the many society folk who might see her display.

After a moment, she wiped her tears and took a deep breath to calm herself. She did not know what would happen next, but she was glad to have done what she could to help his cause. She was glad she could help him.

Evelyn sat in the garden surrounded by her writing materials staring into the distance. Her pages sat unfinished, and her pencil had long since dropped from her hands to the bench beside her.

The letter was printed yesterday. She had feigned interest in the social pages to borrow her father's copy after breakfast. Once her parents were distracted, she had excused herself to her room where she re-read the whole thing.

```
         "What Story Shall
    the Good Man Teach His Son?"


    By Lady Cordelia Fitzgerald


        We all know those who felt the call
of glory and heeded that most honorable of
charges. We see them in our streets, in our
pews, and in our villages. Some returned
whole in mind and body, while others suffer
still the ravages of war. Some returned in
a box to be entombed in our nation's
highest annals of praise. As it is written,
'Greater love has no man than this, that he
lay down his life for another.' And yet,
how do we honor these brave men? We carve
the names of the fallen on tombstones and
```

we etch their names in the history books, but how do we honor those who walk among us? I will tell you, we do not. We look the other way as they beg for alms in the streets. We dismiss them when their injuries make them weak. We send our praise to widows, and then turn our backs on them in their time of need.

What can one man do, you ask? Give work to the pensioners and widows. Make allowance for the injuries in those who have paid with their blood. Support those among us who labor so that these brave men and their families might thrive...

The letter concluded with a brief description of Oliver's plans and his postal direction. She had no idea whether it would have any impact, but she did not regret her actions. She only hoped Oliver received increased support as a result of it.

She sighed. She hated not knowing where he was. She wanted to know what he thought of the letter. She wanted to know what happened with Elizabeth. She knew he owed her no explanation. Their deal had ended when William proposed and Marie delivered her last pages the morning he left for Longwood.

Evelyn forced her thoughts back to the present and began to gather up her supplies. She knew it would be days, if not weeks, before she would be able to follow up with William to determine whether her efforts had any effect. She groaned at the thought.

A sound in the distance made her look up from where she sat. She smiled at the sight of Charlotte, Sophia, and William making their way across the garden to her location. She hurriedly shoved her materials into her satchel before they caught up to her.

"Welcome, my friends," she hailed as they drew closer. "What brings you here on this fine afternoon?"

William leaned up against a column in front of her while Charlotte and Sophia moved to another bench and sat. After their initial greetings, Charlotte and Sophia sat silent, watching William.

Evelyn glanced between them warily, unsure of what to make of their silence. "Is everything alright?" she finally asked.

"I don't know, Lady Cordelia Fitzgerald, why don't you tell me?" William asked with a smirk.

Evelyn froze. "I don't-"

He raised his hand to stop her. "Don't say another word, Evie. I do not know your reasons, nor is it my business, but your secret is safe with me."

She tried again, "I am not-"

Sophia and Charlotte laughed. "We know you better than anyone, Evelyn. You have sneaked off and returned with ink on your fingers and gown for as long as we can remember." Sophia said.

"You have always been a grand storyteller, even when we did scenes as children," Charlotte added.

Evelyn looked down, avoiding their smirks. Rather than deny it again, she posed a question to William. "Have you heard from Oliv...Mr. Marten lately?"

William raised his eyebrows at the use of his name but shook his head. "Not since I last saw you." He looked at her as if debating his next words. Finally, he said, "Forgive my boldness, but did you have an understanding with Oliver before he left?"

She heard Charlotte and Sophia gasp at his question and almost laughed. "No, I did not." She met his gaze as if daring him to question her.

"Why not?" he asked, taking a step towards her.

This time it was she who gasped. His question caught her off guard and she flushed under his scrutiny. "I...I guess you would have to ask him that," she finally said. Though she knew her cheeks were as red as her hair, she looked him square in the eyes as she answered.

"That's what I figured," he said, almost to himself. He shook his head and came towards her, grasping her shoulders gently. "He's a fool." William smiled at her and she felt tears prick behind her eyes.

"He was so intent on his research, he missed what was in front of him the whole time."

Charlotte and Sophia came up on either side of her and looped their arms through hers. Charlotte rested her head on her shoulder.

"We didn't know how strongly you felt," Sophia said. "If we had, we would have made sure things played out differently."

Charlotte echoed her sister, "We knew you were friends, but it was not until we saw the letter and William showed us the pamphlet that we put the pieces together."

Sophia winked at her. "All those trips to the museum were for research, right?" They laughed at her sheepish expression.

Evelyn smiled and squared her shoulders, looking between her three dear friends. "It is no matter. That is all in the past and I only hope he is one day able to have all he dreams of in America."

"You are far kinder than me," Sophia said. "If he had broken my heart, I'd hope his ship sank on the way."

"Sophia," cried Evelyn and Charlotte in unison, but they laughed again as they began to walk back to the house.

"A Mr. William Montgomery to see you, sir" his footman intoned from the doorway of the study.

Oliver looked up from his uncle's desk in surprise at the name. "Show him in," he said. "And call for tea. It is a long ride from London."

He stood up and moved towards the door, eager to both see his friend and hear news from London. He had hoped to return before now but business matters at the estate had kept him longer than he planned.

His face broke into a grin as he saw William enter the room. "Aren't you a sight for sore eyes," he said clapping him on the shoulder.

William returned the gesture and greeting and moved to a chair in front of the desk before falling into it. "What a pleasure to sit in a seat that does not move beneath me," he breathed.

Oliver laughed. "Did you not come by carriage?"

William shook his head. "Not this time. I sought a quick trip with little baggage. Besides, the weather is fine and the scenery is lovely once you're outside of London."

A maid entered with the tea service and the men paused while she poured for each of them. William took several cakes from a tray and wolfed them down quickly before taking his time to savor the tea.

"How long will you stay?" Oliver asked as she exited the room. "You know my door is always open to you."

"Only the night," William responded. "I am here on the orders of my sisters."

Oliver cocked his eyebrows questioningly at his friend. "Are they well? Is Evelyn well?"

Ignoring his questions, William asked, "Have you seen the papers this week?"

Oliver glanced behind him at the desk where a stack of unread newspapers lay. The footman brought them in each morning after his uncle read it at breakfast.

He shrugged. "Did I miss the latest gossip?"

William pulled a folded paper from inside his jacket and handed it to Oliver.

Oliver scanned the page, unsure of what he was looking for until his gaze settled on a name. Lady Cordelia Fitzgerald.

He sucked in his breath sharply. "What did she do?" he asked softly.

William jerked his chin in the direction of the paper. "Read it."

Oliver read the short passage, his heartbeat increasing with each word he read. Her words filled him with joy and sadness at the same time. He felt a deep longing to see her and talk to her.

He looked back up at William. "Did she see the pamphlet?" he asked.

William nodded. "She only learned of it when she went to publish this under her pseudonym and the editor recognized it."

Oliver flinched at this news. He had debated whether to tell her that he had credited her - or her alias - with the pamphlet, but decided it was best to keep his distance. "Was she angry?" he asked.

William laughed at this. "Not nearly as angry as she should be," he replied. His laughter died quickly, and he frowned at his friend. "Far be it from me to tell anyone how to conduct themselves in matters of the heart, but you, sir, are being foolish."

Oliver's shoulders sagged. "I know," he said. He pushed himself away from the desk he had leaned against and circled the room. "I have spent the last month making plans-"

"Oliver stop," William interjected. "Do you not realize that it was your grand plans that got in the way in London? You made plans for yourself with no consideration for the plans of those around you." He stood from the chair and moved in front of Oliver. "Evelyn supported you, wrote for you, maybe loved you even. But all you saw were your infernal plans. What about her plans?"

Oliver shook his head as the irony of William's words sunk in. Her plan had been to marry William. When that did not align with his own plan for America, he plunged ahead on his own. He had used her and cast her aside at the very moment when she needed someone to help pick up the pieces of her own shattered plans.

He looked at William, who was watching him closely. He knew he couldn't tell him everything because parts of the story were not his to tell. Maybe one day they would laugh about her marriage plans, but only if she chose to tell the story. For now, he could share his part in the story.

He held out his hands. "Hear me out, William. I have a new plan."

William laughed, but Oliver couldn't tell if it was sincere or sardonic. "Hear me out," he repeated, pleading with his friend. "This time, my plan is *for* Evelyn, not about her."

By the time William left the next morning, Oliver had managed to win him over. His friend's arrival was unexpected, but fortuitous as he took on a role in his grand scheme.

Oliver spent most of that morning writing letters and invitations. His valet had packed his trunks that evening, and he would relocate back to his townhouse in London the next day. As he stood in his study and stared at the street below, he could not contain his excitement. The last few weeks had passed in a blur of conversations with his uncle, planning, and designing. For the first time in a long time, he had dared to dream of his own happiness amidst his plans.

He looked at the sealed envelope on his desk and frowned. He had debated posting it to Evelyn multiple times each day, but he never did. It was not enough. She deserved better and he hoped to deliver something better this week.

A knock sounded at the door and he looked up to see his solicitor enter.

"Ah, Mr. North, so good to see you. Come in, come in, we have much to discuss before my departure."

Evelyn jumped as the footman entered and announced a guest. Her nerves were taut ever since she heard from Charlotte that Oliver had returned to London last week. She did not expect him to arrive unannounced, but that did not prevent her from spending each morning in suspense until calling hours were over.

She held her breath, but it was not Oliver. A smile spread across her face as Henry appeared from behind the door. She breathed a sigh of relief and stood to greet him as he entered.

"Mr. Holmes, what a pleasure to see you," she said sincerely. She had seen him several times since their visit to St. Paul's and she now counted among her truest friends.

He bowed low over her outstretched hand. "Miss Berkeley, it is always a joy." He smiled at her and glanced around the room. "Where is your dear mother today?" he asked.

She sat back down in her wingback chair as he took a spot on the settee across from her. "She is out making calls today rather than receiving." She looked pointedly at him. "She asked me to come along, but I declined."

He laughed, as she had intended at their personal joke. She admired his cheerful countenance, but she had come to think there was sadness behind his humor in recent weeks. She had asked several times if there was anything on his mind, but he always deflected with a joke. She was determined to be his friend - as was her lot in life with eligible men - and hope that one day he would share his burden. If not with her, then at least with someone who might help bear the weight.

"To what do I owe the pleasure of your visit today, Henry? Have you more entertaining parish stories?" Despite his current hiatus from the pulpit, he clearly loved his former flock and enjoyed sharing their most entertaining stories.

He shook his head and leaned forward. "I am calling in a debt," he said.

She racked her brain but could not think of anything they had discussed that she might owe. "A debt?" she asked. "What do I owe?"

"I would like a personal tour of the British Museum," he said with a twinkle in his eye.

She hid her disappointment with a broad smile. "Of course, Henry, I would be happy to accompany you." She remembered the conversation now, of course. "As long as I must go no further than the second-floor galleries, I shall be fine," she added with a smile.

She had not been to the institution in weeks. She had not been since her last visit with Oliver, although it had not been a conscious decision to stay away. After all, how often must one visit such a place to know its collections? But she knew that she would always affiliate its grand halls with Oliver. The hours they had spent there in conversation, or even quick and covert hand offs, were precious memories indelibly seared in her mind. She would never enter its doors again without thinking of Oliver.

Pushing these thoughts aside, she asked, "When shall we go?"

"I will come tomorrow afternoon if it is amenable to you," Henry responded. "I just left the Montgomerys and William, Charlotte, and Sophia will join as well. We will have quite the merry party," he finished with a smile.

"I look forward to it," she said, attempting to mean it.

She was grateful for their easy friendship and his talkative disposition as he filled the rest of his requisite thirty minutes with casual conversation and storytelling that necessitated very little response on her part. After he left, she sat staring at her blank pages for some time, willing new ideas to flow on the page, but knowing she would be distracted until after their visit tomorrow.

She had no reason to be nervous visiting the familiar halls, but she felt butterflies in her stomach as she stepped down from the carriage. Charlotte and Sophia took up on either side of her and the three moved up the large grand staircase arm in arm.

"It is a testament to how much I love you both that I am here right now," Sophia said under her breath.

Charlotte and Evelyn laughed. "We know, dear, this is not exactly your idea of a fun afternoon," said Charlotte.

"I never tire of this place," Evelyn breathed, admiring the grand building as it loomed over them. "It has been some time since I last visited. I wonder if they have any new exhibits?"

Hearing her question, Henry stepped up in line with the three girls. "It is my understanding that a new exhibit is opening just this afternoon," he said. "It is called, "What Story Shall the Good Man Teach His Son?" He held open the door and ushered the group inside.

"That's an unusual title," Charlotte said. "What does it depict?"

Evelyn's heart raced. It had to be a coincidence. What else could it be? She echoed Charlotte. "What is the exhibit?"

"It is just here, around the corner in the Gallery of Egyptian Antiquities," William offered.

Evelyn glanced around him and saw a series of easels lining the long room with prints on each. The space was crowded with others interested in the new exhibit. She headed towards a few of the images she could see that appeared less crowded than some of the others.

The first panel she saw was titled, "Longwood House" and had a house plan drawn on it. The name was familiar but she couldn't place where she had heard it. She stepped closer to examine it and saw a large house two-story house with symmetrical wings stretching out on both sides of a central facade. The house was surrounded by decorative gardens and markings on the image indicated the placement of orchards, a fishing pond, and a kitchen garden.

The next image was a drawing of the same house with two additional extensions drawn on to the pre-existing wings. The artist had written labels into this version of the house identifying things like the ballroom, dining room, veteran housing, chapel, and a medical wing.

Evelyn stared at the image. Veteran Housing? She re-read the name at the top of the page. Longwood. Where did she know the name?

She did not know her heart could beat so fast. She put a hand to her chest as if to contain it as she moved to the next easel. This panel was not an image, but rather words. She craned her neck around the crowd and nearly fainted as she saw the title.

"What Story Shall the Good Man Teach His Son?" By Lady Cordelia Fitzgerald

She moved quicker now down the line of signs, barely registering what she saw: a portrait of a young soldier who looked a bit like Edwards may have in his younger days, a simple budget proposal for "Longwood House: Home for Our Heroes," a proposed bill for Parliament to increase pensions.

She paused at the end of the row of easels and tried to catch her breath. What did this mean? What was Longwood House? *Where* was Longwood House? She spun around looking for her friends. Where was William? He would know what was happening.

She halted when she heard a loud voice from the front call for attention. "Ladies and gentlemen, welcome to the British Museum, our nation's most esteemed institution." She joined in the round of proper applause while trying to spot the speaker.

Attempting to be both polite and firm, she maneuvered her way towards the front of the exhibit where she had begun and finally identified the origin. A rather short, stocky man with a shock of gray hair sticking out from his head at odd angles spoke from the center of the hall. She immediately labeled him as someone who worked at the museum and did not go outside much.

"My name is Cornelius Baker and I am a trustee of this fine museum." He beamed at the hall around him as a proud father might admire his child.

Evelyn instantly liked the man.

"We are gathered here today to champion a cause very dear to our hearts. We would not have many of the objects within these walls were it not for the actions and exploits of His Majesty's men."

Another perfunctory round of applause followed this statement.

"Our library boasts, among others, the collections of Sir Joseph Banks and Sir William Hamilton, the Admiralty, the War Office, and generous donations from His late Majesty George II and his son, George III. Every nation must protect these stories so our children and our children's children may know from whence they came. Yet, sadly, our books are often better cared for then our heroes themselves." He looked around the room, clearly enjoying the opportunity of a captive audience.

"Our soldiers return broken and are turned away from work, put in prison for debts. They must rely on the kindness of family or friends to survive. Our men deserve better. Their families deserve better."

Evelyn heard a "Hear, Hear," from somewhere behind her as another round of polite applause filtered forward.

"Today, we are here to support the vision one man has to do his small part to make this nation a better home for these men."

Evelyn held her breath.

A voice spoke softly in her ear. "I have missed you, Evie."

She spun around to see him, but he was already moving away.

She let out her breath and could not contain the smile that spread across her face at the mere sight of Oliver. She had missed him, too.

She watched as he moved to the front while the curator introduced him.

"Mr. Oliver Marten has devoted himself to creating a future for these men, but he needs your help. I ask you all to give him a moment of your time and a mountain of your money." The gentleman basked in the laughter of the gathered crowd as he gestured for the guest of honor to take center stage.

Evelyn drank him in as he faced the crowd. She remembered the feel of being held in his arms as they danced. She heard his laughter in her head the night of the dinner party at Colonel Kilpatrick's. She admired his unruly dark curls and deep brown eyes shining bright behind his spectacles. How had she ever thought him too serious? He was passionate and intense, not devoid of emotions. How she longed to share a dance with him again.

She clenched her fists at her side. Her thoughts were running away from her. She still did not know his intentions and did not want to be hurt again if his departure was still imminent. She shook her head as if clearing away the dangerous thoughts and focused on his speech.

"Thank you all for joining me here today. Many years ago, I sat at the knee of my grandfather and uncle while they filled my head with tales of adventure and glory across the ocean. I was in awe of these men and what they had accomplished. Then I began to meet others like them and I learned that not everyone had the same experience."

Oliver looked at the gathered crowd. "You know the ones I speak of, who returned to poverty, injury, and apathy. The more I learned, the more I wanted to help." He gestured around to his signs. "I decided I wanted my own tale of adventure and glory across the ocean."

Evelyn's heart sank. He still intended to go to America.

"I made plans, I researched, and I dreamed. I interviewed veterans, gathered stories, and even had them committed to paper." His eyes met Evelyn's here briefly but he looked away quickly.

"I never lost sight of my goal: to establish a home for veterans in America." He looked down at his feet and paused.

Evelyn realized she was holding her breath again.

"But I lost sight of myself. The plan became more important than the original motivation to help others. I was more focused on what others could offer to me than what I could offer to others." He put his hands out before him, palms up in a gesture of supplication.

"Thankfully, I have come to my senses. My uncle, my friends, and those dearest to me made me realize I had missed the most perfect plan that was right in front of me the entire time." He gestured to the easels and images lining the room.

"By next year's end, I hope to open "Longwood House: A Home for Heroes" at my uncle's estate. We will work to make a place that is safe and encouraging for these men and their families to find confidence and hope rather than shame and hopelessness."

Evelyn thought her chest might explode. She wasn't sure if it was because she was holding her breath or because she was so proud of him.

"I need your help to accomplish this goal. I hope I can count on each of you to support this dream."

Evelyn clasped her hands at her chest, overwhelmed with emotions.

His eyes locked on hers. Though he still spoke to the crowd, she felt as if he addressed her alone.

"I hope that you will walk with me in this journey because I cannot succeed on my own. I cannot do this without you."

Evelyn's heart soared. Her eyes filled with tears as polite applause rippled around her. The crowd began to move but she stood rooted to the spot. Oliver never took his eyes off her as he walked towards her.

He reached out and took her hands in his. "Evie, I am so sorry." He looked around at the crowd, many of whom were queuing to speak to him. "This is neither the time nor place for this conversation. May I call on you tomorrow?"

Evelyn nodded, unsure if her voice would betray her. She felt as if her face might split despite the tears threatening to fall. She was a mess.

He squeezed her hands and smiled down at her. He held her gaze for a long moment before turning to greet an older man next to him.

She moved back through the crowd towards the exhibit images again. She felt as if she were gliding on air. She looked at the pictures but could not focus on them. She watched him move through the crowd, shaking hands and smiling. He caught her eye and smiled at her.

Evelyn felt someone at her elbow. Sophia sidled up and leaned in close. "This was the most fun I've ever had here." She grinned at Evelyn, who laughed.

"Did you know about all of this?" Evelyn asked.

"Not until recently," Charlotte answered. "William paid a visit to the Longwood estate after your letter came out. He went there angry and came home pleased."

"We don't know all the details, but he enlisted our help, along with Henry," Sophia added.

"What did Oliver say?" Charlotte asked.

"Nothing much yet," Evelyn said with a laugh. She could not wipe the grin off her face. "He said he is sorry, and he would call on me tomorrow."

"We shall visit, too," Sophia said with enthusiasm. "When is he coming?"

"We shall do no such thing," Charlotte said with a horrified look on her face. She turned to Evelyn. "Oh, dearest, I am so happy for you."

Evelyn smiled but did not respond. She watched Oliver from a distance. She did not know what tomorrow would bring, but she was happy that Oliver would be a part of it.

Chapter 16

Oliver did not believe a night had ever passed more slowly. The event had gone off better than he could have dreamed. Not only did he see Evelyn again, but people had liked his ideas. More than that, they had pledged funds to see it through.

He marveled again at his progress over the last months. He had languished for years in some type of self-induced purgatory of painful writing, fruitless dreaming, and frustrating rejections. He had wandered around as if in a fog, focused only on a distant goal without the faintest idea of how to get there.

Evelyn had changed all that. Of course, her writing had been beneficial to his overall project, but it was more than that. Her friendship had brightened the process and shone a light through the fog. Dare he dream that she could want more than friendship?

He glanced out the window. The street below was showing signs of life, but it was still too early for social calls. He sighed and leaned against the window frame.

Oliver spent the rest of his morning alternating between sighing at the window, pacing through the drawing room, and smiling for no reason. When the clock on the mantel finally indicated that he could visit the Berkeleys without rousing the household from sleep, he swept on his hat and bolted from the house.

He was shown into the drawing room with no fanfare. He stepped in and saw Evelyn seated on the settee directly in front of the fireplace. Her mother sat next to her in an elegant wingback chair. He moved to Lady Berkeley and bowed low over her hand.

"Lady Berkeley, what a pleasure to see you," he said with a smile.

"You are always most welcome here, Mr. Marten," she returned. "Pray, what has kept you away from us for so long?"

He turned to Evelyn who flushed a pretty pink under his gaze. "I assure you I came back as soon as possible, my lady." He smiled at her and bowed low over her hand as well.

"How is your uncle, Mr. Marten?" Evelyn asked.

He took a seat across from Evelyn and crossed his leg comfortably. "He is quite well, Miss Berkeley. In fact, I have never seen him happier than when I told him of my decision to make my home at Longwood. He has missed having a family about."

"Family?" Lady Berkeley asked with a raised eyebrow. "Are you betrothed, Mr. Marten?" She struck her ever-present fan on her lap "Mrs. Fitzhugh!" she exclaimed.

"No, no, no, Lady Berkeley, nothing of the sort." Oliver rushed, frantic to disabuse her of any such notion. He looked at Evelyn and cast her an apologetic glance.

"I have no betrothed as of yet, Lady Berkeley, I just hope to one day." He again cast his eyes to Evelyn and admired the pink of her cheeks. She somehow looked different and unchanged at the same time. Her hair was still bold and unruly framing her pale face. He thought her dress appeared different, but he could not have explained what was different.

"Were you happy with the exhibit yesterday, Mr. Marten?" Evelyn asked, thankfully changing the subject.

"Very much," he replied. "I have several generous patrons already and I am confident their numbers will continue to grow."

"I thought it went splendidly," Evelyn agreed. "Your presentation was inspiring, and the renderings were so beautiful."

She beamed at him, and Oliver thought he could bask in her

sunshine all morning. He glanced out the window and nodded in that direction.

"Would you do me the favor of a turn about the garden, Miss Berkeley? It is a gorgeous day, and I am collecting inspiration for the gardens at Longwood."

"It would be my pleasure, Mr. Marten," Evelyn returned with a smile. She glanced at her mother. "Will you excuse us, Mama?"

The older woman made a shooing motion with her fan. "Be off with you, I shall take a bit of a rest in your absence."

The pair walked in silence at a slight distance apart as they moved away from the house. It was a beautiful afternoon with no clouds and a slight breeze carrying away the worst of the city's smells. Oliver could not have chosen better weather for a walk with Evelyn. He glanced at the woman beside him, still somewhat in awe that his plan had worked. So far.

He cleared his throat and came to a stop, turning to face her. It was definitely her dress that was different. He looked up at the house and guessed that her mother's face was likely pressed to the window, but he could not see it for the sun's glare. At least they were out of earshot in case he bumbled things.

"Evelyn, it is so lovely to see you again. You look so lovely...what I mean to say is...I missed you." He frowned, frustrated at his inability to articulate. He knew he couldn't write, but at least he could usually speak with some degree of clarity.

She smiled back at him and he relaxed.

"I missed you, too," she said, looking down. "I never left, you know. I was always here." Her smile was gone and she looked up at him intently.

He drew a deep breath and took her hands in his. "I was chasing after an empty dream. I was so focused on getting to America that I lost sight of what was important. I want to help our men, but I don't need to cross an ocean to do it. My own uncle needs me here and there are hundreds of others here that need help." He squeezed her hands. "I thought I would find what I needed in America, but everything I need is right here."

He looked at Evelyn and saw tears pooling in her eyes. *Were they happy tears?* He had never been good at judging women's emotions.

When she spoke, he could hear a slight tremor in her voice. "You left with Elizabeth. Where does she factor in your plans?"

He laughed, relieved that he could so easily assuage her fears on that front. He turned to walk with her again, this time drawing her close to his side with her arm on his. "Elizabeth revealed her true colors while we were at Uncle's estate. He offered a generous amount to help with my endeavor and she offered a similarly large amount. She was quite bold in her insinuations towards marriage between us." He found it easier to speak the next part without looking directly at her. "If I am being quite honest with you, I had resigned myself to marrying her if it meant I could accomplish my goals. I felt that the good I could accomplish was worth a marriage of convenience. Men have done much worse, and she is a generally pleasant woman. I adore her father and I was quite sure we could suit in a comfortable if not passionate partnership." He kicked at the dirt a bit with his boot. "It turns out that her goals were to leave her father behind and use me as a way to reach America and have an adventure for herself."

Evelyn gasped. He looked down at her shocked face. He shook his head and frowned. "I was surprised too, but it made my next decisions much easier. She departed immediately and I had quite a long conversation with Uncle."

"You decided to stay on at Longwood," she said, guessing where he was going before he could fill in the blanks. "You will make *it* your soldier's home."

He nodded, smiling at the memory of the long days and nights he and Uncle had shared as they devised all their plans for the present house and its future conversions. "It will be everything I ever envisioned and more." He stopped again and turned her to face him. "But there is still one part of my plans yet to be completed."

"I assumed I had lost you when I left. After Elizabeth's departure, I threw myself into the planning, designing, and building to make everything a reality. I knew I had no one to blame but myself and I came to terms with that," Oliver explained.

He reached into his jacket and pulled out a folded piece of paper. He unfolded the newspaper and held it out to her. "And then William showed up at my house one day and showed me this. And I dared to hope again."

She took the paper from his hands and laughed. "Lady Cordelia Fitzgerald," she said. He could hear the tremor in her voice again. "She recently published another work as well, did she not?" Evelyn looked up at him smiling.

He nodded. "I owe her everything," Oliver said. He took her hand in both of his much larger ones. "If you see her, please tell her thank you. Tell her that I would not have made it this far without her. If I have learned anything through this, it is that I need her by my side if I am to succeed. Tell her...tell her I love her."

A sound somewhere between a laugh and a sob broke out of Evelyn. He reached up and wiped a tear from her face, caressing her cheek. "Please tell me that I have not missed my chance, Evie."

He felt her lean into his hand and his heart soared. She gazed up at him with watery eyes. "I cannot speak for Lady Cordelia Fitzgerald, but I can tell you that Miss Evelyn Berkeley loves you very much, Oliver Marten."

He thought he might burst. Regardless of who may be watching from the window, he pulled her to him in a fierce embrace. One hand encircled her waist and the other moved into her hair at her neck. She fit into his arms as if she was meant to be there. He bent over her head, breathing in her scent and relishing her closeness.

After a moment her hands came up between them and pushed against his chest. He reluctantly eased his hold on her and leaned back. Her face was wet with tears, but this time he did not worry about their meaning. "I kept up my end of the bargain, sir, but you did not. What are you going to do about it?"

Oliver assumed a look of mock offense but did not release her. "Excuse me?" he asked. "I promised to thank you in my acknowledgments, which I did. In fact, I went above and beyond by using your intended alias, did I not?"

She laughed and wrapped her arms around him. "I could not

believe my eyes when I saw you had published with that name. I still cannot believe you remembered."

"Of course, I remembered," Oliver replied. "It was the least I could do given that I accused you of not finishing when you had."

She frowned and pushed back against him again, though not enough to get out of his embrace. "But I did finish. Why would you think I had not?"

Oliver sighed. "Apparently Marie delivered your last set of pages the morning that we departed." Evelyn nodded. "When Elizabeth arrived, she saw the package on the table and rifled through it. She realized what it was and who had written it and she hid the pages in her trunk. Her father found it by accident and turned them over to me none the wiser as to what he had done to his daughter."

Evelyn appeared to mull over his words and then shook her head. "I cannot believe Elizabeth's duplicity." She smiled with a mischievous look in her eyes. "But her loss is my gain, I suppose."

Oliver threw back his head and laughed. He could not believe how far things had come in just the last few weeks to now be standing here with his arms around Evelyn.

He looked down at her and she was frowning back at him. He tensed, unsure of what had changed.

"You have not answered my question, Mr. Marten. What will you do to fulfill your end of the bargain? You promised me an engagement."

He saw the twinkle in her eye and the flush in her cheeks as she spoke.

He grinned at her and pulled her close. "Shall I go visit with William and try to change his mind?"

She laughed and punched him lightly in the arm. She tried to pull out of his grasp, but he held her tight.

Their laughter died and he held her gaze. "I will not let you go again, Evie."

He put his hands on her upper arms and stepped back, holding her at a distance. He slid his hands down her arms and captured her hands in his. "You are my partner, my friend, my muse. Your words brought my dream to life and your love gave my life new meaning. If you will have me, I will never leave you again." He squeezed her hands and tried to keep his voice from quavering. "Evelyn Berkeley, will you marry me?"

Her face lit up with her smile, though tears filled her eyes. "I never was good at saying no," she said with a choked laugh. She threw her arms around his neck, and he pulled her close, reveling at how perfect she felt in his arms. "Besides," she whispered in his ear, "I could never live with myself if I was the reason you didn't keep your promise!"

He chuckled, thanking God for whatever impulse had led him to read her story.

ABOUT THE AUTHOR

Abbie Grubb lives in Texas with her husband and son, three dogs, and two cats. She is an Army brat who loves traveling, reading, baking, and spending time with family and friends. Her favorite books are those that celebrate friendships, whether romantic or platonic, and she enjoys a good tale of an epic quest now and then as well. A college history professor by day and a historical fiction and romance author by night, she juggles classes, PTO, cub scouts, and many other activities, but there is nothing she enjoys more than being at home with her family.